· A Green Bag

'Some days ago,' P'⬚⬚⬚
letter from some⬚⬚⬚
ex-member of th⬚⬚⬚⬚⬚⬚⬚⬚lty
he had information⬚⬚⬚⬚⬚⬚⬚⬚⬚⬚⬚ty
of serious criminal act⬚⬚⬚⬚⬚⬚hoice
but to find out what the n⬚⬚⬚⬚⬚as, so I
sent an official from the C⬚⬚⬚⬚ Office to
interview him. The official also talked to a
French journalist who was the real source of
the allegation. It was to the effect that you'd
engaged in paedophilia.'

Druitt's expression did not change. Yet the
smile he had maintained throughout somehow
no longer seemed appropriate to it, like a lamp
left burning after daylight fills a room.

Paul Geddes worked for the Government for
many years, in London and abroad, and was
formerly in the Army. He has also practised as
a lawyer. He now lives in East Sussex.

PAUL GEDDES

· A Green Bag Affair ·

Mandarin

A Mandarin Paperback
A GREEN BAG AFFAIR

First published in Great Britain 1993
by Sinclair-Stevenson
This edition published 1994
by Mandarin Paperbacks
an imprint of Reed Consumer Books Ltd
Michelin House, 81 Fulham Road, London SW3 6RB
and Auckland, Melbourne, Singapore and Toronto

A CIP catalogue record for this title
is available from the British Library
ISBN 0 7493 1738 8

Printed and bound in Great Britain
by Cox & Wyman Ltd, Reading, Berkshire

For Pegitha

· One ·

Glancing up from the folder, he saw with surprise a familiar sight on the roadside, the Scots pine with the broken arm, gaunt survivor of the storm of eighty-seven. Bogged down in Patrick Welcroft's marshy prose with its lame excuses for the cock-ups in the prison building programme of his Department, he had failed to notice they had almost reached Kilndown.

Already the unchanging pantomime ahead was being advertised. A constable stationed in the hedgerow had begun speaking into his handset. Round the next bend a group of police cars awaited him, crested, colour-striped, and quartered for the avoidance of all doubt. A barrier across the road would be denying passage to disgruntled locals coming from the opposite direction. Then the star performer would step forward; gesticulating for the drive gates to be thrown back, the superintendent would erect his grand salute against a frieze of minions.

Irritation could be vented by ignoring the salute, returning the gaze to the folder. But that would achieve nothing, might even lose a vote: hardly the time for that. Elephantine security arrangements were inseparable from life, particularly when, as now, a county force was panting to show it was up to all the tricks. He oughtn't to let it annoy him.

The car rounded the final bend. As Evatt slowed to turn into Kilndown's entrance he composed his features to patient civility and pressed the window button.

'Evening, Superintendent, all well?'

'Good evening, Prime Minister, all in order. My officers are in the grounds as usual.'

'Thank you very much.'

The helicopter that had followed the car from near the county boundary was swinging away. He tapped the glass for Evatt to drive on. Possessed of the energy and relish for interference of someone like Churchill, long before now he would have fired off a broadside: 'Pray inform me this day in what manner the security of Mrs Blackmer and myself is improved, on arrival at our country house for a stay intended to be unpublicised, by the local superintendent of police and his men exposing themselves with such abandon at the gates.' Something like that.

That was also the way of commanding posterity's attention. Not by solid political achievement: not by getting a Cabinet of prima donnas to work together, far better than anyone had forecast before he became Prime Minister; not by finally settling into Europe on terms most people could live with; not by establishing with an American President what really could be called a special relationship; probably not even by making the country a more civilised and compassionate place to live in. Rather than these things, he should have written more quirky, quotable minutes, cultivated a speech mannerism, worn a curious hat.

Glancing back, he saw that a tractor driver from the nearby farm was being held up along with the rest of the traffic. Terrorists, he supposed the Superintendent had argued, could be hidden in the hay.

He muttered and closed the folder on Welcroft's minute. Beside him, Diana smoked impassively. Since leaving Downing Street, they had not exchanged more than a dozen words.

'What did you say?' she asked.

'The antics whenever we arrive are ridiculous. The police down here always overdo things. I'm sick of it.'

'I don't recall you taking that line the time those students were trying to break into the car.'

'The situation was totally different. This is a rural bloody backwater. Our journey wasn't announced in advance. All that man should have laid on were cars front and back. No barriers, no fuss, nothing else.'

She yawned. 'Have him shot. The firm smack of government. Everything makes you irritable these days.'

'I suppose I'll have to talk to the Chief Constable.'

But he wouldn't do it; and she knew he wouldn't.

On the walls of rhododendron that lined the drive to the house, the buds were barely coloured; it was the latest spring for years. He became aware that she was studying his face, frowning slightly.

'What is it?'

She expelled smoke in a brief rush. 'The hair that's begun growing out of your ears – I was wondering when you were going to do something about it.'

Investigating with his fingers, he discovered bristle round the front edge of both. It was strange that he hadn't noticed it when shaving, there was at least a quarter of an inch.

She said, 'The lights caught it when you were on the box the other evening. I don't think the Farmer Giles look is what the country wants. It certainly doesn't go with those new spectacles.'

'You might have told me before.'

'I imagined you knew. Anyway, Trevor Walden should have told you. He's responsible for your image after all.' She articulated the word venomously. 'Whyever did you let him talk you into those spectacle frames? If I'd been consulted, I'd have said they were a great mistake.'

Diana had always loathed Walden, believed in any case that when it was a question of his appearance, she knew best. And that had always been true in their early years in politics, when operating as a team had been as natural as breathing. She was right that Walden should have noticed. They'd met the day before the television interview and discussed style, presentation. Walden had been rather quiet, shooting his cuffs more sparingly than usual. Most of the time he had talked about his ideas for the general election campaign. He had brought along a design for a new motif, to be used in the background for press conferences. But the huckster patter had been low-key. Like others, no doubt, he had been reflecting gloomily on what the autumn might bring, wondering whether his annual fifty thousand would survive the holocaust.

The rhododendrons fell away and there was Kilndown, its façade glistening creamy white on the gravel curve. Once upon a time, this sight had always lifted his heart when he drove down from London on Friday nights, however bloody existence had been during the week in the Commons. In those early backbench days, when the cost of pulling the house together had threatened to cripple him permanently, he had almost sold the place several times. But once it was in shape and not eating its head off, he had come to believe, increasingly as he progressed in the party, he might keep it forever. As they endured the interminable Thatcher years together, he had been sure Diana felt the same about the house.

When, a little to his surprise but not Diana's, he had become Prime Minister and was able to use Chequers, he had continued to think of Kilndown as the real haven from the treadmill of No 10, the place where he could hope to rediscover who and what he was, to the extent that was any longer possible. And with the arrival of Hilda Morrisey as house-keeper had come miraculously a solution to the problem of caring for Esther.

They still managed to come here half a dozen times a year, even if only for a single night's stay, as now. Diana would ride a horse lent by the farmer next door and sometimes sketch or paint. For him it was an opportunity to relax, mess about in the garden; most of all to spend time with Esther, away from the world for which she now had a skin too few. It was a haven still. Yet, in recent months, although he never failed to register Kilndown's special charm, to marvel at the way the seasons' brisk revision of shrubberies and flower beds never diminished the welcome offered by the first glimpse up the drive, he had become aware that he was no longer beguiled to the extent he had been. A flatness seemed to be entering the relationship. *Affairs* with houses were perhaps subject to the same declensions as those with women. Either that or he was experiencing a symptom of a deeper malaise.

Hilda Morrisey, shoulders hunched against the sharpness of the air, was at the open door of the house. 'Hello, Hilda,' Diana called. 'Do you call this spring?' West, his detective, was reaching out the red boxes beside his feet. As West withdrew, Diana thrust across him to follow. She was wearing a scent he did not find familiar. But that was hardly uncommon now.

In the hall, he squeezed Hilda's arm, assumed the mask of teasing jocularity, least demanding of disguises. The aroma of apple logs burning entered his nostril agreeably. He glanced towards the study. 'Chimney all right now?'

'Mr Grattan said there was a loose brick which he's dealt with. He refused to be paid at first saying it was an honour to do it.'

One vote still solid, anyway. 'Anything else new?'

'Ames says the pruning of the limes by the stables was finished yesterday. Rather bare now but he thinks they'll be all right by the summer.'

He feigned enthusiasm. 'Fine. I'll go across and look before dark.'

Diana had disappeared upstairs. Taking off his overcoat, he glanced into the drawing room. 'My sister not about?'

'She's in her room. She knows you're here.'

'Is she . . . all right?'

'Oh, yes.'

It was the voice of reassurance, robust, confident. Her efficiency in caring for the house he admired but it was her manner in speaking of Esther, that comforting tone, he valued most. 'She felt a little jumpy earlier on but she's fine now.'

'Good.' He was fighting a familiar sense of inadequacy, felt only in these circumstances, never back in London. 'Should I go up to her, do you think?'

'She was dressing when I looked in. She'll be down. No need to worry.'

He accepted her advice without hesitation. He believed in her more than he believed in any of the doctors who had dealt with Esther with the possible exception of Reeves. They had offered no more than bland variations on the theme of despair. It was when Esther had been in the private hospital partly owned by one of them that Hilda had entered his life to look after Kilndown. Her only credentials had been her service as housekeeper to the Chairman of his Constituency Committee who had just died. But later on he discovered she had also worked as a hospital sister. When they finally got the balance of the drugs right at the hospital, Esther had come to Kilndown for a visit, to be handled by Hilda with a cool compassion that later grew into affection. On the second visit it had been agreed Esther should stay there with her, to the end or very near that.

Hilda went off to the kitchen. Washing his hands in the cloakroom, he studied his face in the mirror. The hair at the rim of the ears became noticeable only with his head at a certain angle. Diana's gibe about the Farmer Giles look had been an exaggeration. But the effect *was* disconcerting; she had been right in saying it sorted oddly with the modish spectacles Walden had prescribed when he was being attacked in the press as fuddy-duddy.

He took off the spectacles to examine his eye whites: clear enough. The skin colour around was good too. Nose and teeth regular, mouth firm, no sagging at the jowls. Even the hair had hardly begun to turn grey. The rest of him, apart from shortness of stature, was presentable enough. A bit foxed perhaps, a shade worn; but better that than the plastic appearance of so many in the Parliamentary Party. In general, not bad for fifty-four. Not bad at all.

Also, he felt well. Over a year had gone by since a panic over symptoms that had proved harmless had taken him to Reeves for another check-up. All in all, he would probably pass a fitness test with ease. The drained feeling he had at the moment, he knew to be psychological. It would disappear come the autumn; an election campaign always acted like a shot in the arm.

Emerging from the cloakroom, he called to Evatt, still lingering in the hall for possible orders. 'There's nothing else, Fred, you can go.'

Evatt raised a hand until it was at the level of his cheek. The movement never quite developed into a proper salute. Anything smarter would have struck him as ostentatious, too close to toadying. He went off, heavy-footed, ponderous as an elderly Labrador at times; but an admirable driver also, obliging without being servile, uncommonly shrewd whenever consulted, whether about the state of the weather or the current mood in saloon bars. If a kitchen Cabinet had held any appeal for him, he would have found a place for Evatt in it.

Watching him go, Blackmer thought: in a few months from now, barring a miracle, Evatt and I will have parted forever. Evatt belonged to the category of aids and comforts taken for granted in the past few years, which the election would remove. Minor consolations would arrive if he became Leader of the Opposition. But even that he couldn't hope for with confidence.

He went into the drawing room and poured himself a brandy and soda. Diana appeared, having changed into sweater and trousers. She had brushed out her hair; it clung against the cheeks like black silk. Despite a tiredness about the eyes, she was still beautiful. Patrick Welcroft could be said to have sponsored a notable glow these past months. Once, perhaps, he had done the same.

The private line phone went as she was passing it on her way to the drinks table. She raised her eyebrows wearily but didn't pause. Once she would have grabbed the receiver before he could reach it, determined to protect him from any call that wasn't vital. If he let it ring, Hilda or West would pick up an extension. But he would no doubt have to speak in the end.

It was Rainsborough, calling from Central Office, an unlikely location for him on a Saturday evening. Some occasion of real importance, like a flyfishers' dinner or regimental reunion, was perhaps scheduled for later on. 'Charles,' he said, 'what are you doing there?'

'I just looked in for half an hour. There's a little news you'd probably like forewarning on. I have the poll results the *Observer* will be carrying tomorrow.'

Rainsborough's voice had a graveyard quality at such times; he would be a perfect midwife for defeat. 'They now put us ten points behind.'

'When was the poll done?'

'Thursday.'

'One point better than our own poll three days before.' He watched Diana rearranging the flowers Hilda had placed in a bowl on the coffee table. 'However, hardly a consolation, I think.'

'Things can still change. A fine summer, an upturn in the employment figures. . .' Rainsborough was hunting for crumbs. 'And your personal rating has gone up. Druitt's credentials for PM are now considered to be only four points better.'

'My ear whiskers may have had appeal after all.'

When Rainsborough fell into a baffled silence, he said, 'Private joke between Diana and myself, Charles. Any other news?'

'A little unrest among the northern tribes. The Scottish Party appear to think that when you had to cancel attending their conference this year, some later date was going to be found for you to do morale boosting. I said I'd mention it.'

'I see. I'll think about that.' He sighed. 'Go home, Charles, you may need to get more used to it soon.'

Putting the phone down he thought: that might be interpreted as a threat of the sack from Party Chairmanship rather than a reference to the likely outcome of the election. But if so, it would do no harm for Charles to sweat a little.

He returned to his chair. 'The Chairman of our Great Party, anxious to improve the Happy Hour.'

'He's been a big mistake,' Diana said. 'Going back to having a knight in that job was wrong. Particularly one with nothing between the ears.'

'He was the only candidate with broad support when Benskin had to go, you know that. Anyway Charles is shrewd enough.'

'Patrick would have been right. If you'd supported his candidature, others would have gone along.'

'So you've said before.'

'You shouldn't have panicked over Benskin. In the event there's been no publicity. What he was involved in may never come out. Not to an extent that's really damaging.'

He poured himself another brandy. 'There was no way I could take the risk. And you can hardly claim to be entirely impartial in advancing Patrick's claims.'

'Impartial enough.'

She was right of course. She was a political animal before she was anything else. Sex just happened to come a good second.

He watched her light a cigarette with that slight flourish that seemed to say something of a more intimate nature would follow shortly. Often it had done so in the past, the distant past. He felt irritation growing inside him; or perhaps it was something more primitive, like jealousy.

A trivial thought came to his aid. 'By the way, this month's *Tatler* has a photograph of you, lighting up at the Toulmins' wedding reception. I wish you'd avoid giving photographers and the press in general that sort of chance. It clashes rather inconveniently with the speech I made at the Royal College of Surgeons' dinner.'

She drew back the corner of her mouth, then looked at him blandly. She was hoping to convey that she supposed he'd made the remark because of their exchange about Welcroft. 'I didn't know they were circulating the *Tatler* to you these days.'

'The photograph was in some clippings sent over from Smith Square.'

She smiled. 'How efficient! I wonder if Charles cut it out of his daughter's copy himself. What did he want on the telephone by the way?'

'The *Observer* poll tomorrow will show us ten points behind.'

'Pay no attention.'

'Polls have done for elections what Packer did to cricket.'

He went to the window that gave on to the side of the house. The first of the red-twigged limes by the stables was just visible. It looked as though it had been savaged, was little more than a trunk with thalidomide limbs. 'I hope those tree people Ames got in knew what they were doing.'

She wasn't listening. He turned back. 'So are you definitely not coming on the visit to India?'

'Not unless you insist it's vital.'

'You know it couldn't be that.'

'If I go with you on the Far East trip, won't that do?'

'I suppose so.' At least she was prepared to do without Patrick Welcroft for that long. 'Is that definite? Can I tell Giles Grice – the Far East but not India?'

'Yes. I hope he's coming too.'

In the past she had had an idle interest in Grice, attracted by that graceful willowy form, the Foreign Service smoothness, the effortless flow of courtesies and amusing comment on other trips. But Grice remained intact. A Principal Private Secretary, with sense, acquired the footwork to dance him out of danger. And officials were not really Diana's game.

'Giles'll have to be in the party. You'll be less pleased to hear Judith Lang will be as well. The Foreign Secretary told me yesterday she hasn't got jaundice after all so he's bringing her.'

'God,' she said, 'more of those *hats*! What a wife for a Foreign Secretary!' She stubbed out her cigarette in a resigned way. 'Hilda's cooking venison for dinner, I hope you don't get indigestion. She asked about tomorrow morning. When do you want a call?'

'Six. I'll put in a couple of hours on boxes before breakfast. If it's reasonably fine afterwards I might clear some of the brambles at the end of the lawn. Ames seems to be avoiding them.'

A footling task of course. Ames would view the result with heavy silence or say he had been waiting for some important related event before doing the job. But afterwards the azaleas would be properly visible again. It would quite likely be the last summer of seeing them.

'We shall have to sell this place, you know,' he said.

He had startled her. 'Kilndown?'

'Yes. After the election.'

'Because you think you're going to lose?'

He shrugged.

'To hell with the polls! There are still four months before you have to go to the country.'

'I see no real chance of turning things around in that time. We could start a war somewhere, I suppose, as long as we could be sure of winning it. Do you suggest I ask the MoD if they've got a contingency plan for one of those? Because short of that, the only hope is if the Opposition make some really lunatic blunder. And I regard Druitt as much too shrewd to allow that sort of mistake.'

He looked at his watch. Still no sign of Esther. Perhaps she was worse than Hilda had let on. 'Did you see Esther when you were upstairs?'

'Briefly. She was on the way from the bathroom. She said she'd be with us soon.'

'How did she look?'

'Pretty tense. Let's hope we're not going to have a repetition of the weekend last autumn when Reeves had to come down in the middle of the night.'

He shook his head. 'Hilda said she was all right.' He didn't want to think about it. 'Anyway, what I was going to say is that we have to reckon with the likelihood of being out of No 10 by mid-October. I may not even be leading the Opposition if the Party Conference later persuades my dear colleagues someone else should do it.'

'God, you're dreary today.'

'Just being realistic.'

'I still don't see why that should mean we have to sell this place.'

She was giving the impression that Kilndown still meant a lot to her. Yet for ages, it seemed, she had been getting cooler about their visits, complaining of the journey or the absence of good riding or the impracticability of having people to stay with Esther around.

'We have to sell because we need somewhere in London if we lose No 10. I don't want a flat in Dolphin Square or anywhere like that, I want a decent-sized house. That will take all the capital we can get for this and more.'

'We could sell the apartment in Switzerland.'

'I wouldn't like to give that up. We need somewhere to escape to. I might start on my memoirs on the terrace there.' It was the first moderately agreeable thought he had had since morning.

She was pinching the skin on the back of a hand, a sure sign of unease. 'And Esther?'

'She'd be in London as well of course.'

'You're relying on Hilda, most of whose relations are down here, agreeing to come with us.'

Before he could reply, she went on, 'Because I couldn't cope with Esther by myself. You know that's not on.'

'I expect Hilda will agree to come. The sort of house we'd buy would enable us to make a flat in it for her.'

Diana was staring at the wall ahead. He knew what she was thinking. Even with Hilda around she would never be free of Esther. Everything would be subordinated to the fact of her presence: Esther, sometimes displaying all her sweetness, infinitely touching, sometimes, when the drug failed to control her, a shouting, raging stranger. And getting worse.

'We might sound Hilda out this weekend,' he said.

She lit another cigarette. 'And what about *you*?'

'Me?'

'How are you going to cope with not being top dog after all this time? Not being anything, since you seem to expect the Party to ditch you as well.'

'I've survived on the back benches before.'

'Not for a long time. No decisions, nobody to summon and bully. No more of those bloody boxes I've had to watch you with every night.'

Not, he thought grimly, on the nights you make your escape to Patrick's when Lorna's conveniently left behind in darkest Northumberland with little more than a choice of game-keepers for company.

But she had a point all the same. He had allowed himself fleeting reflections on losing Evatt, on life without the other perquisites that went with the job. Yet he hadn't truly faced up to the shape of Afterwards.

He would presumably need to learn the part of Elder Statesman, consulted now and then for decorum's sake, deferred to in the tea room by the more civilised in the Party, rising occasionally in the House for senatorial pronounce-ments, seasoned with a touch of *cafard*. In suddenly gigantic stretches of empty time, he would be driven to work at his memoirs, for serialisation in the *Sunday Times* and, all too soon, remaindering in the shops. Others had survived as Yesterday's Men, so no doubt he could. But the brandy intake would certainly go up.

'You'd better win somehow,' she said. 'You'll be intolerable to live with otherwise.'

He was suddenly impelled to an act uncharacteristic of their relationship now – to impart a true confidence.

'A second term would mean a great deal to me. I wouldn't necessarily want to go to the full five years. Perhaps three. But I know with absolute certainty there are things I could do in a second term that nobody else in the country could manage.'

'Three years, you say?'

'About that.'

She shrugged. 'Long enough to dish Kenneth Cridland's chance of succeeding you. Isn't that all you care about now?'

She opened the palm of a hand and angled it as though releasing something towards the ceiling. It was one of her gestures when enjoying malice.

'It's your mind I love,' he said, 'your mind above all.' He grimaced. 'Anyway, I owe it to humanity to keep Kenneth out of No 10. He could start World War III.'

She had stopped listening. 'If you insist on selling this place and buying a London house instead, I won't have Esther there.'

'With Hilda we'd manage things perfectly well.'

She was shaking her head violently. 'No!'

'You're not suggesting I put her in hospital again?'

'There must be nursing homes that would take her.'

'She's not ill enough for that yet.'

'Then you'll have to find another solution. Don't think I shall change my mind about this, I won't. We're not going to have Esther with us if we're living in London.'

He drained his glass. She would change; she would have to. 'I'm going to look at what they've done to those limes.'

He was almost at the door when it opened and Esther came in. The appalling thought came to him that she had perhaps heard something of the exchange. But the door had been closed, and eavesdropping she despised.

She was walking quite well, with only the smallest hint of awkwardness. She stiffened for the effort of greeting them, but that wasn't unusual. After she had kissed them, she sat in the other chair by the fire, stroking Bron, the spaniel, who had followed her in.

'How are you, Est?' he asked.

'All right.'

'Really?'

She nodded. 'I was having a bath when you arrived, I didn't hear the car. Hasn't it been terribly cold?' She was driving herself on. 'Did you notice how dead everything still looks? All except the cherries. They've been beautiful.'

'Hilda said you'd spent the morning in bed.'

'I was a bit jangly early on. But it's better now.'

'You look fine.'

She again gave the over-emphatic nod. 'Are you staying all tomorrow?'

'Yes.'

'In the morning you can come and see the duck houses Ames has rebuilt. And we're going to plant some primulas along the edge of the pool. The nursery were supposed to have delivered yesterday but I don't think they came in the end.'

He was conscious of Diana's eyes briefly upon him. She was signalling that surely he could see how ridiculous it was to think of selling the place.

Esther had taken Bron on to her lap. 'I'm rather worried about a lump on his side, it's quite noticeable. Can you see? Ames thinks it's probably a growth.'

The dog was fourteen. They had always taken him on visits to the hospital. He had experienced everything from the beginning and always stayed the same.

'We'll get a vet to look. It may be nothing to worry about.'

'I don't want him put down.' She spaced the words very carefully. 'If we can possibly avoid it.'

'We're probably a long way from that. Don't anticipate the worst.'

The cause of the morning crisis, he guessed, could have been Ames' remark. He stared at her bowed head, his feelings a mixture of annoyance with Ames and despair at her vulnerability.

Diana said, 'How's the tapestry going? Were the wools I sent what you wanted?'

He would have said the tone was too bracing by far. Diana could never get it right. But Esther looked up and produced a smile. 'I'm working on a cushion with them, they were perfect. I thought it might go on the divan over there.' She put Bron on the floor again and went out to fetch the cushion. She had pulled herself together. Surely, he thought, that's actually an improvement on a year ago.

Diana looked at the end of her cigarette. 'It's a knife edge. One's always just waiting, wondering if she's going to fall into another black hole.'

'We simply have to go on making her feel secure,' he said doggedly. 'And loved.'

'Then keep this place. Get an advance on your memoirs to help pay for the London house. Or borrow. There must be somebody in the Party who'd stump up the cash.'

Esther returned. After she had handed the cushion to Diana, she took an envelope from the pocket of her dress and placed it beside his drink. 'A letter for you, David, it came yesterday.'

He glanced down. 'But it's addressed to you.'

'There's another envelope inside.'

The first envelope was addressed to Miss L. E. J. Blackmer. The stamp and postmark were Italian. He frowned. He'd taken care never to include her in any reference book for which he'd supplied an entry. In none of the profiles printed about him had she figured even briefly. The few people in the world who knew of her existence as his sister would not easily call up her initials in their correct order – or the fact that she was now here at Kilndown.

A note attached to the inner envelope read,

Dear Miss Blackmer,
I would be most grateful if you would hand the accompanying letter to the Prime Minister when you next see him. It contains a very important

communication. As he will understand when he
reads it, it was necessary to avoid putting it
through official channels where it might be seen
by others. Please forgive my troubling you.

Yours sincerely,
Edward Syce

The second envelope had only his name on it, together with
the words, Strictly Personal. The letter inside, like the covering
note to Esther, was decently typed on good paper.

c/o Hotel Villani,
Poggibonsi,
Province Siena,
Italy.

6th May

Dear Prime Minister,
I hope you will excuse this unorthodox means of
communicating with you, chosen in order to
avoid any risk of the letter being opened by
others. My reason for this exceptional precaution
will be explained in what follows.

If I am to believe the press comment I see here,
there is a strong possibility of the Labour Party
led by Mr John Druitt gaining power when the
next general election takes place. I have no
ideological or other objection to the Labour Party
taking over the government, although I would
regard the loss of your personal leadership as a
blow to the country where I was born. But I think
you should be aware that Mr Druitt has engaged
in criminal activity of a character that even in
these liberal times would not be acceptable in a
Prime Minister if they were known to the British
public. I can also say, from direct knowledge, that
information about this activity has already been

passed to a senior official of yours but is being withheld from you.

Unfortunately I cannot travel to London but I am ready to tell what I know and provide the name of the witness to the activity to someone carrying your personal written authority. My only request, based on what I know has already happened once, is that I should not find myself dealing with an official. Perhaps someone from Conservative Party Central Office in whom you have absolute confidence could come here.

To assure you I have some understanding of delicate issues of this kind, perhaps I may add that the circumstances in which you had to call on Mr Benskin to give up his chairmanship of the Party are known to me.

A telephone message to the above hotel will reach me. Since I am unlikely to be available immediately, your representative should leave a number for me to call back.

Yours sincerely,
Edward Syce

Blackmer dropped the letter on the table beside him and half-closed his eyes. He was conscious after a few moments of Diana reaching across for it.

'A nut?' she said eventually.

'Not completely a nut, I fancy. You'll notice he seems to be aware of the background to the Benskin business. God knows where he picked that up. It's not likely to have been in the Hotel Villani, Poggibonsi. He must have a very good contact somewhere.'

'So there could be something in what he says?'

'There might.'

Their eyes met. For a brief moment they were thinking the same thoughts, a team again. He rose and went to the telephone.

At No 10, the only Private Secretary still about was Wyeth.

'I want you to find out if the police or the Security Service have any record of a person named Edward Syce. At present he seems to be staying at the Hotel Villani, Poggibonsi. That's in central Italy as far as I recall. Although I doubt it, he could be mad or a hoaxer, so I also need any special records of people like that looked at.'

'Do you want the Italian police asked as well as our own?'

'I doubt if that's desirable at present. In any case I'd like an answer tonight. And get Sir Norman Pagett to call me.' He put down the receiver.

Esther said, 'Is the letter important?'

'It might be. It's something I have to take seriously anyway.'

'Does the writer say how he knew my name so that he could send it through me?'

'No.' For a moment he had forgotten his own puzzlement over the fact. It was something he might have to explore further, once Syce had been identified.

He remembered he hadn't looked at the cushion. He reached for it. 'Where did you get the pattern from?'

'I more or less made it up.'

'It's good.' He put his arm round her shoulders. At once she became hunched. He guessed she was hardening against the possible onset of spasms. Once touching had been a natural, instinctive thing for them both. It remained for him something he had been able to turn to advantage in politics. He had come to rely on pressing flesh to evoke a response, a current of warmth. With Esther, now, it never happened. Yet he knew she loved him more than anything else in the world.

She broke away from him. 'I think I ought to feed Bron, it's after his normal time.' She went out, moving in that jerky way that made him sick at heart.

Pagett came through on the telephone as the door closed behind Esther. He had been summoned, it seemed, from carpentry in the attic: suitable therapy for a Cabinet Secretary at the weekends, Blackmer reflected. 'Norman,' he said, 'that man you brought back from retirement to head your new investigation unit in the Cabinet office – what's his name?'

'Fender, Ludovic Fender.'

'I may have a job for him.'

'I'm afraid he's away sick with back trouble. The forecast is that he'll be bed-bound for a month or more.'

'Then I'll want a reliable member of his team.'

'Fender thinks well of a man named Egerton. We brought him over from the Central Crimes Bureau when it was disbanded.'

'Would I have met him when I came round your people last year?'

'Very probably, Prime Minister. Tall, dark-haired, about thirty, good manner – came into the Civil Service from merchant banking.'

'He'll have to be exceptionally discreet.'

'I'm sure he's that.'

'He'll also need to wear a hat you won't like. You'll understand why when you hear the facts of the case.'

Pagett said politely, 'I see.' His voice was conveying the message that he reserved judgement on whether he *would* understand. Getting him to allow one of his minions to pretend to be a Party Office worker was not going to be plain sailing.

Diana had picked up the letter again. 'Surely if something *really* serious had been reported, you'd have been told? The Civil Servants wouldn't dare hold that back, would they?'

'Why did I have to hear about Benskin first through the American Ambassador? I shan't forget that in a hurry.'

She turned to look out of the window. 'If there's anything at all in the story, it could make quite a difference to us.'

He gazed at her back, allowed himself briefly to reflect on the gracefulness of the shoulders, the gentle curve downwards from the neck, the hips still as slim as when she was a young girl.

All no doubt a source of pleasure to Patrick Welcroft nowadays. But he had known these things before him, known them in their perfection. He could recall the moment when he had seen her body for the first time. Lying beside her, he had marvelled at the contrast with his own heavy limbs, the forearms so unattractively darkened by hair that when Walden had advised against photo-opportunities in short sleeves, he had not grumbled but meekly complied.

The way Diana had spoken about the possible advantages the letter might hold had lifted his spirits a little. He could tell that already she was thinking of the election campaign. Despite her railing at the endless round of functions, the entertaining, the speech-listening and the speech-giving – despite it all, she wanted to stay at No 10 as much as he did.

Before they went to bed, she said, 'About India – I'll come. I don't want you doing it on your own.'

So they had something left.

· Two ·

Glancing into the bath en route, to check that the volume of filth bubbling from the waste was no worse, Egerton went back to Gail in the bedroom. She was dressing as she drank a second cup of coffee. 'Who was that on the phone?' she asked.

He sat on the bed to watch her. 'The plumber. Not only calling back but swearing he'll arrive within the hour. Can you believe it?'

'It's your overwhelming charm.'

'Perhaps I paid him in cash last time.'

Gail's head was bent over in grim inspection of a hole in her tights. She said, 'You go to the office – I'll hang on for him. I'll ring Bristow and tell him he'll have to get there himself if he wants the gallery open on time.'

He shook his head. 'My appointment with Pagett isn't until 10.15. I'll let the plumber in and leave him to it.'

She straightened up. 'Why does the Secretary to the Cabinet want to see you? Doesn't he normally deal with Fender?'

'Ludo's still sick. He's not expected back for ages.'

'Perhaps Pagett wants to promote you – to take over from Ludo.'

'Hah,' he said. He went back to his own coffee in the kitchen. Gail appeared in the doorway after a while. She looked pale but no more than usual these days. He worried that the gallery and the late work it often involved was pulling her down. He drew her to him and kissed her through muffled protests. Disentangling herself, she said, 'Aren't you pleased Pagett wants to talk to you rather than anyone else in the

· 21 ·

investigation unit? He could have asked for Jessop instead, couldn't he? Isn't he more senior than you?'

'Yes.'

'Well? Perhaps he *is* going to promote you. Tell him from me *I* think you ought to be promoted. That if you're not, you'll . . .'

'I'll what?'

In a moment they'd be back on the dreary and intractable subject of money, shortage of. But she was looking at her watch and groaning, 'I'll have to fly.' She kissed him and was gone, to another day of trying to flog Bristow's ludicrously-priced paintings.

He switched on the radio news. Druitt, the Leader of the Opposition, had made a speech criticising the Government for clinging to an American military presence in Europe. We all know, Druitt had said, that the threat it was here to counter has vanished. For too long, the Government has made reliance on the Americans a substitute for a defence policy. Why must we be always out of step with our European partners? We should be joining them in saying to the Americans – Thank you, but go home now! Europe – and Britain within Europe – will take care of its own security.

A couple of political journalists were wheeled on soon afterwards to discuss the speech. They were in agreement that Druitt was effectively reinforcing his claim to understand the realities of the post-Cold War world while the Prime Minister's thinking remained trapped in the past. Also that the line was likely to help his chances when the General Election came.

By now the mail would have arrived. Egerton went down to collect it from his box in the hall of the apartment block. Most of the envelopes were the sort that spelled only tribulation. Seating himself at the desk in the living room, he filtered final demands from routine accounts, noted the dentist's change of address, tore up the offer of porcelain figures of characters in the novels of Charles Dickens. The white foolscap envelope he kept until last as appearing reasonably benign.

But it was a wolf in sheep's clothing. The letter inside was from the managing agents for the apartment building. He would remember, it said, the regrettable extent of the wet rot that was destroying the roof timbers; in the accompanying schedule he would find the itemised costings of the repairs shortly to be carried out; he would also recall the liability arising under the terms of his lease: £1800 was the amount that was down to him, and a cheque would be looked for not later than the end of June.

He crushed the letter in his fist, threw it in the furthest corner of the room, then went to the window overlooking Battersea Park to communicate to the ducks on the lake the sheer impossibility of everything. Below him, parked next to the Mini, was a Jaguar he knew. It belonged to the computer salesman who made a weekly visit to Deirdre on the top floor. Their relationship had endured since he had first moved into the building. Then there had been a modest Sierra where the Jaguar now stood, and a certain furtiveness from the salesman during chance encounters on the stairs. Now the Armani suit and gold-chained shoes passed him with a confident nod. The world had looked on the salesman and pronounced him good.

Deirdre too, it seemed, had also found success in post-industrial Britain. Letters came from an investment bank. In a lock-up garage round the corner, safe from vandalising by the envious, a smooth white soft-top waited her bidding when no clients were expected. Sometimes, from behind the wheel, on the way to visit Mum, she waved to him.

Something about the progress of the salesman and Deirdre seemed to hold a lesson, although he found it difficult to identify what it was. He wished nothing bad to either of them; only that he was not still driving the Mini.

The plumber appeared, not quite within the hour, but early enough to rule out the need for a cab to get him to the Cabinet Office in time for the appointment with Pagett. He left him whistling through his teeth over the bath waste and hurried out into Prince of Wales Drive. Sunlight was breaking across the Park, yet the air remained chilly. Spring had still not sprung, although the leaves said it was definitely on its way. He looked up at widening slivers of blue sky and forgot the letter from the managing agents.

Entering Pagett's lair, he found him reading *Private Eye* with neatly pursed lips. He waved Egerton to a chair. 'How are you, Egerton – all well?'

'Very well, thank you, sir.'

'Excellent.' Time for showing concern was allocated by Pagett in the same meticulous way the rest of his encounters were organised. Yet it was not wholly mechanical: civilised courtesy was bred in him, was never quite forgotten even on days when Whitehall's roof seemed to be falling in. 'And your wife – how is she?'

No special meaning to that, perhaps, but he still disliked the enquiry. That Pagett had been told of his own brief spell on heroin before joining the Civil Service he had accepted as reasonable; but that he should also know about Gail had stuck in his throat and still rankled. He had complained to Fender that it was no business of Pagett's, the more so because the clinic in Somerset had pronounced her cured of the addiction. Fender had replied simply that it was best to hold nothing back. And there was something in that.

Gnome-like behind the too large desk, eternal cigarette between the lips, Pagett had begun unfolding a sheet of paper taken from his pocket. He said without glancing up from it, 'The PM wishes you to carry out a delicate interview in unusual circumstances. It arises from this personal letter sent to him at his country house. He received it at the weekend. Apparently it arrived inside another letter addressed to his sister.'

'I didn't know he had a sister.'

'She stays very much in the background. Rather delicate, I believe.' Pagett paused briefly. It was possible he was withholding something, or he might simply have been struck by another thought. 'The letter was sent through the sister because the sender felt he must avoid all risk of it being intercepted and read by an official. His stated reason is that the information it deals with has been passed on before to an official and then wilfully withheld from the PM. There could, you see, be some sinister *plot*.' He articulated the final word with a weary resignation.

Without looking, Pagett reached inside the box at his elbow and took another cigarette. Throughout the day, the movement would be repeated with hardly a variation in its pattern. Lighting up, he said, 'Belief in plots, I find, is on the increase again. Like astrology. There's probably a connection.'

'What is the information?'

'In essence the writer is saying the Leader of the Opposition is guilty of criminal acts that render him unfit for office. He wants to talk about it and to supply the name of a witness to these acts.'

'The PM can't really believe that anything of that kind would have been withheld from him?'

'Unfortunately a recent experience which the writer also seems to know about has made him rather sensitive to the possibility. It concerned the last Conservative Party chairman, Benskin. You'd better know about this since the person you'll be interviewing clearly does. The police, investigating, at the behest of the Americans, the laundering of a large amount of drugs money through London, found that much of it had gone through the bank of which Benskin was Managing Director. They told the Police Department in the Home Office. An Assistant Secretary there decided since there was as yet no legal evidence the bank had knowledge of the origin of the money, he would wait for something harder before passing the information on for his Minister to see.

'The evidence was never in fact obtained and the Home Secretary never informed, although there was eventually no room for doubt that Benskin was privy to the facts. All this could be deduced from the report the police passed to the American Drugs Enforcement Agency. The Ambassador, meeting the PM at a dinner, remarked how much the Drugs Enforcement people had appreciated the Yard's exhaustive enquiries and went on to express sympathy at the embarrassment the involvement of Benskin must be causing him.'

Propriety seemed to call for a strictly neutral response. 'I see.'

Pagett went on, 'I had a disagreeable ten minutes with the PM about the shortcomings of the Assistant Secretary, whose future position in the galleys I have still to settle. However the Home Secretary bore the brunt of his anger – which, since it was Patrick Welcroft he was dealing with, he will not have had any inclination to restrain.' He looked at his cigarette's smoke trail with obvious pleasure. 'Because of the danger of the story getting out, the PM decided Benskin would have to resign at once from the Party chairmanship. His statement for the press about health problems was written in No 10 the same night.

'You can imagine that the PM is rather sensitive to the possibility that this is another occasion when he has not been told all he should be.' Pagett held out the sheet of paper, smiling bleakly. 'Happily you and I appear to be exempt from suspicion. So perhaps you should now read what this says.'

Egerton read the letter. When he looked up he found Pagett watching him closely. He had a strong sensation of being on trial. 'The writer specifically asks for a Conservative Central Office contact. Shouldn't someone from Smith Square be going?'

'You may well ask. However the PM believes there is a possibility that a plan to cause him political embarrassment lies behind the approach. Should that turn out to be the case, the fact of having handed the letter to officials to deal with will provide a good riposte to any criticism. He says he'll arrange for you to carry Smith Square credentials and rather reluctantly I've agreed to that. If something genuinely serious affecting Druitt is revealed it can be pursued through the proper channels. With due regard to the calendar and the approach of the election.' Pagett raised and lowered his eyebrows, not so much for Egerton's benefit but as an accompaniment of thoughts unspoken. 'I shall then have the task of discovering where in the machine the earlier information became stuck. And why.'

Coffee and biscuits appeared. Pagett poured from his silver pot. 'Syce by the way couldn't be identified in any of the records which the PM consulted over the weekend. The police and the Security Service had never heard of him and he doesn't seem to be one of the regular letter-writing cranks. The PM says he can't be traced in Conservative Party records either. And there's no record of any Civil Servant, past or present, with his names – I checked this morning before you came in.'

Egerton shook his head. It was difficult to believe anything really substantial would come out of the interview. Genuine information somehow never emerged like this. If Syce wasn't simply trying to damage Druitt out of enmity, he was likely to be a credulous busybody peddling gossip picked up in a bar. But that wouldn't altogether explain his knowledge of the Benskin business.

There was a question that had to be asked. 'Is there anything about Druitt it would be helpful to know before I see Syce?'

The pause lasted perhaps five seconds. Pagett brushed away biscuit crumbs. 'I don't think so.' His tone was casual. 'I find him very agreeable to deal with. Have you read the novel he wrote before he set his sights on leading his Party?'

'I've a vague recollection of doing so when it came out.'

'Perhaps you should refresh your memory. I thought it quite good. He's unmarried of course. Seldom a wise condition for a politician in this country.' His smile was impenetrable.

A head belonging to one of his Private Secretaries appeared round the door and spoke words Egerton did not catch. Pagett acknowledged them with a nod and reached for a folder. 'Given the present standing of the Government in the polls, the implications if something comes out of this could be considerable. On the other hand the facts, while fruity, may not be as serious as Syce would like the PM to accept they are. But let's at least have no mistake over what the facts are. No assumptions, no facile deductions. You'll make sure of that, won't you, Egerton?'

The tone of the voice was as urbane as ever. But if Pagett could ever be associated with anything so impolite as a threat, one had now been uttered.

Egerton bought a bottle of wine on his way home. Gail was preparing a salad when he arrived at the flat. He opened the bottle of Chilean white before he told her his news – the flight booking to Pisa (first class on account of no cheaper seats as prescribed by Auntie Treasury being available), the reservation in the best hotel in Certaldo. He watched her covertly as he spoke, but her smile was unshadowed. 'Sounds marvellous,' she said.

While he was in the living room, trying to find his passport and the paperback of Druitt's novel, she called, 'What do they want you to do there?'

'Interview a man who may or may not have earth-shattering news.'

'An Italian?'

'No, English apparently. He says he has evidence Druitt is guilty of serious crimes.'

'The Leader of the Labour Party?'

'Yes.'

She made sounds of mockery. 'I expect it's a rabid Tory with a fairy tale. What do you know about him?'

'Hardly anything. He's very coy about his whereabouts too. To make contact I had to telephone the receptionist of a hotel in Poggibonsi. She'd obviously been briefed to say he wasn't immediately available but she could have him call me back. He's not supposed to know I'm in the Cabinet Office, so this meant using one of our unlisted numbers. I had to wait a couple of hours before he came through. The upshot is he'll be at a particular bar in Certaldo tomorrow night at six o'clock.'

'Does he live there?'

'He claims to be farming somewhere close by. It'll all prove to be moonshine I expect.' He went back to the kitchen. 'How was the great world of Art today? Did you sell anything?'

'Not a single person came into the gallery until twelve o'clock and then it was only somebody trying to sell his own work. The market's going dead.'

An idea came to him. 'If things are that quiet, couldn't you take a couple of days off and come with me? Liza could surely hold the fort with Bristow as well as doing his typing. Ring him at home now and ask. He'll probably agree.'

He kissed her neck as further encouragement. Under the perfume her skin was cool and sweet. She had let her hair grow long again. She looked exactly the person he had first met, pushing a cycle too large for her out of that Oxford college, a slight figure with hair that seemed like the palest gold and lips slightly parted as though about to smile.

'Call him,' he said again.

'How would we pay my fare?'

'With plastic.'

'We agreed we wouldn't use plastic until we'd paid off what we owed from before.'

'An exception – just this once.'

'Two hundred pounds at least.'

'What's two hundred?' he said.

Through the blur made by her hair, he stared at grime pencilled along a counter top where it met the wall tiles he had fixed one rainy Saturday. He had still not adjusted to this change in Gail. In the Oxford days she had treated money as instantly disposable, infinitely replaceable. Her extravagance had had a spectacular quality to it. With some apprehension he had seen himself when they married as the accountant of their union, applying his own mixture of irritation and despair to the impossible monthly balancing act.

It had not turned out like that. His expectation of a struggle to persuade her of financial realities had proved wildly wrong. Now she was far more realistic than he was. When the Mini needed its new gearbox, she had been the one to define the economies to be made. He felt half-relieved, half-cheated.

Nowadays, they both knew what two hundred was. 'All right,' he said. 'Forget it.'

· Three ·

The journey to Certaldo from Pisa took less time than he had expected, barely an hour. Syce had told him he would find the Bar Miranda in a street leading out of the main *piazza* and he saw the sign almost at once where another street crossed. He was twenty minutes ahead of the time agreed for the meeting; but that might not be enough of a margin for searching out the hotel, leaving his bag and then returning. He decided to park the hire car in the *piazza* and stroll the town.

It seemed to have developed in two parts, the older houses built on the side of a hill, the remainder sprawling along the banks of the river. In a square higher up the hill, he found a woman seated on a kitchen chair before an open door, knitting and singing softly. There was no traffic noise. The woman's fingers flickered as they moved in a shaft of sunlight. From the grocery behind where he had paused to watch came the mingled scents of cheese and herbs. He thought of the crabby chill of the London he had left behind that morning, a crossed-legged city still with May half-gone, and already it seemed unreal.

At the Bar Miranda, he took a pavement table and ordered an *espresso*. The arrangement for the meeting had been less foolproof than he would have chosen. His suggestion of an exchange of physical descriptions had been dismissed with a laugh by Syce, who had asserted it was unnecessary. Syce had also turned aside a request for means of contact other than through the hotel receptionist in Poggibonsi. He had politely made it plain that any conditions governing their contact would be his.

From his table, at the foot of the street leading from the *piazza*, Egerton could see a courtyard flanked by a dusty villa and buildings of more utilitarian design. People had begun to emerge into the courtyard from a corner of one of the buildings. He caught the glint of glass in coaches sliding by behind and realised this must be the town's railway station.

It was perhaps the way Syce would arrive; on the telephone he had spoken of never driving unless forced to do so. But the few men among the travellers who made their way up the street were unmistakably Italian; the remainder were young girls carrying books, possibly returned from a college down the line. A pair of them took the table alongside his own. When they had ordered their coffee, they sat in silence, their faces dull with boredom. They were waiting for something, but their posture and listlessness announced that the wait could never carry a reward to match their dreams.

He failed to notice until it was quite near, the figure that approached him from the direction of the *piazza*. The man was dressed in a bright orange shirt, khaki shorts and a broad straw hat of a type he had seen worn by workers in the fields on the way from Pisa. He was perhaps in his late fifties, untidy and rather bent, as though an upright carriage had already become burdensome. The features, the whole physical conformation, were unmistakeably North European. It had to be Syce.

He stood to signal his presence at the bar but Syce was keeping his eyes down; he might have been climbing a hill. Only as he reached Egerton's table did he raise his head. His manner now acknowledged he had been aware of Egerton some way back; it was as though their meeting was a tryst not to be acknowledged until the last moment. 'Mr Egerton?' He extended a hand. 'Well met.'

Seating himself, Syce placed a shabby document wallet beside him. He was panting, obviously not in first-class condition. His face showed he was no longer a reliable shaver, either. But his eyes under the straggly ginger brows were sharp and full of life.

'You hired a car at Pisa as I suggested?'

'Yes.'

'Not the most attractive of drives. Too many lunatics on the road. Soon there'll be the main tourist invasion. We don't get the worst of the British, thank God, but they'll still be about the place like ants. Most of them revoltingly well-heeled.'

'Can I order you something?' Egerton had started to beckon the waiter but Syce waved him away, reinforcing his gesture with a volley of ornate Italian that caused the girls at the nearby table to stare. 'I've told him we'll order our drinks a little later. There are a few preliminaries I'd like to get out of the way first.'

He had kept on the straw hat. He pushed it back now to mop his forehead with a handkerchief marked by what looked like a mixture of oil and bloodstains. The hat didn't suit him but he was plainly attached to it, his symbol of honest toil perhaps.

'I expect you've been to this part of Italy before?'

'I spent a short time in Florence as a schoolboy nearly fifteen years ago. But that's all.'

'It's still Arcady, you'll be glad to know – for as long as they allow it to survive. That may not be too long. Florence has already become impossible.' He was back to tourists again. 'Vast, moon-faced armies, wandering everywhere, clicking their cameras, eating as they go, and chattering, always chattering. You have to have stillness to absorb what Florence has to say about our civilisation, and, God knows, we need to listen. Only in mid-winter are you likely to find you can.'

A man went by, pushing a handcart full of picture frames. Syce paused to watch. 'The lesson the Florentines could teach the modern world, if it *were* capable of listening, is how to strike the balance between the pursuit of money and the achievement of the cultivated life. Thatcherism with a Human Face, one might once have called it, I suppose.'

He gave a throaty laugh. He sounded like a fugitive schoolmaster, sick of tiresome and ungrateful youth.

'Perhaps I shouldn't have said that!' He was grinning. 'Were you working in the Party's Central Office in those days?'

'No.'

'Ah.' The blue eyes were putting an age to him, forming more queries. 'What were you doing?'

'I began in a merchant bank when I came down from university.'

'And you went to Central Office from there?'

'Yes.'

It seemed to satisfy him for the time being. 'Clearly you must know the Prime Minister pretty well for him to have sent you. I hope he's quite fit.' When Egerton had responded, he went on. 'And his sister? Or perhaps you don't know her?' There seemed an odd nuance to the enquiry.

'No, I don't know her.'

'Anyway I appreciate his responding so quickly to my letter. You've seen it, I suppose.'

'Yes.'

'I feared he might think I was just an old fool with a bee in my bonnet.' Syce was still holding the handkerchief with which he had mopped his forehead. He stared without embarrassment at its condition before tucking it into the back pocket of his shorts.

'Although I've never had dealings with him, I admire the PM greatly; it would be a tragedy if he were not re-elected next time. And rather a frightening tragedy in the circumstances.'

It seemed they were at last getting down to business. 'However,' Syce said, 'before we go further perhaps I could see the authority I asked you to bring. We shall be dealing with very delicate matters. Odd things can happen to arrangements made by telephone.'

He conveyed to a remarkable extent a conviction that he was in charge of the entire proceedings. During their telephone conversation yesterday he had made great play of his insistence that Egerton should bring with him not only Central Office credentials but also a letter from the Prime Minister, personally authorising him to tell Egerton what he knew. Pagett, when informed, had displayed extreme irritation but had finally secured both requirements.

Syce read it with the aid of wire-framed spectacles taken from the document wallet. When he had finished, he placed it under a corner of the wallet. 'I'm sorry to appear fussy. I needed to make absolutely sure I was getting the Prime Minister's ear. You'll have gathered from *my* letter, the story has already failed to reach him once.'

'You implied it had been suppressed.'

'Yes.'

'Do you actually know that for a fact?'

'I do. Nothing was done about it.'

'Wasn't it believed?'

'I'd rather not comment on possible reasons except to say lack of belief couldn't reasonably have entered into it. The Prime Minister will no doubt make up his own mind on the motives of the person concerned when he conducts an investigation, which I assume he will.'

He smiled again. He had sharp, rather irregular teeth, obviously neglected. 'I think we should now have a bottle of wine. You have come to the most splendid region in the world for honest red wine.'

He went inside the bar and was gone some time. Through the open door, Egerton could see him in conversation with the proprietor. His expression and gestures had become extravagant, he was almost the caricature of an excitable local. But he was not comic, he was too serious about whatever he was saying for that.

He returned looking triumphant. 'Not my first choice, but an excellent *classico*. You will be delighted.'

They drank, had almost finished the bottle before Syce's story was over. Egerton was aware before they were half-way through it that he would need to fight against becoming over-relaxed. An openness seemed to suffuse the atmosphere as the shadows lengthened and more people appeared on the streets to greet each other. Even the girls at the next table had lost their gloom. Joined by a third, they had started to talk and laugh.

Syce had begun almost hesitantly, the fingers of one hand constantly returning to fidget with the stem of his glass. 'Doing this gives me no pleasure. I realise it can only have the result of destroying the career of someone who seems personally likeable. But living abroad doesn't remove one's concern for one's native country.'

He took the straw hat off to mop the crown of his head. He was nearly bald, with just a few strands of ginger hair straggling across the scalp. 'What do you *know* about Druitt?'

Deciding how best to answer was difficult but Syce saved him doing so. 'I suppose at Party Headquarters you keep a fat file on him along with all the rest of the Opposition Front Bench. Does the word Pugwash ring a bell in that connection?'

The bell was nearly audible. 'Wasn't it an unofficial disarmament movement started by Bertrand Russell and others in the fifties?'

'Not really a movement, although it acquired some of the characteristics of one. Pugwash was a curious phenomenon that grew directly out of the Cold War. Some quite distinguished scientists, including Nobel Prize winners, issued an appeal to other scientists in the East and West to meet and discuss the dangers from atomic weapons. The first meeting was held in a small village in Novia Scotia called Pugwash, and the name stuck during the subsequent meetings.

'Pugwash spawned study groups among people who weren't scientists. One of the longest-surviving of these groups – it seems to have gone on into the middle eighties – was formed by writers. It met in different European capitals and was open to authors, journalists and pretty well anybody involved in the media. A short time ago I was in Paris on business and I met a journalist there, a Frenchman who was at a number of this group's conferences. His name was Pierre Massenet. He's now retired and lives in an apartment in the VIIth District. He told some amusing stories about the mental acrobatics needed at each meeting to produce a communique acceptable to both sides. However the really important thing he had to say was about the activities of a British delegate to the 1979 meeting in Vienna. This was Druitt.'

Now that he was getting into his stride, Syce seemed to lose his ex-schoolmaster manner. He had a way of telling a story that was compelling. 'On the last evening of the meeting Massenet was unwell and stayed in his room, which was next to Druitt's. He became aware that Druitt had visitors, another man and a child. After a certain amount of conversation which he couldn't catch, he heard noises from the child, as though it was in a certain amount of pain, followed by reassuring sounds from the men. There were other noises later, but not from the child.

'Massenet was curious about what had gone on. When he eventually heard Druitt's door open he looked out of his own. The visitors were standing in the corridor while Druitt said some parting words to the other man. He noticed the child, who looked rather bored and knowing, was a boy of nine or ten. Druitt happened to glance sideways and saw Massenet. He went rather pink and made a show of saying goodbye to the man and the boy in a very formal way.'

'So what did Massenet believe had happened in the room?'

'He didn't have any doubt that the boy had been brought there for sexual purposes.'

'But Massenet didn't see that happening – you said in your letter that he was a witness.'

'Massenet says the noises he heard were consistent with only one thing – the boy was being sexually abused. He's sure of it.'

'Did he speak to anybody else about it?'

'Not until after he'd discovered by chance the identity of the man who'd brought the boy to Druitt's room. A year or two later he came across an item in an Austrian newspaper which he took for professional purposes. It was reporting the conviction in an Austrian court of the director of a children's orphanage. He'd been found guilty of procuring children for prostitution. The case had had political overtones because two Austrian politicians had used the man's services to obtain children for sexual purposes.'

'How did Massenet know this was the man he'd seen?'

'His photograph appeared in the newspaper. He was a very distinctive-looking person.'

'Do you know what his name was?'

'I believe it was Reinholdt – Alois Reinholdt.'

'So what did Massenet do then?'

'By this time of course Druitt was a rising star in the Labour

Party and already tipped for the leadership. Massenet decided that on the assumption that the sexual abuse of children was not yet an acceptable pastime for senior British politicians, he ought to pass on what he knew to someone in Whitehall.'

'Was it to somebody in the Foreign Office, the Home Office . . .'

Syce was holding up a hand. 'I've done my stuff. Better for you to see Massenet now.' He took a sheet of paper from the document wallet. 'I've typed out his address and telephone number. I've also told him I'm telling you what I know. He's expecting you to call him. He knows you're someone who's been sent from London to make sure the information is properly handled this time.'

'Did you mention the Prime Minister as having sent me?'

'No, I just said you'd have the right authority.'

A deep sense of anti-climax overtook Egerton. What this was boiling down to was gossip about a single event that had happened – if it happened at all – over ten years ago. Even if Massenet proved convincing when seen, the chances of getting corroboration for his story seemed non-existent.

The sun had dipped further, a shaft was entering his eyes. As he shifted in his chair, his gaze was caught by a woman standing in the shadow of a shop entrance some yards down the street towards the railway station. She was holding a camera which seemed pointed towards himself and Syce.

He touched Syce's arm. 'What makes us so special?'

Syce swivelled in his chair. After a few moments, he said, with apparent amusement, 'Perhaps this bar holds a nostalgic memory for her. Either that or she can't resist my hat. Few can.' Moving it further back on his head, he turned towards the woman.

But apparently she was no longer tempted. Slinging the camera on her shoulder she sauntered up the street toward the *piazza*, occasionally stopping to glance in shop windows as she went. Now that she was out in the sunlight Egerton could see that she was a tall blonde, attractive enough to turn the heads of some of the male strollers. She was dressed in dazzling lemon trousers and a sleeveless white top. He judged her to be in her late thirties. She didn't look back before disappearing in to the *piazza*. It had been a mildly disconcerting happening but it seemed harmless enough.

Another knot of people emerged from the railway station. One or two of the men carried document cases. 'Where would they have come from?' he asked.

'Empoli. Or Florence – it's only twenty miles or so away. Commuters probably.' Syce poured out more of the wine. 'I suppose you do the same to London each day. Or have you a London house?'

'I live in a flat in Battersea.'

'Battersea!' Syce smiled. 'Think: if you lived here, in Boccaccio's town – did you know that's what Certaldo is? – you might travel by that train to work in the most wonderful city in the world.' He had apparently forgotten his lament about the state of Florence. 'In your apartment on the hill behind us, you would be at the heart of the civilisation that produced you.'

'Opportunity is all.'

'You must make your opportunities. As I have done.' He sat back, still smiling.

On the hand and arm with which he had gestured towards the houses behind them, there were blue stains. He caught Egerton's glance. 'Copper sulphate – I was spraying my vines before I came to meet you. Rather late I'm afraid. There are always too many things to do, even on a *podere* as small as mine.'

'Is it nearby?'

'Not too far.'

'Before you came here, were you living in England?'

'Yes. One day the year before last I reached a decision. I decided it was stupid not to attempt something I'd always dreamed of doing before age made it impossible. So my wife and I upped sticks. We return to Britain very occasionally, to visit our daughter who is handicapped and in hospital there. As long as she's alive we shall do that. But this is where I want to die. I have twelves acres, enough to provide a basis for existence. A little arable, a cow, a few pigs and hens, vines and olives of course, the odd fruit tree. Not a particularly good position and the house is a little gloomy. But I knew I had to have it when I saw the *cantina* which is *immense*! I was going to be able to make my own wine! There was no turning back then. I couldn't wait for my first *vendemmia*.' He was over-fond of using Italian, elaborately enunciated; but on the tide of his enthusiasm, the effect was not irritating.

'What were you doing before?'

Syce studied the stains on his skin. 'If you don't mind, I'd rather not go into the past. It involves painful memories.'

'I ask only because I'm sure the Prime Minister will ask me. He will naturally be interested.'

'I'm sorry, but there you are. Massenet is the man you want. My only purpose is to bring you together. Perhaps when the PM has taken the necessary action, we can talk more. Come for this year's *vendemmia*!' He was steering the conversation away fast. 'Have you ever been to one?'

'No.'

'Magical! Every day I go to break the crust on the vats. Below me this mysterious bubbling is going on. I stay just listening, sharing the anticipation of everyone who has ever made wine since the world began. Have you read Virgil?'

Egerton smiled. '*The Georgics*? Yes.'

'So you know *The Georgics*! Splendid!' His delight was plainly genuine. 'I taught Latin when I was younger.'

So he *had* been a schoolmaster at some time.

'I can't remember enough of them to quote. But the flavour's stayed with me,' Egerton said.

'Virgil becomes extraordinarily real in this country. I find he's also very reliable on most aspects of farming. I can think of him as living over the hill from my place. I can see him walking among the vines, saying they'd be better if they were tied in such and such a way.'

Where affectation took over from genuine feeling was hard to tell. Syce was intent on giving the impression of a man totally fulfilled. But there was also something working away inside him that Egerton found impossible to identify, but could be bitterness.

Syce looked at his watch. 'I ought to get back. I think I told you the man who helps me is ill.' He gathered up the document wallet. Upright again, he cut an ungainly, almost comic figure. The hat didn't suit him at all, and the khaki shorts were too wide; from beneath his kneecaps, the flesh drooped to the edge of brown woollen stockings. There was only one nationality he could possibly be.

They shook hands. A woman with a child in a pushchair veered in front of Syce as he moved off. Removing the straw hat, he stepped back elaborately. About him was the same rather florid courtliness that Egerton associated with Ludo Fender.

Watching Syce's figure recede, he faced up to two disconcerting thoughts. The lesser was the realisation that at some moment Syce had slipped into the document wallet the Prime Minister's letter of authority which he had intended to recover. Presumably Syce was planning to keep it as a souvenir of his dealings over Druitt. That was tiresome but not disastrous. The more disagreeable thought was that he had succeeded in discovering nothing substantial about Syce himself. It might be irrelevant to the main issue of what Druitt had or hadn't been up to, but detail, comprehensive and meticulous detail, would be what Pagett was expecting to be told about all aspects of the affair. Syce's current address would be a minimum requirement. And who exactly was he? To report merely that he seemed to be an intelligent, if mildly affected, creature passing on the result of a chance meeting in Paris for others to explore further would not be enough by a long chalk. Somehow, Syce had to be housed as a preliminary to more investigation.

Syce had come from the direction of the *piazza*, so in all probability he was on his way to a vehicle parked there. Following in his footsteps up the same street was ruled out in case Syce looked round. But in his earlier walk round the town Egerton had noticed a parallel street not far from the bar which led to another corner of the *piazza*. If he ran hard he could hope to reach his car in the *piazza* before Syce got away.

Luck was with him. He arrived to see Syce climbing into a

blue three-wheeler truck on the far side. He watched until the truck turned down towards the river then followed. Outside Certaldo, Syce took a minor road winding through open country. The difficulty now in keeping discreetly on his tail lay in the snail's pace of the three-wheeler. Egerton found himself unique among cars approaching from behind in declining to pass. When the risk of being observed began to seem great, the day was saved by the appearance ahead of a heavier truck loaded with bricks which even Syce's truck was able to get in front of.

The brick truck still between them, they skirted the edge of a walled town which Egerton guessed must be San Gimignano. At a junction on the outskirts they passed a sign marked Poggibonsi but Syce and the brick truck both took a different road. After another minute or two the brick truck began to pull into the side and Egerton saw with relief that only a hundred yards further on Syce was swinging off the tarmac too. He had taken a track along which was visible a small *podere*.

Egerton waited until Syce's dust cloud had settled then walked cautiously up the track. There had been the decaying remnants of a gate at the entrance but no name board. A little way ahead he saw a clump of cypresses which might give cover from which to observe the place. He advanced to the cypresses.

Even in its palmier days, the *podere* must have had a dour look. A plain stone box, it was frogged by square shutters of which the wood was badly in need of paint. In a yard that had only now come into view was the truck. With it was another car, similar to the one he was driving himself, and also with Pisa plates. Beyond the yard were outbuildings, dilapidated to a point where collapse seemed an imminent danger. Syce had obviously spent nothing on the place since moving in.

A woman emerged from the house carrying a tray; on it were three glasses and a bottle of wine. She looked about Syce's age. The blouse and skirt she wore were black, the skirt voluminous and long enough to sweep the ground, yet her quick movements somehow didn't suggest a local. Crossing a strip of rough grass, she disappeared towards the other side of the house. Presumably Syce and, perhaps, the driver of the other car were there, enjoying the cool of the evening.

At least he knew where to find Syce again. He decided to withdraw and consider when and how to tackle him once more and in the process discover where he'd acquired his knowledge of the Benskin business, which the Prime Minister would certainly want to know. Returning to his car he noticed a sign beside the road announcing that a straggle of houses to which he now saw the *podere* could be said to belong, was San Donato. So this was Syce's piece of Arcady.

At his hotel in Certaldo he ate his evening meal and made notes. An initial plan to surprise Syce the following morning gave way in favour of seeing Massenet first. He might after all turn out to be so unconvincing a witness that pursuing the enquiry further would be pointless. If not, there was a possibility he would have picked up something about Syce that would be useful in having a second go in San Donato the following day.

His call to Massenet's number was answered by a man-servant speaking a curious, glottic French. Massenet, when he came on the line, sounded bored but polite enough. They agreed on six-thirty the next evening as the time for Egerton to call at his apartment.

The manservant who opened the door of Massenet's apartment was an Oriental, which explained the liquid quality of the French in which the telephone had been answered the previous evening. Lithe and handsome, he looked as though he might be Vietnamese, although taller than most of his race. He led the way across the parquet of the entrance hall to a corridor from which several doors led off. The apartment was clearly very large. Studio photographs which, from the clothing worn by the subjects, reached back a century or more covered the walls of the corridor. Massenet obviously relished reminders of his forbears, unlovely though most of them seemed to be. Elaborate coats of arms were incorporated in some of the frames.

They entered a library. A small man, immaculate in a black

pincord suit worn with a roll collar shirt of dazzling whiteness, rose from an armchair and greeted Egerton with rather languid enquiries about the comfort of the journey from Pisa. His manner was ironical, tending towards fatigued patience. The prospect of anything approaching warmth in the discussion to come was already inconceivable.

The room was shadowed and indistinct in its corners, the only illumination coming from a standard lamp beside a desk and the pencil of light suspended over an oil painting portrait, presumably of another ancestor. The books lining three of the walls were backed by mirror glass and had, as dividers, polished metal strips. Apart from two armchairs, the furniture was black lacquer, trimmed here and there with metal strips like those on the bookshelves. The effect was severe, a calculated match for Massenet's own appearance.

Massenet had paused behind the desk to reach something inside a drawer. Then he seemed to change his mind and raised a hand for the servant who had been waiting by the door to advance and take orders for drinks. At a guess he was in his early sixties. His blue-white hair, slightly bouffant, had plainly been sprayed to remove any risk of disturbance. The eyebrows were equally neat. Only an area of donkey-coloured whiskers in his short beard quarrelled with the starkness of definition that was obviously a passion with him.

When their drinks had arrived he told his story of the incident in Vienna as convincingly as Syce had forecast and with an expert's gift for clarity and relevant detail. It matched the account Syce had given in every detail. Egerton said at the end, 'How can you be so sure the sounds you heard meant the child was being used in a sexual way?'

Massenet shrugged, allowed Egerton a brief, weary smile. 'The musical score for copulation has a monotonously narrow range. The sounds were unmistakeable, I assure you, Mr Egerton.' Suddenly he turned his head sideways to stare at the manservant who had remained in the shadows. Some silent message was being conveyed and apparently resisted by the other. Massenet flicked with the finger of one hand. Still the servant made no move, his eyes fixed on Massenet. A crisis of an emotional character had been reached. Then with the same abruptness of movement Massenet had shown, the servant turned on his heel and went out of the door. Massenet continued speaking as though nothing had happened, 'What else can I help you with?'

'I understand you've already reported what you saw and heard.'

'Yes, about two years ago.'

'This was after you read the newspaper item of the prosecution in Vienna of the man you saw with the child outside Mr Druitt's room.'

'Yes.' Massenet took a folder from his desk and extracted a cutting from an Austrian newspaper. It gave a summary of the trial of Alois Reinholdt, the Director of a children's orphanage, for procuring children in his care for prostitution. Two members of the ruling party in the Government had been separately convicted for offences against boys who had been in Reinholdt's care. From the evidence quoted – which referred to Reinholdt arranging orgies for pederasts, some of whom came from outside Austria for the purpose – the sentence of four years' imprisonment seemed extraordinarily light. Noting down the details, Egerton was struck by a thought. 'You said it was two years ago you contacted somebody in London about this. But I see this news item is more than eight years old.'

Massenet made a gesture of impatience. 'It was two years ago that I had the need to contact British Security. That was when I passed on my information.'

It was the first discrepancy between Syce's account and Massenet's. Plainly he had not bothered about telling his story when he saw the news item. He had kept it to use at a later date when he found personal advantage in doing so. 'Could I ask why you needed to see British Security?' Egerton asked.

'They had information I wanted. I have been writing a biography of my father, who was a pilot during the First World War and a member of the Resistance in the Second. In 1943 he was captured by the Germans at a dropping point for weapons from England. He and all the members of the cell he controlled were shot. Some historians have alleged this was because he had been indiscreet, but I am sure he was betrayed by someone you are too young to have heard of, Henri Dericourt, who had been a trusted friend. Dericourt was an agent of the British SOE, who were careless of the fact that he also had links with the Germans.' Massenet inspected his fingernails with an expression of scorn. 'At the end of the war he was tried by a French court for treachery but the betrayal of my father was never brought up in the proceedings and the truth has therefore never been published. However I discovered that on an occasion when he was recalled to London for interrogation because of French Resistance concern about his German links, he was questioned about my father's betrayal. It occurred to me I might find out what he had said from the department which had carried out the interrogation, the British Security Service.'

'So that's where you went with your information?'

'Yes. I was thanked warmly and told it would be reported to the Director General, Sir Richard Goble.'

'Did you hear any more?'

'A week or so later, a Mr Bridewell, who I understand is a senior officer in the Security Service, wrote to me.' Massenet took another paper from the folder and handed it to Egerton. It was a handwritten letter from what seemed to be a private address in Pimlico – some outpost of the Security Service when dealing with the public, perhaps.

Dear Monsieur Massenet,

I am pleased to enclose some extracts from the report you spoke of when you called recently. They are the only references to your father it contains. Although I am unable to give you permission for their verbatim use in your biography of your father, there would be no objection if they are paraphrased and attributed to 'British official sources'. I would welcome your letting me see the form of words you intend to use.

I confirm the information which you were good

enough to give to my colleague has been passed to
the Director General. Your desire to be of assistance
is much appreciated.

Yours sincerely,
Jeremy Bridewell

Egerton handed back the letter. 'And you heard no more?'
'Nothing.'

The manservant reappeared to offer fresh drinks although
their glasses were only half-empty. Withdrawing in frustration, he shot a smouldering glance at Massenet as though he
was in some way to blame. This time Massenet ignored him.
Egerton picked up the newspaper cutting again and studied the
photograph of Alois Reinholdt. 'You're in no doubt this is the
man who brought the child to Mr Druitt?'

'No doubt at all. I have an excellent memory for features.'
And to forget that heavy-lipped mouth and the fleshy cheeks
surmounted by wire-rimmed spectacles, Egerton reflected,
would not be easy.

'I suppose you haven't heard anything of Reinholdt's
whereabouts since he left prison?'

'Out of curiosity I made some enquiries when I was in
Vienna earlier this year. It was said he went to Mexico as soon
as he was released.'

Massenet leaned forward in his chair, at the same time
raising his eyebrows. It was the clearest possible signal that he
regarded the usefulness of the interview as now exhausted.
Egerton put down his glass. 'Mr Syce sent you his regards. A
very interesting man – you know of course about his farm?'

'I believe he told me.'

'Quite a change from his earlier life. I expect he told you a
little about that?'

Massenet stood up. 'I did not discuss Mr Syce's interests
with him.' Either he knew nothing of Syce's background or
Syce had asked him to avoid the subject. He was not a man
who would often be tempted to take a fly cast over him.

There didn't seem more that could usefully be pursued for
the time being. Egerton put away his notes and Massenet rose

to his feet to speed his departure. 'You know Sir Richard Goble perhaps?'

'Only by sight.'

Massenet smiled enigmatically. 'But you will now be reporting to your Prime Minister of course. Perhaps you will remind him of an occasion when we met. He was good enough to give me an exclusive interview during his visit to United Nations headquarters when I was working in Washington. Please give him my good wishes.' Syce had obviously told him more than he had admitted and Massenet was keen to have it known that Prime Ministers were nothing out of the way for him.

He accompanied Egerton across the hall to the apartment door. The manservant reappeared from another door and stood watching with an expression of sullen resentment. Perhaps he was aggrieved at being done out of what he regarded as his proper duties, but the reaction was obviously excessive. As the door closed behind Egerton, he heard Massenet's voice raised in cold anger, followed by the man-servant replying at an even higher pitch. Then the voices faded as another door closed within.

· Four ·

It was late in the afternoon of the following day when he made his way toward the house in San Donato to which he had tailed Syce. Sweetcorn grew untidily in the field that separated the house from the road; in amongst the corn were what looked like barren pear trees. All the shutters on the house were closed, but he was relieved to see the three-wheeler truck in the yard, a small tractor alongside. Presumably that meant Syce was at home although, apart from quarrelling fowl in the shadow of the truck, there was no sign of life around the yard or outbuildings.

No-one came to his knock on the door of the house. Pushing, he found it open and began a cautious reconnaissance inside. Syce and spouse were conceivably still having a siesta; the atmosphere of the afternoon had an enervating quality likely to discourage an early return to labour. But, all the same, the time was past four o'clock.

Calling up the stairs raised no response. After he had checked the rooms below, he went to look in the outbuildings. It was as he emerged from the last of these that he saw them. At the rear of the outbuildings, rows of vines growing in soil the colour of milk chocolate stretched away for perhaps two hundred metres until halted by a cypress-covered hill. At almost the furthest point along a row, a figure in a straw hat and orange shirt was engaged in tying-in vines. As Egerton watched, another figure moved in front of the first, also straw-hatted but wearing a long black skirt. It was the woman he had seen carrying a tray three days before.

About to advance, he paused, then went back inside the

house. The window at one end of the living room looked round a corner of the outbuildings sufficiently to provide a view of the rows of vines. By pushing its shutters a little further ajar, he would be forewarned of any move towards the house. Not to take the opportunity of discovering whether the desk beneath it or the cupboards elsewhere in the room offered information about Syce would be foolish.

A quick glance in cupboards showed they held nothing more than china and glass. He looked about the rest of the room before tackling the desk. The general effect was spartan. A settee and armchairs in a lavender-striped material that went uneasily with the bare plastered walls and ceiling beams were the only concessions to comfort. He guessed they had been brought from England and from a suburban lifestyle. There was a rough bookcase which held a fair range of classics, some works on modern political history, but no novels. Farming magazines, English and Italian, were stacked untidily on the bottom shelf.

He turned back to the desk. A studio photograph of a young woman, with the same set of jaw as Syce's gazed at him. She had forced herself to smile, almost to laugh, for the photographer; but the eyes looked beyond to something that was no laughing matter.

Alongside, secured by a bulldog clip, a collection of letters recorded a correspondence with an Italian government body apparently empowered to make grants for agricultural purposes. A request for financial assistance in setting up a pig-rearing unit at the *podere* had been made by Syce. The latest letter, now several weeks old, was from the grant body and refused all help. Its language was unusually brusque for Italian officialdom; patience had worn thin; the writer had even managed to spell Syce's name wrong, addressing him as Sisson.

It was the first drawer of the desk that yielded gold, a passport. Opening it, Egerton saw that the writer at the grant body had not been careless after all. The holder of the passport and, from the photograph inside, the correct name of the man who had come to the bar in Certaldo, was James Everard

Sisson. He had been fifty-five when the passport was issued two years ago and employed as a government official. Underneath was another passport, issued to Aileen Jessie Sisson. A face looked out from the photograph that was cheerfully plain, the grey hair drawn tightly back to the neck, the features, without question, a cosmetic-free zone.

None of the other drawers proved interesting until he reached the bottom one. Among a collection of bills and mail shots was a large buff envelope. The letter inside had come from a bank in Ealing, and stated that, in accordance with Sisson's instructions, the mail redirected to the bank during the past four weeks from his previous address in Ealing was enclosed.

Sisson had apparently found the other contents of the envelope of little interest and stuffed them back inside after tearing the covers open. All were circulars apart from one letter, a printed advice note from the Paymaster General's Office in Hounslow. It stated that the sum of £672, being pension due for the previous month, after deduction of tax, had been paid to the credit of Sisson's account at the bank. The name of the sponsoring department shown at the foot of the note proved the best piece of information of all. Sisson had been a member of the Security Service.

He had closed the drawer again and was wondering whether to look in any of the other rooms when a telephone bell made him start. He went to the instrument in the hall and stared at it. Sisson was too far away to have heard the bell. The call could be ignored. On the other hand, by lifting the receiver he might pick up some more useful information.

A woman spoke. 'Everard, have I dragged you away from something important?'

He made a non-committal sound. She came back, more cautiously this time. 'Everard, is that you?' The accent could have been American.

There was no point in fencing. 'No this is a friend. Who's calling?'

'It's . . .' she began, then stopped. 'Perhaps I'll call back.'

'Can I give him a message? Or I could fetch him? I arrived

and found the door open but I see he's working among the vines. Just tell me who it is.'

There was a pause before she said decisively, 'Don't bother, I'll call again later.'

He returned to the living room, closed the shutters and went outside to walk to the head of the row of vines down which Sisson and the woman were working.

The woman saw him first, raising an arm to wipe sweat from her face. He was certain now this was Aileen Sisson. She touched Sisson's shoulder and they came towards him, stumbling a little on the uneven soil.

It was not until they were about twenty metres away that Sisson finally recognised him. He looked satisfactorily disconcerted. 'Egerton!'

He hurried forward, surprise and anxiety equally mixed in his expression. 'How did you get here?'

'By car.'

'I meant — how did you find me?'

'It wasn't difficult.'

He had halted now, searching Egerton's face for some hint of the answer. Aileen Sisson came and stood beside him. She was carrying the basket of tools and twine they had used in their work on the vines. The unliberated air hinted at in the passport photograph seemed amply confirmed by her manner. Sisson said, 'Aileen, this is Egerton, who was sent by the Prime Minister to see me the other day.'

The hand she held out was as large as his own. She was not unlike Sisson, raw-boned and tending to clumsiness. Like the skirt, her blouse was an unrelieved black. Plainly she hoped to be indistinguishable from women in the other farms around, to be absorbed into the background she and Sisson had chosen for their new life.

Sisson pointed to a stone table that stood in an arbour covered by wisteria. 'Shall we sit in the shade?' This, Egerton guessed, was where he and his visitor had been when he had watched Aileen Sisson carrying the tray from the house on the last occasion.

They moved towards the arbour. 'You saw Massenet?' Sisson said.

'Yes.'

'And you got the story, the full story?' He was still trying to overcome an unease at Egerton's unheralded appearance. 'What was the Prime Minister's reaction?'

'He's abroad until the weekend. I've been making further enquiries in the meantime. That's why I'm back.'

'What enquiries?'

It was the moment to be firm. 'I want to know why, among other things, you withheld from me the fact that you'd been a member of the Security Service. And that your name isn't Syce, as you signed your letter to the Prime Minister, but Sisson, James Everard Sisson.'

For a moment he looked utterly cast down. 'I suppose you've talked to Goble.'

'No. But you'll understand the Prime Minister will expect a full explanation.'

'You mean you've had no contact with the Security Service about what Massenet and I have told you?'

'Not so far. Why?'

The features relaxed somewhat. 'Thank God for that.' He gestured towards one of the benches beside the table. 'So I can still hope to get the truth through.'

Aileen Sisson was standing beside them, looking uncertainly at Sisson. She said in a rush, 'I'll bring some tea.' She went away. Sisson continued. 'I know I owe you and the Prime Minister an apology. After we parted in Certaldo I felt increasingly it had been a mistake not to have been frank with you. I'd been obsessed with the need to be sure that nobody had a chance to try and discredit me before I got the facts to the Prime Minister. I knew that would happen if my identity was known.'

'You knew about the Druitt story from your employment . . .'

'Yes.'

'In fact you were the officer who received Massenet's

information in the first place.' Sisson's expression told him his guess had been right. 'Why weren't you prepared to say so the other day?'

Sisson wiped his face with what looked like the same handkerchief that had served in Certaldo. 'I had a good reason.' He sighed. 'How did you find out where I live?'

'It's not relevant now. But you have to give me *all* the facts this time.'

'Of course. I'm glad there's no more need to hold back. You're right that I discovered there'd been a cover-up of the case when I was in the Security Service. I finally decided I had to speak out by telling the Prime Minister what I knew. But I faced a dilemma. I wasn't in England and in a position to reach him directly.

'I had to write. But I knew he would take no notice of my letter until he'd checked police and security records to discover if I was known as a nut or worse. Any reference to my past employers that identified me would have produced a report intended to persuade him that nothing I had to say could be relied on.

'After thinking it over for some time I decided to alter my name in the letter just enough to remove that risk. We stayed at a hotel in Poggibonsi for a week or so when we first came to Tuscany and I used that address. I told the manager and the girl who sits on the switchboard there would be calls for me from somebody who might have got my name slightly wrong. I asked that nothing should be said in reply but that I should be called here with whatever message was received.'

'And what about your insistence that you shouldn't be visited by an official?'

'I reckoned I had to keep officials out of this. Eventually there would have been a closing of ranks to protect one of their own.'

'Druitt isn't one of their own.'

'I wasn't thinking of Druitt.'

He was almost at ease now. 'Look, why don't I give you the whole story over tea? Come and see my domain while we're waiting for Aileen to bring it.'

He led Egerton back to the yard, explained his use of the different outbuildings in enthusiastic detail and then drew him to a corner of the garden where the land fell away. Over a valley geometrically divided into vine and olive plantations, with a single startling field of sunflowers at its edge, were softly rounded hills, cypress-covered. Beyond and above the hills, as though suspended from the sky, a ghost city hung behind a gauze of humid heat.

'San Gimignano, city of towers,' Sisson said. '*Della bella torri*. Less poetically, my local market town.'

The over-careful enunciation of the Italian words seemed to have less affectation to it this time. There could even have been a slightly mocking quality.

'You've probably heard the story of the towers. Each great medieval family in San Gimignano had to have its own watch tower. One-upmanship was the deciding factor when it came to how high they went. When the sun's in a certain position they can look rather magical. Otherwise I'm not so sure. In fact sometimes I'm reminded of the old Battersea Power Station.'

He gave a short cackle of a laugh. It was a relief to discover there was a limit to his infatuation with his surroundings. He went on, 'Don't you think I've chosen the most beautiful place to live? There's nothing more Aileen and I could want for ourselves. Extra money would be nice of course, for improving the place. But if you're doing what you want, it's not important.'

Aileen came to call them to the arbour. As they sat down again, Egerton said, 'Before I forget – when I got to your house earlier, the telephone rang. I thought I'd better answer it. It was a woman.'

Aileen's face became suddenly anxious. 'Was it a call from England? From a hospital?'

'She gave no name and said she'd call back. I thought the voice could have been American actually.'

They looked relieved. Sisson said, 'Forgive us if we seemed tense. We tend to dread a call from England. Our daughter in hospital there was well enough when we visited her last. But she can have rather worrying relapses. When there's a major crisis one of us tries to go over and be with her.'

'I'm pretty sure it was nothing like that.'

A fresh round loaf lay on the table, together with butter on a dish of ice, honey in an earthenware pot. Aileen had placed a bowl of wild flowers alongside. The scent rising from the teapot mingled with that of the flowers. It wasn't exactly Arcady, perhaps, but with that sensuous landscape stretching before them, near enough.

Sisson said, 'Well, let me fill you in. A couple of years ago I was working in Bridewell's Division in the Security Service – in fact I was his immediate deputy. He came into my office one morning and said he wanted me to interview a French journalist named Pierre Massenet who wanted some information from us but also claimed to have some facts we would find important. Well, I did just that and learned what Druitt had been up to in Vienna all those years before. Having checked with a French contact that Massenet was regarded as a scrupulous reporter, I prepared a report and passed it to Bridewell for onward transmission to Goble, the Director General. Bridewell went off with it, saying that Goble would find it a hot potato and he wondered how he'd handle it.

'As you can imagine, I was curious to know the outcome. Eventually I asked Bridewell what Goble had decided to do. He shook his head and said, "Forget about that story." When I pressed him he went on that Goble had decided no action was needed.'

A line of ants which had appeared from a corner of the table was breaking into teams to bear away crumbs from the loaf. Sisson scattered them with a forefinger and then sat watching the teams reform. 'I told Bridewell I couldn't believe it. He gave me a tired look – he was already being pulled down by cancer although none of us knew then – and said, "If you can't see why – I'm not going to tell you." '

'What did that mean?'

'I had no idea. It was only much later I realised he was referring to the fact of Druitt and Goble being very close.'

'In what sense?'

'They were friends at university. I fancy they discovered they had similar sexual tastes when they were there.'

'Have you any evidence regarding Goble's sexual tastes?'

Sisson looked up from the ants. 'Let's just say one wouldn't think of Goble as the marrying kind.' There was a bitter edge to his voice. It was clear he hated Goble.

He continued. 'The conversation with Bridewell I've told you about was our last on the subject. He died in hospital five weeks later. A nice man – one of those people who serve their country to the limit and nobody gives a damn about.'

'Like someone else,' Aileen Sisson said. It was almost the first time she had spoken without prompting. She looked away with a sudden jerk of her head. When she looked back at them, Sisson shook his head at her, smiling. He carried on. 'I mulled things over after Bridewell went into hospital then decided to tackle Goble direct. One evening when I knew he'd be working late I bearded him in his office. I won't bore you with the whole conversation, which became a flaming row. The only thing I could get out of him was that, having known Druitt for a very long time, he was satisfied the visit of the child to his room had an innocent explanation. When I suggested that at least we ought to try to trace and interview the Reinholdt character, he said it was entirely unnecessary. I lost my temper at that point and said some foolish things. Goble replied that I could either accept his judgment or resign. Either way if he found I'd repeated Massenet's story anywhere else I should expect no mercy. That seemed to make my position intolerable. I resigned soon afterwards.'

'You felt he was simply covering up because he and Druitt were friends?'

'Yes.'

'Surely if you believed that then, it was the moment to go to the Prime Minister. Why wait two years?'

'At the time I knew only too well what would happen if I formed up at No. 10 for an appointment. One of the Private Secretaries would be told to check my record with Goble. Even before I got into the PM's study he would have read a note calculated to destroy my credibility – either by suggesting I was unbalanced or was working off spite against Goble. When Bridewell went into hospital Goble moved someone else into his post which most people had expected me to fill. So the spite angle could have seemed persuasive.'

'So you just resigned and did nothing?'

'Not very admirable I know. I felt I wanted to forget the whole bloody business, start a new life that had nothing to do with the past. But after I'd been here for a while I realised I couldn't live with myself if I allowed the situation to develop in which somebody with Druitt's disgusting habits could become Prime Minister, with his chum Goble at his side. So I located Massenet, told him what I planned to do and asked him to co-operate in concealing my background from whoever came to see us until I could be sure the Prime Minister would see the report without having been prejudiced against it.'

From within the house came the sound of the telephone bell. Pressing Aileen back onto the bench Sisson went off to answer it. Aileen's large hand reached tentatively across the table for Egerton's cup. When he handed it to her she thanked him. Her deference was embarrassing. She was deeply impressed, it seemed, by his credentials as Blackmer's personal envoy. But he also sensed that she would be a determined antagonist if she felt Sisson was not receiving the respect he deserved.

Birds were noisily disputing in the wisteria above them. 'Now, now,' she said warningly, looking upwards. The noise stopped. 'I don't allow quarrelling. My blackcap friend never quarrels. I don't think he's about at present. But he sings to me so sweetly some evenings, here or in the cherry tree over there.' She pointed. 'I shall make my flower garden beside that tree if we stay.'

'If?'

She became slightly embarrassed. 'Everard will decide when he can see ahead more clearly than at present.'

From the house drifted the sound of Sisson's cackling laugh. His caller was amusing or pleasing him. 'He's a brilliant person,' Aileen said. 'Others took advantage of that to advance their own careers. They took the praise, his reward was humiliation.'

'I'm sorry.'

'But he would never stoop to their level by complaining, or

paying them back. I hope that now you are able to give the Prime Minister the true facts, he will recognise there's been injustice, very grave injustice.'

Sisson returned. He made no reference to the call but it had obviously pleased him. If Aileen was curious about it, she gave no sign.

Egerton said, 'To revert to what you were saying – I understand of course your concern that your approach to the Prime Minister shouldn't be rubbished by Goble or anybody else before the facts were seen by him. I hope you realise, nevertheless, that by doing what you did, you were bound to raise suspicions of your motives.'

'I see it now of course. I'm afraid I was obsessed with the problem of keeping Goble out of the chain. He's a very influential figure in Whitehall as you must know. Also, although I don't want to sound melodramatic, I couldn't rule out some action being taken against myself. Living abroad doesn't remove the risk of that!'

'And I have your assurance now that you've held nothing back?'

He gave a twisted, apologetic smile. 'You do. I'm sorry to have put you to the trouble of this second visit.'

Aileen began to clear away the remains of the tea. 'Are you driving back to Pisa tonight?' Sisson asked.

'No, I've booked a hotel room in San Gimignano.'

'I hope you'll forgive me if I do a little more work on those vines before it gets dark. We're still behind with the tying-in.'

As he was about to leave them, Sisson produced another bottle of wine for him to take away. 'And for your wife' – he turned towards the bookshelves and made a choice – 'Petrarch, the most civilised of Tuscans.'

He turned a few pages of the book. 'Read it to each other in bed. And always remember this about Petrarch. He was the man who realised that mountains were not simply barriers to movement. They were there to be climbed simply to celebrate their existence and that of the climber. For our civilisation mountains acquired a different meaning once Petrarch told us that.'

Aileen produced a crumpled paper bag for protecting the book. As she was putting it inside, she was looking at Sisson, almost but not quite asking a question. He gazed back sharply but then seemed to grasp something. 'I wonder if we could ask a personal favour of you?'

'Of course.'

'It would involve calling in at a hospital in Wimbledon – with a gift for our daughter. Is that too much out of your way?'

'I should be happy to do it.'

At the hotel, he took Druitt's book from his bag and lay reading it in bed. The second time round it was not as compelling; but it remained impressive. All those years ago, when the critics were talking it up, its themes of public and private morality had been hardly fashionable. Yet it had somehow captured and held people's attention. It had also been a factor in propelling Druitt forward in the Labour Party. He had seemed above all the model of an unscruffy politician. That perception of him might be about to change.

· Five ·

Sweetwater was already in the bar when Louise entered. He was seated in the corner booth where their previous meetings had taken place. Securing it each time was the kind of coup he would relish, a symbol of influence and mysterious power. Removing his pipe from his mouth, he held the stem erect until she showed that she had sighted him.

She had not forseen on the flight from London, that she would be saddled with this before escaping to bed and oblivion. Having gone straight from Kennedy to the office, expecting to do no more than provide Hal Mencken with a run-down on the trip before she headed for her apartment, she had found herself checked by Hal's moist palm on her wrist as she rose at the end of her account.

'One thing before you go,' Hal had said. 'Brad Sweetwater called me last night. He asked if I knew what flight back you were catching. It happened I'd just had your message from London. He said he was coming down on the shuttle today and he might as well get your news before he went back to Washington.'

Fatigue was already affecting her; in a couple of hours she would feel like a zombie. She shook her head. 'There won't be any real news until Egerton gets back to London.'

Hal had produced a pained look. 'I think we have to play ball, Louise. Having a drink with him won't take long.'

When she sighed, he added, 'Get a cab straight home afterwards,' as though it was a treat she probably hadn't thought of.

Sweetwater was poised, half-risen, as she approached. She

took the seat across the table from him, instead of the space he was indicating alongside him in the booth. This way she would be spared the language of the thighs he had begun to offer the last time. He showed no discouragement; his posture, inclined slightly towards her, seemed to gather her into a protective orbit, his personal castle. 'Great to see you, Louise,' he said.

She lit a cigarette while he was catching the waiter's eye for her drink. On the table before him was what she knew would be a straight scotch, Bell's. Like the Church's shoes and Aquascutum raincoat, it belonged to his category of things the old world should concentrate on, instead of still trying to keep a place in the big league. The pipe was back in the corner of his mouth. She could imagine he had once seen Walter Pidgeon in an old movie and told himself, 'That's it!'

'How was Paris?' he asked.

'As usual.'

'And Italy?'

'The tower of Pisa is still leaning. Otherwise it looked fine, what I saw of it. I didn't have much time.'

'Helen and I got over to Italy when I had a posting to Spain in the mid-seventies. We missed out on Pisa. But we covered most of the places up north – Florence, Venice . . .' He waved a hand to spare her the list.

The place was filling up. A couple hovered by their table. They were considering whether to bid to squeeze into the vacant corner of the booth. Sweetwater shook his head at them, making a gesture indicative of an imminent arrival. They turned away, meek tourists from the look of the them. With its bogus Tiffany lamps and mirrors that were too new and too cheap, and waiters who looked either distraught or on the point of flouncing out, this was a bar for tourists, out-of-town people. It was listed in the popular guides, recommended in the airline magazines – a place nobody who worked in New York, or could claim to know it well, would therefore think of as a rendezvous.

That Sweetwater had chosen it for their meetings said things about him he would be mortified to hear. Whatever show he put on in Washington, he was a non-metropolitan creature, deeply provincial and not bright enough for the fieldwork needed to conceal the fact. For someone in the game he seemed to be in, he could with profit take lessons in a course she could prescribe herself. But she wasn't planning to do so.

'I hear you stopped off in London,' he said.

'I had to spend a little time with people there.'

He was expecting her to say more on that; if Hal had told him about Tom and where Tom now was, he could be jumping to the wrong conclusions. She added, 'Hal's taking over a British publisher — perhaps he mentioned it?'

'Not that I recall.'

'He asked me to drop in there. I went for drinks at their office. Not exactly a festive occasion.'

In fact it had been like a wake at which the Irish had failed to put in an appearance to make it bearable. Hal hadn't yet made up his mind what to do with the British company. No-one there knew yet who would be in, who would be out. The atmosphere reflected it. She recalled grimly the halting introductions, the leaden jokes, the faces expecting sentence palely glimpsed over the shoulders of the more confident. The bald man in the pink bow tie whose name she should have remembered when Hal asked, watching her hesitate as the canapés were offered, had murmured it wasn't the plate with the poison pill. Later he had taken her on to a freezing roof top to see a view of St Paul's; or perhaps it had been Westminster Abbey. There he had tried to pump her for information. But since Hal had told her nothing of his plans, he had been unlucky.

'So tell me what happened in Italy,' Sweetwater was saying.

Hal had said, 'We're not going to hold anything back from Brad,' when she had once expressed mild misgivings. So she told him everything. While she talked he made notes with flattering thoroughness.

'This guy from the Party Office in London — you say he's called Egerton?'

'Mark Egerton.'

'What sort of rank — senior or junior?'

'I'd say neither, from what I could see. He's around thirty, perhaps a little younger, quite good-looking.'

'And now he's gone on to see Massenet?'

'Yes. After which I suppose we wait reaction.'

He nodded thoughtfully and carried out some restructuring in the pipe bowl with the aid of a match. He seemed about to speak when somewhere inside his jacket a bleeper sounded. He smiled an apology and went off to the payphones.

Not for the first time she wondered about the wisdom of the game Hal had embarked on with Sweetwater. It was true her own feelings were already soured by dislike of Syce and Massenet, of her own role in having to deal with them. She had noticed that even Hal, although immune to these reservations, showed signs of misgiving about Sweetwater. His general line had become that they had no choice other than to keep Sweetwater posted. That conveniently ignored the fact that it was he who had tipped him about the project in the first place.

He had known Sweetwater at college but had lost sight of him when he went into the Army. Then, a few weeks ago, at some old buddies' meeting, Brad had reappeared. Impressed on hearing of his attachment to some mysterious section of the White House staff, Hal had decided there and then to tell him what was in the works.

Mention of Druitt's name had excited Sweetwater, had probably caused the pipe to elevate. A week later he had taken Hal to an expensive lunch and asked to be kept informed on progress. According to Hal, he had said the project was viewed benignly at the highest level possible. It would be serving a more virtuous end than just profit.

'Has he really the authority to say that?' she had asked. 'Or is it just a line? Is he thinking he'll ride along with us because he might pick up something that'll help him increase his own influence? It's only what everybody else in that town is trying to do.'

Hal had shaken his head and tried to look confident. But she guessed he was uneasy.

When he returned, Sweetwater said, 'So now you're waiting . . .'

'Yes.'

He reached out a hand to squeeze her arm, offering

reassurance with an option of further benefits if desired. 'Maybe we can be a little help on that.' He squeezed again.

She had known from their first meeting that he had seen the prospect of sleeping with her as a possible bonus. Three or four years ago, on the downswing from the divorce from Tom, she might not have resisted it. She was cool about the large ears and puritanical haircut but otherwise he had enough going for him for it not to seem out of the question. The features were good, the grey eyes lively and attractive. A certain lazy grace in the way he crossed a room suggested he'd be more than the bang-bang lover his background usually guaranteed.

The price to be paid, even ignoring unseen defects, would of course be a level of conversation before, after and possibly even during, that would amount to Washington gossip and Army memories at best and the trouble with Helen back in Virginia at worst; and nowadays, no longer in need of proving anything to herself or the world, she had adopted a more astringent view of new relationships. Imagining the taste of his mouth from the constant incineration of tobacco, the stubbled side of his head against her own, she thought: never.

She reached for her glass, withdrawing from his grasp at the same time. 'How would you help?'

'I work with someone who is passing through London quite soon. He'll be in a position to make a discreet enquiry in the right quarter.'

She raised her eyebrows. 'He'll talk to the Prime Minister?'

'Maybe not directly. But he has a contact in the Cabinet there who'll know what's happening on the story Egerton takes back.'

For the first time it seemed there would be some worthwhile dividend from these dealings. 'Won't you tell me who this someone is?'

He smiled. 'One day hopefully you and Hal will meet him.'

Being mysterious gave him a charge. She wasn't disposed to let him think she was intrigued or even particularly impressed. 'And if nothing at all is happening?'

'He might drop a hint.'

'Of what kind?'

She could tell he was being pressed more than he wanted,

but vanity kept him talking. 'Well, he might let it be known the President also knew the story and wouldn't like to think it was being ignored.'

Although this seemed an important moment, she was conscious of having to force her mind to concentrate on what he was saying. Tiredness was getting on top and the drink wasn't helping. She pushed her glass away. 'That would certainly be something I know Hal would appreciate.'

He once more touched her arm. 'It's a great project, all you have to do is stay with it!'

She shook her head. 'The flavour's too heavily British. The book'll sell well in England but I don't see it getting hot here.'

'Why not? You've the magic ingredients — sex, politics, spies. *And* a Lord!' When she looked puzzled he went on, 'Goble, the head of MI5, he's a Lord.'

'Goble's a knight.'

'Nobody'll know the difference in Columbus, Ohio.'

His enthusiasm on top of her fatigue and her own reservations about the project only made her depressed now. She told him she had to leave. He looked disappointed. 'I thought perhaps you'd have dinner with me. We could make a night of it, if you liked. I don't have to be back in Washington before tomorrow.'

'Won't your wife be expecting you?'

'She understands I don't have a fixed time-table down here.'

She shook her head. 'I'm sorry, Brad, dinner's the last thing I want, I'm going straight to my apartment to sleep.'

She let him drop her off in his cab. His eyes studied the facade of the apartment house as she opened the cab door. He was wondering which her window was, thinking that next time, with luck . . . 'Thanks,' she said. 'So I can tell Hal, can I, that you've promised to pull something out of the bag if needed?'

He laughed a shade uneasily. 'Sure, if we can help, we'll do all we can. Give Hal my warm regards. And tell him I think you're doing a great job.'

In the apartment she read her mail, took a couple of pills and looked at her watch. A resolve had come to her in the cab; it had to be implemented tonight and before she was too tired to make sense.

In London the time would be exactly 1 a.m. Most people she would hesitate to call at this hour. But unless since the divorce Tom had abandoned the habits of all except the first two years of marriage, he would not be in bed. He would be pushing the night away, either by reading stuff that wasn't too hot to be brought to the house on Berkeley Square or by watching TV.

Unless of course there was now a woman in his life again. Then things might be different. But if there was, the thought of interrupting something didn't cause her pain.

Although he had put it in a letter when he first got to London, she didn't have his private number at the house now. A call to London directory enquiries wouldn't produce it. She had to call the Embassy.

Cold persistence got her through to the Agency duty officer. It wasn't a voice she recognised but, after all this time, that would have been too much to hope for. He was predictably evasive, inclined to be unhelpful.

'Listen,' she said, 'I'm Tom Busch's ex-wife, Louise, and in case you're in any doubt, we do still speak. I need to talk with him urgently. All I ask is that you contact him now because from what I remember, which is still a great deal, he's unlikely to be in bed yet. I would like him to call me back on the number I'm going to give you.'

She thought it hadn't worked because half an hour went by. When the telephone finally rang, she was already in bed.

'Louise?' Tom sounded cautious but also, she was flattered to detect, concerned. 'Are you all right?'

'Fine. I was beginning to think you must have been in bed after all.'

'No, there was someone here.'

'Has she gone now?'

'The person's gone,' he said. He was going to keep her guessing. His privilege, of course. She reached for a cigarette. This line of thought was childish, a pointless hangover from the past. 'I came through London yesterday. I'd thought of looking in on you at the Embassy but got caught up in something Hal wanted me to do and there wasn't time.'

He sounded genuinely disappointed, then went on to ask

after Hal. 'I see he keeps managing to get his name in the papers. I hope his woman pornographer they're making all the fuss about isn't really you in disguise.'

She was amused he was still sour about Hal. He had offered her a job after Tom had said she was being too ambitious and ought to try a smaller house. 'No. I haven't sunk to that. Yet. But I do have an idea for a black comedy soap. It'll be called Agency Wives. Do you want to buy me off?'

His laugh sounded on the thin side; but it was after all quite late over there. 'Where were you coming through London *from*?'

'France and Italy. That trip's partly why I called. I was wondering if you planned to visit Langley soon and could stop off here. I think we ought to meet.'

'I haven't fixed anything. Is this urgent?'

'There's something going on that maybe ought to concern you. Professionally, I mean.'

'Can you tell me what sort of thing?'

'I don't want to say much now but I'm working on a project Hal is very keen on. Some of it concerns two men in the place where you are now. One of them is big politically, the other is an official, also big. If things go as I expect, these two will be hit by scandal in the very near future. Not just hit, forced to resign, destroyed. Somebody in government here, an old friend Hal talked to about the project, is taking a close interest. He even talks of helping it along if it shows signs of running into the sand. He won't say exactly what he does. But I know he's nothing to do with Langley. And he has an unlisted extension off the White House switchboard.'

She had his interest now. 'Can you tell me anything else about this guy?'

'He's an Army colonel, or has been.'

'But what's his name?'

'Sweetwater, Brad Sweetwater.'

The hissing on the line she realised was Tom's breath being released. 'You and Hal are in bed with Sweetwater?'

'If you want to put it that way.'

He swore unpleasantly. Once she would have complained. 'You're right,' he said. 'We certainly have to meet.'

· Six ·

Observing Tom as he wandered about the apartment on a tour
of exploration, exclaiming politely now and then ('Two
closets!' he called out from the hall. 'In New York? Is it allowed
these days?'), Louise noted with the barest twinge how well he
looked. The limp bequeathed by the mad operation that Ray
Brooks had dreamed up in Vietnam was perhaps more
marked; and she couldn't recall that his hair had been
uniformly grey when they last met. But ignoring those things,
his appearance was years younger than during the months of
blood-letting that preceded their divorce.

The puffiness beneath the eyes which had made him appear
like a bottle-a-day man was gone. The eyes themselves once
more had that politely amused expression she had thought of
as debonair when she first met him and had ended convincing
herself was simply a mask for non-commitment to feeling.

He had arrived with flowers and scent. It was not the scent
she had used when they were married. In her new existence she
had abandoned it, deciding the signal it would send to others
about the self reborn was too bland. But he was not aware of
that decision. The scent he had brought she had never heard
about. 'I thought this might be you, now,' he said enigmatically, when handing it over. She concluded it was not the
moment to tear away the wrapping and discover if insult or
indifference lay inside.

She was setting the table for their meal when he finally
abandoned his reconnaissance. No doubt he had been unable
to resist some inventorising of the artefacts which had
provided the background to their lives together. It would not

have been done meanly; the nostalgia of possessions had always plucked at him more than her. She wondered how he had reacted to the acquisitions of her new life mingling with the other stuff on equal terms. Indulgently he would wish her to suppose. And perhaps it *had* been like that.

'Nice,' he said. 'You certainly haven't lost your touch.'

'My Pollyanna gifts.'

'*And* it's tidy!'

She shook her head, unprepared for so unqualified an encomium from him, this man who growled if he found the toilet paper didn't unroll against the wall. 'It still has the feel of a chopped-up warehouse to me. The windows are impossible. But I couldn't have afforded anything else as big elsewhere in New York.'

'What decided you on the East Village?'

'Hal claimed it was the only place left if I wanted room to breathe. *What* one breathes of course isn't too great. They never get round to clearing the trash properly on this street. On the other hand if Ukrainian cobblers are what you want, I can offer you three no further away than you can toss a shoe. Match that in Knightsbridge. Or is Berkeley Square in Mayfair?'

'Mayfair.' Before she could ask more about the London house, he said with edgey heartiness, 'Clever old Hal. And he helped you find this?'

'He knew the developer who'd bought the warehouse and called him for me.'

'What does he think of the way you've done the place over?'

'The one time he was here, he'd lost a crown from his teeth so he wasn't concentrating very well. He brought that vase. It's eighteenth century. One way and another he's been quite supportive.'

Digesting that and perhaps more than was actually there, he revolved his glass to make waves in the scotch and soda, a habit not yet defused of irritation by time and separation. 'I didn't see the lacquered table we bought in Saigon.'

'There was nowhere it would go.'

He was waiting for more, reluctant to ask outright if she had sold it, but she stayed silent. He gave the impression of being unwilling to abandon conversation related to themselves and to get down to the subject that had brought him here. The silence went on; he was simply watching her move about the table. In a moment she might have to say, well what have been the recent warm-up topics at your London dinner-parties – Japanese rearmament, the prospects for world cereal production under the greenhouse effect or Is AIDS Mutating? It certainly won't have been us and our lacquered table.

'I like your hair like that,' he said. 'You're growing it longer.'

'It's just as it used to be.'

He accepted the pronouncement meekly, unaware of the extent of the lie. She had never quite got over her surprise that a man who could fabricate with such convincing elaboration in his work, who would never listen to an agent's report without scepticism, could be so unsuspecting of the small untruths of marriage.

The larger untruth of their marriage had not gone unsuspected by either of them, but had been pushed away, unwanted. They had entered into an unspoken pact against believing what was happening to them. In those final months in Washington, the act played out to all and sundry had announced things were fine in the citadel. That had exacted a special price. By the time they'd been forced to face the truth, the walls were crumbling fast, repair was out of the question, the place was doomed and no amount of shoring up would alter things.

'I suppose we'd better get down to business,' he said at last. 'This project of Hal's, do I deduce it's a political exposé somebody has managed to sell him?'

'Yes – or it will be when it's written.'

'It's not a book yet?'

'We have a synopsis so far.'

'Who is the politician?'

'John Howard Druitt, leader of the British Labour Party.'

'And the official you mentioned?'

'The head of MI5, Sir Richard Goble.'

He raised his eyebrows, more impressed than he cared to show. 'Go on.'

'Although there'll be other stuff showing Goble in a poor light, the main theme will be how he protected Druitt from an investigation into his having sex with a child. The main section of the book's going to cover the way our brave author has brought it to the notice of the Prime Minister. The rest of it, which Hal insisted on in order to have an American flavour, will consist of what the author knows about MI5's joint operations with the FBI over the years. Unfortunately I can't get on with putting the material into shape until we know the Prime Minister is moving against Druitt and Goble. Hal needs to be sure he isn't risking a couple of major libel actions.'

'Where does this child molestation story come from?'

'A journalist who was at a conference with Druitt and observed it happening.'

'*Observed*?'

'Not literally, but as good as – the journalist saw them together with the man who brought the child to Druitt's bedroom. He told the story to the author when he was on Goble's staff two years ago. According to the author Goble refused to do anything about it because he and Druitt are old buddies and share the same sexual tastes. The author has now reported this to a special representative of the Prime Minister, who went out to Italy for the purpose and has also checked with the journalist as well. We're going to have photographs of the author briefing the Prime Minister's man – which I took because I was watching nearby – and a tape made by the journalist of *his* meeting with him.' She grinned. 'History as it's happening – see? Hal's great idea for making the book *different*.'

'How did he get onto this?'

'The author wouldn't risk approaching a British publisher in case it got back to Goble. The journalist who's taking a share of the advance and royalties put him on to Hal, who'd once published a book of his when the journalist was working in the States.'

'And Hal's sure their story's genuine?'

'Yes.'

He adopted his casually amused manner. 'So now tell me who the two are.'

'No.'

'Why not?'

'You don't need to know. All I wanted was to warn you that Brad Sweetwater seems to be planning to play on your pitch and he's not somebody I'd trust to avoid burying everybody in the process.'

He was plainly about to press her further then changed his mind. 'All right, tell me how Sweetwater comes into it.'

'Hal knew him at college and discovered not long ago he was on the White House staff. Quite why he let him in on the book I'm not sure – he may have hoped for something in return. Anyway Sweetwater came back, saying a lot of interest was being shown in the White House and please keep him posted. The night I called you he'd gone as far as to suggest that if the British Government wasn't showing signs of using the information to fix Druitt, the man he works for could bring pressure to bear behind the scenes in London.'

'Jesus!' Tom stretched both arms down the sides of his chair in a sort of paroxysm of fury.

'I thought that would interest you.'

He stayed silent, communing with her ceiling. She decided they'd better eat if the chili wasn't going to be dried up. After a minute or two it seemed he had calmed down and he came into the kitchen to offer help.

'Isn't it about time you told me what Brad Sweetwater does and who for?' she said. 'Is he anything to do with the National Security Council?'

He shook his head. 'It wouldn't be so bad if he belonged to the NSC, they're ball-and-chained these days, or were when I last heard. No, Sweetwater is one of Lew Rothman's cavalry.'

'Whose cavalry?'

'Lew Rothman's. He runs something called the President's Contingency Research Staff.'

'Should I have heard of him?'

'You should if you're interested in who's got power in

Washington at the moment. When this President got to the White House, he decided to create a job along the corridor for his old buddy, Lew Rothman. He'd been a broker on Wall Street then went to Europe for a spell to run his firm's business in London. He came back convinced he was an expert in foreign affairs. I met him once at Langley soon after he was appointed to the White House and realised he was going to be bad news. Anyway the President created this Contingency Research outfit with Lew in charge, to look at the foreign policy problems that could arise in the future and present him with options to add to all the others he'd be offered by those who really knew. At first people said it probably didn't matter, it just meant the President would have someone around to exchange stories with. But they didn't allow for Lew's ambition which is limitless. He now has the President taking his advice all the time. And he's also using his Research staff for things which, if they should be done at all, ought to be left to Langley. He's somehow even acquired an intelligence source which is so hot nobody else is allowed in on it. In other words we're back watching an old movie. You say surely they're not repeating *this* again? But they are.'

'How is it an old movie?'

'Because a man has to go through purgatory to become a President. It makes him feel that if he ever gets there, he'll have won, he can have his own way. But he finds that if he works inside the system, he can't. When he isn't busy trying to fix Congress, he's getting tripped by the judiciary or oversight committees or a hundred and one other things that combine to make him wild. Lying awake at night, he thinks there's got to be a way of getting more of the action to myself. Then he thinks – suppose I put Lew into executive mode? He'll need to touch base with the others now and then, but he can handle that quietly enough. Sooner or later Lew decides that touching base only fouls things up and futhermore that he now knows the President's mind well enough to make even consulting *him* unnecessary. That's the way the movie runs until the day it just twists up in the projector and comes apart.'

They took the food to the table. Tom uncorked the wine

she'd bought at lunchtime. He filled her glass in a solicitous way before he sat down. It was like life before marriage, she thought.

'I understand about the movie,' she said, 'but are you saying you really don't care that Druitt might have his political career destroyed? Or is it Goble you worry about?'

'To hell with Goble,' he said. 'But Druitt matters. Even if he does enjoy sexually abusing children, it doesn't mean he'd make a bad Prime Minister.' When Louise raised her eyes to the ceiling, he went on, 'All right, but *listen*. The bottom line is this: are the interests of the United States going to be served by stopping Druitt winning the next election in the UK? At Langley we don't think so. A government led by Druitt is far more likely to be accomodating to what our policy towards Europe ought to be over the next decade than one led by David Blackmer or any other Tory for that matter. Much faster reduction of force levels and weaponry plus a fixed date for total withdrawal from Europe is what we need. All the economic indicators say so. The fact that for his own reasons Lew Rothman keeps pressing the contrary on the President is something we need to fight in every way we can. And the Europeans have to learn to get on without us.

'Druitt has faced this and got his Party to adopt a policy for Europe that matches our interests. The Tories still hang on to their mid-Atlantic fantasies. Blackmer is quite a nice guy personally but he'll be a balls-aching nuisance if he gets re-elected because this cosy relationship he's got with the President results in him always reinforcing the crap Rothman keeps spewing into his ear. And there's another reason why it would be better if Blackmer didn't get another term.'

'What is it?'

'I'll tell you one day.'

Once he would have told her now. He had told her everything once and she had never let him down. Now, if not exactly like somebody met on the sidewalk, she was in the same bag as journalists and visiting Senators. It was a deprivation she had learned to live with. 'Why does Lew Rothman view things so differently?' she asked.

He was looking annoyed again. 'He'll give you a whole bag of reasons. He seems to believe in some Pax Americana concept which involves having regional forces permanently deployed in Europe and most other continents of the world. He also claims to know there's cheating going on in Russia over the destruction of weapons and has managed to persuade the President the threat from the East is growing again. Lew isn't happy when we're not playing Rambo.' He shook his head at the cheese she pushed towards him and glanced at his watch. 'I must go for the shuttle soon.'

'Where will you stay in Washington?'

'Ray Brooks is giving me a bed.'

Speaking of Rambos, she thought; but there was an old loyalty there she knew there was no point in arguing against. 'Is he going to have another overseas post?'

'Probably not. Anyway he and Betty are buying a farm in Maryland close enough for him to drive into Langley each day.'

The echo registered with her as he must have known it would, because he went on, 'It's not far from a place we looked at once.' He was watching her face for a reaction. She looked away and went to start the coffee machine.

As they drank the coffee, he said, 'Why don't you tell me who these two guys are who are providing the material for the book?'

She frowned. 'Have you got some special reason for wanting to protect Druitt that you haven't told me about?' He shook his head but she went on. 'Because in case you have, I'm certainly not going to tell you. How do I know Langley won't send somebody to persuade them to forget about exposing Druitt and waste all the time I've put into this book? I just wanted to warn you about Brad Sweetwater or his boss muscling into what ought to be your territory.'

'All right,' he said. 'Don't tell me. I was only curious. Blackmer probably won't use the information anyway. Then you've the libel problem to worry about if you publish. I can't see Hal taking that risk.'

'But Blackmer will *have* to use the story in some way if he wants to beat Druitt in the election.'

He blew out his cheeks but didn't try to argue. Instead, glancing round the room as though back to the task of noting what she had done with their possessions, he said, 'Do you see anything of Cord these days?'

'No.'

'How's that?'

'It was over a long time ago. We both knew it wasn't a big deal.'

'That wasn't how it looked once.'

'It looked the way I wanted it to. You were having an affair. Did you expect me just to sit back and take it?'

'Even though I hadn't started sleeping with Kate when you and Cord . . .'

'You were going to. As soon as she'd let you.'

'So you just wanted to make damn sure you weren't going to come second. Isn't that it?' When she raised her eyebrows and smiled, he grimaced then smiled also. Neither of them looked away. The moment took her back a long time.

'Looking back, does it strike you now as a god-awful waste?' Tom said. 'A waste of something we could never do as well again with anybody else?' It was his utilitarian approach surfacing.

'You look as though you've survived it all right,' she said. She wanted to see the new woman, smell her, observe all the things he had persuaded himself were desirable in her. She was sure now that she existed, came if he whistled, applied the balm when he returned from a terrible day at the Embassy.

He went on probing. 'So, no Cord these days. Are there *any* interesting men in your life?'

'New York contains no interesting men who are unmarried, free from disease and capable of conversation not exclusively focussed on themselves.' She wanted him away from the subject of her own life. 'How much longer are you going to do in London?'

'Two years probably.'

'And then?'

'I've no idea. If Langley want me to retire I might stay on in London. It's close enough to the parts of Europe I like. It's reasonable still as capitals go and the English countryside is pleasant. The pace is civilised too.'

He was dissembling, she concluded. Talk of pace being civilised was so far removed from his style as she remembered it, she almost laughed aloud. It must come back to the woman again: a gel from the shires perhaps, big in the bottom; from saddle to bed and back to the saddle again.

She said, 'Do you mean you see Europe differently these days? You always said it was a *dying* world. Living there would be like watching another sort of old movie, wouldn't it? Is that what you want?'

It hadn't twisted his tail as much as she had expected. He looked merely thoughtful. 'I still feel much the same about the British. They're like a combat division that's been in one battle too many. They've seen too much and they don't believe in victories any more. But what they've hung onto is quite seductive. I could get to like it quite a lot. And if it meant never having to meet people like Lew Rothman and Brad Sweetwater any more, that wouldn't be bad either.'

'So you'll stay?'

'I might.'

She felt a little chill that in such an event she might not see him again. Even ex-husbands around in old age could be better than no-one.

He rose. 'I really must go and catch that plane.'

At the door, he kissed her twice, once on the cheek and once, tentatively, on her mouth. She could tell he was hoping she would respond. But there was no future in that.

After he'd gone, she went to the bedroom and opened the scent. It was very good.

Loading the dishwater she reached a provisional conclusion. He was having an affair, yes. But he had a problem — or anyway the woman did; because he was still in love with herself. She'd finally been sure in the last ten minutes of his visit. How much, however, she couldn't tell; nor what, if anything, it meant to her.

· Seven ·

By this time in the afternoon, the terrace of the High Comissioner's house offered relative comfort – as well as a pleasant view of the garden. Delhi in May, Pagett had said, will be like a furnace. As usual Pagett had been right. The heat had been shrivelling whenever during the day Blackmer had to move out of air-conditioned buildings. The sound man of one of the television crews from London had fainted during a five minutes' interview in front of the Parliament.

He took off jacket and tie and sank into the wicker chair most favoured by the ceiling fan. 'I wonder what it is out there – hundred and ten?' He waved towards the lawn.

Beads of sweat clung to Wyeth's hairline. He made no move to take off his own jacket. He lacked the easy confidence some Private Secretaries displayed from the moment they started. Wyeth had joined the party in place of Giles Grice. He still hadn't realised that while formality might be necessary in public, it needed softening in private if everybody was to stay human.

'Why don't you take your tie off? It looks as though it's strangling you.' It was difficult not to be mean to him. 'That was an awful meeting! I didn't come here expecting to be lectured about subversive Sikhs in Rochdale.'

He felt heat generating inside as well as on the parts of his skin the fan didn't reach. It was stupid to let irritation affect him like this. 'I take it we've time for a couple of drinks before I have to change for the dinner with the President?'

'About an hour.'

'Good, find one of those bearers. I'd like a large brandy and soda.'

'You haven't forgotten you said you'd call Sir Norman Pagett about the new Permanent head for the Treasury? The announcement's due in the morning.'

He sighed. 'All right, see if you can raise him. But after we've had the drinks.'

He watched Wyeth go. He was limping a little and a patch of what was presumably heat rash had appeared on his cheek: clearly one of those fair-complexioned people who always wilted in the heat. He was a nice enough boy – man, rather, since for all his coltish air he must be over thirty – a swift draftsman, conscientious, even capable of a little wit when some antidote to the tedium of a programme was wanted. But it wasn't enough. A Private Secretary needed stamina for every situation, to be still on his feet while others slept if that was necessary to keep the machine running smoothly. Here in Delhi that had just about been achieved but with signs of flagging. There had been a moment too, at the Red Fort reception the previous evening, when Wyeth had almost lost his head, shouting and pushing Indian security men out of the way. They had happened to be blocking the line of sight of the London press corps intent on a particular succulent photo opportunity – Blackmer being garlanded by a local maiden, her Page Three proportions set off by a clinging *sari*.

True, Cusack, the Press Secretary, helplessly trapped on the wrong side of the dais, had been signalling to Wyeth to save the day. But not like that. On return to London, he might have to tell Pagett there should be a change, Wyeth returned to his Department and some more robust and emotionally secure creature brought into the Private office in his place. Pagett wouldn't like his judgment in choosing Wyeth for No. 10 to be faulted like that. But his defeats were few enough.

Blackmer narrowed his eyes, trying without success to identify something in a tree on the far side of the High Commissioner's lawn. The shape was too geometrical to be part of the tree. There seemed to be a curtain of sorts involved in it. He thought of sending Wyeth to look, but he was still absent, summoning the drinks. Giving up, he put his head back to bathe in the fullness of the fan's sweep.

A slight weariness apart, he felt in good shape, despite having been transported from London's chill spring into the atmosphere of an oven. Physical fatigue was still something he rarely experienced unless he induced it by violent exercise; ox-like, had always been Reeves' verdict on that side of his constitution. Moreover, the *accidie* which had been consuming him in England had lifted, at least temporarily. The prospect of defeat in the autumn no longer soured. He could draw the unaccustomed smells of this Indian garden into his nostrils and feel satisfied he was still putting on an impressive show.

Tonight he would be the focus of attention that was neither hostile or derisive, unlike his experience in Westminster these days. At the dinner in the President's Palace, he would make a speech from notes he needed to glance at only once more to know by heart. In private conversations later he would, unprompted, press the points agreed with Holderness, the High Commissioner, as insufficiently resolved at earlier meetings. Then he would return here for an hour or more's dictation to one of the girls in the No. 10 party; a glance through telegrams, a final round-up with Holderness — all on no more fuel than the occasional brandy and sofa.

At the end Holderness would be lingering, hopeful of his company being desired, an unlikely contingency with so arid a creature. He would wave him away politely, smoke a last cigar and retire to the bedroom. Against the faint hum of the air-conditioning, he would look down in the moonlight at the blind, sleeping goddess, Diana in her face mask. He would feel no inconvenient desire, time had quenched it long ago; unless, perversely, he imagined behind the mask the features first seen at Palam airport two days ago, those of Teresa Holderness.

Wyeth returned. Behind him a turbanned bearer, twitching with obsequious pomp, carried their drinks on a tray. Blackmer raised his glass in Wyeth's direction. His thoughts about him earlier had perhaps been over-harsh. 'Why not get something for that cheek from the High Commission's doctor?'

Wyeth shook his head. 'It's nothing, thanks.' He sounded more relaxed now. 'Incidentally, your wife and Lady Holderness have just come back.'

'From what?'

'Tea with junior female grades at the High Commission.'

Diana would have found that a monumental drag, of course; but nobody would have suspected it. By now she had perfected the sub-royal manner – the brilliant opening smile, the succeeding frown of sympathetic concentration, the swift nod of understanding. More carefully rationed would have been the blessing of her laugh, delightful and quite un-mechanical. The reluctance to be moved on, to keep abreast with programme timing would strike observers as beyond reasonable doubt. They had learned the game together in his first constituency, unsparing in their comments on each other in the post mortems over dinner or in bed. Now she beat him at it every time.

'Are they coming out here for a drink?'

'I think they've decided to bathe and change first. They're having drinks sent up.'

He was mildly disappointed. Reflected in the surface of his brandy and soda he saw the outline of Teresa Holderness, stepping into her bath, twisting slowly under the shower. The image was vivid, took its teasing conviction from something that had happened the morning after his arrival in Delhi.

A quarter of an hour had been allotted to glad-handing staff in and around the High Commission offices. He had been to the swimming pool, where, obviously by design, infant offspring were being instructed in keeping afloat by some of the wives.

Teresa Holderness had paraded for the occasion, leading her troops from the front. He vaguely recalled from gossip with Roger Lang before leaving London that Holderness had acquired her in Hong Kong during a secondment to the Governor's staff some years before. She was an astounding prize to be secured by someone resembling a stick insect; a ravishing half-Chinese, still in her thirties, the hair as black and silky as Diana's, the figure and skin even better, only a grating cadence of the voice, familiar from his own visit to China, diminishing her appeal.

Stripped down to a minimal bikini, she had been running to recapture a fugitive from the swimming class as he arrived alongside the first of the wives. Shaking hands, head on one side as though offering his best ear to her observations, he had found his gaze locked on the movement of buttocks beneath the horizontal strap of the bikini bottom, was eventually aware of an access of lust so violent he lost the thread of the response he was trying to make. Too long unused to the directness of simple messages, he had felt entirely undone.

Afterwards, when alone for a short time, he had reflected on the singularity of this revival in sexual feeling. There was a paradox somewhere. After he and Diana had ceased sleeping together, while all was going well for the Government, at a time when his reputation in the Party and the country was still unchallenged, sex had left him alone, acknowledging it could not compete with other entrancements.

Yet now, with influence slipping away, reputation at an all-time low, with that supposedly compelling aphrodisiac, power, being watered down with every week that passed, he was discovering himself in thrall again. A comforting flicker of desire to remind him of past splendours he would not have minded. But this was something less convenient, a summons. Perhaps it was a warning to rediscover this other path to self-assertion before the axe fell in the autumn.

Satisfying that requirement would no doubt be easy enough, would certainly be applauded by Diana as validating her own diversions. But watching Teresa Holderness these past two days, he had identified a danger. The pleasure would be enhanced or muted in direct ratio to the discretion displayed in pursuing it. Risk, that cocaine companion of every single day in government, had become a necessary thing.

He turned to look across the lawn again. 'That tree,' he said to Wyeth. 'There's a thing inside the foliage, high up, I can't make out, a sort of structure. Can you see?'

Wyeth went to the edge of the terrace and stared. The

turbanned bearer had noiselessly materialised behind Blackmer, was reaching forward to take his glass and also to speak.

'Sir.' He was excited to be offering a double service. 'High Commissioner hide there.'

'*Hide*?'

'Sir, yes, hide.' There was no doubt he meant it, he was nodding solemnly, big with certainty.

'I see.' He laughed. 'Well, thank you.' After the bearer had gone, he said, 'What the *hell* was he talking about?'

Wyeth had turned, smiling. 'I've remembered – Lady Holderness told me last night the High Commissioner has taken up bird-watching. That must be his hide.'

He gazed again at the tree. It was fascinating to imagine Holderness's six feet plus compressed into the hide, eyes a-glitter through minute round spectacles for another bout of voyeurism. All for birds! While in the house, Teresa Holderness twisted and turned . . .

Holderness himself appeared as Wyeth was leaving the terrace to raise Pagett on the telephone. His appearance was as refrigerated as ever, the pale grey suit miraculously uncreased. He was cool in every way, the skin apparently never provoked to sweat, the eye wintry, the manner expertly courteous but remote. A significant shortage of all bodily fluids seemed to be signalled. But one would need the testimony of Teresa Holderness fully to explore that.

The tall glass being brought to him by the bearer would contain only fresh lime juice. Except for a little wine, drunk for politeness' sake at lunch and dinner, he was reputed to be sustained by nothing stronger than that. Cigars too, Blackmer had noticed, were always declined. He was a man who picked his way round the marshes of indulgence, hoping a righteous tread would carry him to the Permanent Secretary's chair at the Office in three years time. The conjunction of age and seniority would in fact be favourable. But if Blackmer was still around to have his way, someone else would succeed. The bloodless priesthood he had found dominating the mandarin scene when he got to No. 10, would lose more ground. He would find a warm-water creature instead to take over that tiresomely self-satisfied Department.

Holderness sat, delicately adjusting his trouser knees in a way reminiscent of Pagett when about to volunteer a confidence about some Minister's foolishness or worse. 'I think it's gone extremely well so far, Prime Minister.'

He grunted and reached for his fresh brandy and soda.

'I was struck by the warmth that came through at the Red Fort reception. Sen Gupta said the same thing to me at lunch.'

He could let it pass as the small change of sycophancy. But that would be letting Holderness off too lightly. 'Experience has taught me that applause, particularly in the Third World, has an exact correlation to the size of the free circus laid on by the host government. Are you saying that hasn't been the case here?'

'I think it went deeper.' Holderness was standing his ground. 'Your reputation is very high with educated Indians.'

'Perhaps we could ship a few hundred thousand of them over in time for the next election.' A bougainvillaea was twined about a column near his chair. He plucked a bloom. With the scent of the flower he thought once more of Teresa Holderness. 'The Home Minister is impressive.'

'Highly intelligent, totally on top of his job. He'd succeed anywhere.'

He smiled. 'World class?'

'Absolutely.'

It conjured an agreeable fantasy, politics going the way of commerce and professional football. Gigantic transfer fees would waft the stars from government to government. Returning to Heathrow at the weekend, he would step into a press conference with at his side the roly-poly figure of Narayan in Nehru cap and *dhoti*. He had bought him, he would announce to the assembled hacks, to take over the Home Office, where there had been a certain weakness in the team lately. White-lipped with fury, Diana would have slipped away before he added that Welcroft was being given a free transfer.

'How did you find the atmosphere during your stop-over in Brussels?' Holderness asked.

'They're still hell-bent on quicker American withdrawal. It's depressing.'

'They have to reckon with an American President who apparently doesn't agree.'

'Thank God.'

'He seems to have become exceptionally hawkish in the past twelve months. Do you know what brought about the change?'

'I don't think I do. I agree it's interesting.' He drained his glass and looked away. He wasn't disposed to get more closely into his private dealings with the President. If he did, the details would almost certainly filter back to Roger Lang, making him more po-faced than ever on the subject. And in any case the change had been a puzzle he was irked not to have got nearer to solving.

Wyeth was signalling from the terrace door that he had Pagett on the line. He went into the study.

'Norman, you want to know what I've decided about the Treasury. I prefer Cushman. I recognise he's the second choice of both yourself and the Chancellor. But there you are, I think he's the sounder.'

'I see.'

Pagett's tone had tightened almost imperceptibly. Disapproval he would never register. Irreversible defeats he accepted without waste of emotion or tongue. His mind would already have ranged ahead, working on the adjustments needed to handle awkwardness among his troops.

'So you'll go ahead tomorrow . . .'

'Yes. Will you be saying anything to the Chancellor yourself?'

'I'll send him a personal telegram tonight with my reasons.'

'That would be helpful.'

'Is there anything I should know about while we're on?'

'You'll have heard I suppose that your press coverage here has been exceptionally good. You led the middle of the day news on ITN, being garlanded.'

'Beauty and the Beast?'

'Always a compelling image.'

A rare event, Pagett venturing on a liberty, close though they were now. He could imagine the faint smile coming and going behind the cigarette smoke. 'Nothing else?'

'Only one thing . . .' Pagett was hesitating. 'A little difficult on this line. You'll remember the personal letter you received at Kilndown, through your sister?'

He had to reach for it at the back of his mind. 'Yes, was there anything in that?'

'There may be. Fender's man has seen the writer twice. Also the Frenchman who is the actual source of most of the story. We shan't know exactly what to make of it until there have been further enquiries this end.'

'Involving whom?'

'Goble. The writer was on his staff some time ago. He says Goble was given the story and decided to suppress it.'

'What was being reported?'

'Personal conduct of a rather unattractive character,' Pagett said primly.

'But was it *criminal*?'

'Oh, yes – criminal if there's anything in the story. But this can only be cleared up by talking to Goble. You may like me to do that myself now. Then the whole story can be available to you immediately on your return.'

He almost bought it, stopped himself assenting just in time. He trusted Pagett far more than any other official, was reasonably sure he wouldn't double-cross him. But Pagett had a special interest, a concern to protect his bureaucratic machine. Those hordes of acolytes who kept it running looked to Pagett to shield them; politicians weren't wanted in the engine room. He couldn't absolutely put it past Pagett to decide his special concern called for helping Goble off a hook. And in the process, the facts of what Druitt had or hadn't done might also be watered down, even rendered useless.

'Thank you, Norman, but I'd prefer to see Goble myself about this.'

'As you wish.' He detected the disappointment in Pagett's voice and knew he had been right.

'Presumably Fender's man is writing up his interviews in

detail. I shall also want to see him after I've read them. It had better be at Kilndown on Sunday morning; I plan to drive down on Saturday night. As regards Goble, I'll arrange my meeting with him myself. I'll be glad if you'll ensure nothing is mentioned to him beforehand.'

As he returned to the terrace, he felt a mild elation. It was too early to feel confidence. But was luck, after all, on the turn? Out of all this, there might yet come a famous victory in the autumn.

Teresa Holderness had arrived and was talking to Wyeth. He glanced at his watch as he went over. She had noticed and placed a hand lightly on his forearm. 'Don't worry, I came down terribly early. Time for another drink at least.' She called to a bearer.

Even in its higher register, her voice retained its rather harsh quality. He would not want her to talk much in bed. But in every other respect she was delectable.

'Good session with the staff this afternoon?' he said.

She touched his arm again, this time near the wrist. 'Your wife was *marvellous*, Prime Minister. They were genuinely pleased. It makes so much difference when someone shows a really involved interest.'

She had a fair line of patter and could put it over effortlessly. All in all, watching her these past days, he rated her a polished performer, an undeserved asset to Holderness. There were clear signs of an expensive education in England or elsewhere in Europe; and she had learned how to dress well in the process.

'Have you yet seen the *sari*?' she asked.

When he shook his head, frowning, she went on, 'Perhaps you didn't know about it. Your wife asked me to go shopping with her this morning. It's gorgeous. But not for her apparently! She said she was buying it for someone else on your behalf. Whoever it is will be thrilled.'

Wyeth made his excuses and went off to change. She moved closer to Blackmer and as she did so perfume, lightly floating on the odour of her skin, rose from the hollow beneath her chin.

He wanted her with a ferocity that made the hand holding his glass tremble. He touched her necklace and told her it was attractive, all as a pretext so that he could have her skin even briefly under his fingers. Over her shoulder he saw Holderness talking to a member of his staff who had brought him a piece of paper to look at.

Palmerston would not have hesitated: taking Teresa Holderness by the arm, he would have steered her to the nearest bedroom. That would be a little cavalier of course. Minimum politeness would require at least a few words to Holderness en route. 'High Commissioner, I find I need to have your wife before we leave for dinner. Would you be so kind as to send the bearer in with another brandy and soda and whatever she herself normally prefers?'

She went on talking sbout the *sari*, remarking that it must be for somebody very special. 'Won't you tell me, Prime Minister? Or is it a state secret?' She was being provocative, not caring about the words, aware that he desired her and eager to let him think she was far from out of reach.

The thought that he had revealed himself so plainly was a shock. He found his appetite abruptly stifled. She was, he saw now, an impudent, dangerous woman. He drained his glass. 'My secrets, I fear, you must allow me to keep.'

He saw her flush as he turned away. Putting her down was a poor substitute for satisfaction; but it had to suffice.

· Eight ·

As Rainsborough sat down, Blackmer noticed the buttonhole bloom was secured by a tiny gold safety-pin; a service presumably performed by one of the Filipino slave force employed to run that monstrous house in Hampshire.

'Nice to see you back,' Rainsborough said. 'I thought it best to drive over this morning so that we could discuss the problem before trouble develops in other constiuencies.'

He was in full weekend rig, Harris Tweed jacket and plus-fours worn with the famous puttees, favoured targets for the tabloid photographers when they hunted him on the grouse moors. To have arrived here at Kilndown as early as this, he must have started out before eight o'clock. So church had been cut.

'Are you *expecting* trouble from anywhere else?' Blackmer asked.

'No but Farquharson is a stirrer. If we put the boot in now, I'm sure any movement to support him will collapse. There's enormous loyalty towards you among Party workers as a whole. I certainly don't know of another constituency chairman who would have voiced criticism of this kind.'

'But you're saying there are some who might be tempted to do so now . . .'

'A couple perhaps.'

He sighed. 'Nothing like news of a little mutiny in the ranks to make one feel at home again. What are you recommending we do?'

'I'll deal with Farquharson, he was a rather bumptious subaltern in my regiment at Suez. But it would be helpful if you could see your way to going round the country a bit in the next few weeks. The constituency parties would appreciate enormously receiving a little chocolate from you. Take Diana whenever you can.'

'I have the Far East trip, remember.'

'I hope you might get something in beforehand. I'll make it known you're planning this. It needn't be anything elaborate. But it will spike guns. The sort of programme I had in mind . . .'

He droned on, referring to notes made on the back of a bridge scorecard. It all sounded sensible and also rather futile. 'Thank you, Charles,' he said when he'd finished. 'You're absolutely right. Put it on paper and I'll have a look tomorrow.'

Watching Rainsborough dab away the moisture that appeared on his upper forehead as from a spring, whenever confined indoors without every window open, Blackmer wished he could feel kinder. The telephone call about Farquharson's chatter to local press on the need for an inspiring lead from the top, followed by this bustling arrival so soon after breakfast, when he had been hoping to have got through at least two boxes by now, had been profoundly irritating. All the same, here was a loyal old thing, to the extent that loyalty could ever be said to exist in politics. Cleverness and drive might be lacking; but they weren't everything. To head a Cabinet at this time without a Rainsborough around would be like sitting alone at a camp fire, dying for want of fuel while in the darkness the wolves circled.

More gently he said, 'Actually there could be a break in the clouds soon. How would the prospect of a major scandal on the Opposition Front Bench appeal to you?'

'How major?'

'Druitt.'

Rainsborough's straggly eyebrows lifted. 'What sort of scandal?'

'Sex. Child sex.'

He watched it sinking in. Rainsborough had acquired the appearance of someone trying not to become hopeful in case what he saw was a mirage.

'There is one inconvenient factor – assuming any of this is true. The head of the Security Service is claimed to have received the information and suppressed it. The suggestion is that he and Druitt have sexual interests in common. If Druitt goes to the stake Goble will have to go with him, and Goble, you'll recall, was a Tory appointment. However, that would be a small price to pay for what we'd gain.'

He glanced at the clock in the corner of the room. 'You'll have to forgive me if we leave it there for the moment, Charles. I'm about to see the fellow who interviewed the two men responsible for providing the information.'

'I find it difficult to imagine Druitt ever getting caught out in anything like this,' Rainsborough said.

'So do I. It could well turn out to be moonshine.'

Standing beside Rainsborough's Jaguar to exchange final words, Blackmer saw a tall young man walk up the drive and ring the doorbell. Later he found him in the hall studying the pictures.

'Egerton?'

'Yes, Prime Minister.' He had a firm handshake that seemed to claim a better status than junior official. When they were seated in the study, Blackmer examined him more closely: well-made with lively brown eyes, a straight nose and reasonably firm chin; the dark hair grown too thickly near the collar for his own taste but giving the head a graceful shape. Diana would look twice, perhaps more.

'Sorry to have broken into your Sunday. You drove down from London I take it. I hope not to keep you long.'

Behind the chair in which Egerton sat, dust was dancing in a shaft of sunlight. 'Spring seems to have arrived at last,' Blackmer said.

'The blossom on the azalea across the lawn looked magnificent as I walked up the drive.'

'It gets better every year. You have a garden?'

'No, just a view across Battersea Park. It can look surprisingly pastoral beyond the street lamps and the joggers.' He seemed intelligent and assured enough; Pagett's confidence about his suitability to pursue the Druitt story had probably been justified. He might go a long way in the Service.

He opened the folder Pagett had sent down. 'I read your reports last night. Very clearly presented. Do you believe the Frenchman at the end of it all?'

'I don't disbelieve him.'

'That isn't what I asked.'

'I felt by the end of my meeting with him that he *had* witnessed what he described.'

'And Sisson?'

'I find him rather a complex character. I'm not sure he's come completely clean even now. On the other hand *he* isn't providing the evidence against Mr Druitt.'

'Only against Sir Richard Goble . . .'

'Yes.'

'A disaffected employee obviously — should that give us pause?'

'He certainly feels strongly that Sir Richard acted wrongly. He's quite frank about wanting his conduct exposed. But if his reading of the situation is correct, his attitude is hardly surprising. Apart from that he seems mostly moved by concern for the country.'

'A patriot! One of that endangered species! Is that *really* it?'

'He gives that impression.'

'Notwithstanding the fact he chooses to live abroad and drools about the delights of it?'

'He and his wife do come back from time to time. They visit a daughter in a private hospital in Wimbledon. I went to call on her yesterday — Mrs Sisson had asked me to deliver a parcel.'

'What hospital is that?'

'The Holgate.'

'*The Holgate?*'

'Yes.'

A coincidence, he told himself, surely no more than that. And yet there had been the sending of the letter via Esther . . .

'How long has the daughter been in that hospital, do you know?'

Faint surprise at the question crossed Egerton's face. 'I'm not sure. From my conversation with her, I'd say several years. Although she was quite rational talking to me, I gather she can have alarming relapses.'

He returned his gaze to the folder; to pursue it any further would seem odd. 'Well, let's get on. If all you've been told is true, we seem to be faced with a grave problem. Also a sad one. Although Mr Druitt is my political opponent, I've held him in high regard both as a Parliamentary colleague and as a man.'

The phrases flowed almost mechanically from his lips, drawn from some contingent obituary filed at the back of his mind. Yet they were true. He would rather have Druitt with him in a tight spot than most of his own Party.

'Have you met him yourself, Egerton?'

'No. Apart from seeing him on television and reading his novel, I don't know him.'

'The novel's well thought of, I gather.'

'Yes, I re-read it the other day. It still seemed pretty good.'

'Did it offer any illumination in relation to what we're now faced with?' When Egerton hesitated, gathering his thoughts together, he went on, 'Tell me about it.'

'The book?'

'Yes.'

He smiled at his discomfort. He would certainly not have prepared himself for this. It would be interesting to see what sort of a fist he made of it.

'It deals with the lives of perhaps a dozen people in a small North of England town, taking them up to the late seventies.'

'A saga?'

'Of a kind, but dealing with just one generation. The main characters are two women, painters who live together. Their work's sufficiently well-known for them to be local celebrities. The town views them affectionately, treats what is guessed to be their relationship with amusement.' Egerton paused, still uncertain perhaps about what details to select.

'So what happens to them?'

'A crisis occurs after they become involved with the Women's Liberation movement. This happens largely through the elder, Helen, an enthusiast for causes of all kinds. They hold exhibitions of their work in support of the movement, make platform appearances, eventually decide on a public declaration that their relationship is lesbian.

'The town is affronted, feels let down. It can accept the implicit without difficulty, it won't tolerate the *explicit*. Under the hostility the relationship deteriorates and breaks up. Helen leaves, the other, Grace, stays behind. Grace is now largely ignored in the town, her painting no longer admired. Some time afterwards she's visited by a journalist interested in her work who becomes taken with the idea of writing an article exposing the town's hypocrisy. She wants it condemned for making an act of simple and harmless honesty an occasion for ostracism. When Grace hears this, she's violently opposed to the idea. The journalist thinks it's because she's apprehensive about the local reaction. But under pressure Grace says the article would be built on a lie she now regrets – there had never been a lesbian affair between her and Helen, a physical relationship of that kind would have been repellent to them both. The public declaration had been a purely political act. The journalist goes ahead with the article. In the atmosphere of bitterness that follows, Grace commits suicide.'

'Is that all?'

'So far as the two women are concerned. Other characters face different sorts of crisis.'

It sounded dreary, nothing like Druitt's private conversation.

Egerton said, 'Essentially it's a study of moral attitudes, of society's behaviour in a variety of situations. I suppose it's also a plea for tolerance.'

Perhaps Druitt had had a vague premonition that one day he might be faced with a situation like that involving the two women. In the northern town where he grew up and to which he occasionally referred with cynical affection, advertised lesbianism might not be too uncomfortable to survive nowadays. But child abuse was something else.

'Have you anything to add to what you said in your report?' he asked.

'Yes, I've been able to discover more about the reasons for the light sentence Alois Reinholdt received at his trial. According to the Austrian police, it was largely on account of the number of people who had been in his care as children and who came forward to testify to his kindness and efforts to give them a decent start in life. Reinholdt seems to have had two distinct sides, one as provider of child prostitutes for men who shared his own tastes, the other as a genuinely caring social worker.'

'Do the Austrian police know his present whereabouts?'

'Only that he went to Mexico after his release from prison.'

'So there's no chance of getting hold of him?'

'Apparently not.'

He pursed his lips; firming up the evidence seemed out of the question. 'Anything else?'

'No, Prime Minister.'

'Then I needn't keep you longer. Thank you for your work. Please continue to regard this as very delicate. I see Sisson asked you at one point to be told what was being done. I don't know that will ever be desirable. On the other hand I don't want him to become a problem. Ex-officials with strong feelings develop an itch for the limelight and have to be watched. I rely on you to keep him sweet. Understood?'

He was being unfair in demanding that; but people tried harder, he found, when required to achieve what might be impossible. He took Egerton to the front door. 'If you drove down from London, why did I see you walking up the drive?'

'My wife came with me. The police at the entrance lodge made rather a fuss because they only had authority to admit me. We arranged she'd come back in an hour. She should be there by now.'

He went off, a pleasant man, better-mannered than most of his contemporaries without being servile, possibly a little too serious for his own good. He seemed to have conducted himself competently. An appreciative note was perhaps warranted together with, in Rainsborough's favourite phrase, a little chocolate for that balloon-like creature Fender, with his brooding eyes and enigmatic manner.

A radio news bulletin was due but he needed to spend time in the lavatory. He took the radio with him. Farquharson's grizzling had already been downgraded to a minor item. After he had heard it, he realised he was listening with only half an ear to the rest of the news. His mind was focussed on the Druitt story, impatient to learn whether it was going to stand up, and for the interview with Goble that should resolve the affair. For a few moments he toyed with the idea of telephoning him to come down to Kilndown, instead of to No. 10 later as already arranged. But only a few hours would have been gained and there were other things to be dealt with before he and Diana went back to London.

Behind the newscaster's voice he had been conscious of noise which he had put down to interference. But coming out of the cloakroom, he realised it was inside the house. The sound of screaming was being replaced by sobs. The drawing room door opened and Esther emerged, apparently having broken away from Hilda who was just behind her. She was weeping, her head tilted grotesquely to one side as she moved. The *sari* bought in Delhi lay on the floor.

He reached out. 'Esther!' She evaded his grasp; head still at its extreme angle, she groped towards the stairs. He had not seen her moving in such a terrible way since Reeves had stepped up the drugs dosage. Her lurching and thrusting forward had a macabre, dancing air. Then Hilda had got her by the waist and was helping her up the stairs without resistance now.

He went into the drawing room, picking up the *sari* on the way. Diana was standing by the fireplace, white-faced. He raised his eyebrows. She gave a long defeated sigh. He felt very tired.

'What happened?'

'She'd unwrapped the *sari*. We were helping her to drape it over her dress. Suddenly her fingers failed to do what she wanted and the whole thing became too much. She started lashing out and screaming. It was as though she wanted to kill Hilda. Afterwards she said that most of all she wanted to be dead herself. She'd begun to calm down when you saw her.'

'What caused it? It's been months . . .'

'Hilda suspects she's secretly cut down on the tablets. Presumably she's tried to manage on less than Reeves prescribed. Hilda's going to talk to her about it.'

'I'd better call Reeves.'

'Give it a few minutes, see what Hilda says.'

He got them both a drink. He noticed her hand was bleeding slightly from a scratch.

After a while she asked, 'Was that Egerton you were seeing?'

'Yes.'

'I caught sight of him when he came in. Quite attractive. Are you pleased with him?'

'He seems to have done all right.' He went to the window. 'This fellow Sisson in Italy . . . . Something Egerton said this morning suggests a rather disquieting explanation for why he thought of sending his letter via Esther. His daughter is a patient in the Holgate.' He told her what Egerton had said.

She was frowning. 'But you made absolutely sure that none of the records showed Esther under her own name. Whenever we visited, we always . . .'

'There could have been a slip-up. And we can't altogether rely on Esther's word that she never confided in people. I suspect she has no recollection of some of the things that happened at the hospital.'

'What will you do?'

'There's nothing I *can* do – only bear in mind that Sisson may have information it would be better he hadn't.'

'Only if he's been digging.'

'He was an Intelligence officer before he bought his bloody farm in Tuscany.'

She drew on a cigarette then gave another sigh. 'Gloom and doom. You've got to stop expecting things to go wrong.'

His eyelids were heavy. The tired feeling had not just been a reaction to witnessing another of the crises with Esther; his time clock hadn't adjusted after the trip to Delhi. He had to try to get an hour's sleep after lunch.

'Egerton believes the Frenchman's telling the truth, does he?' she asked.

'He seems to. I now have to discover why Goble sat on it. He may tell me he found out it was an invention, of course.'

She shook her head. 'This is your lifebelt; handled in the right way, it's going to guarantee you another term in No. 10.'

'I'm not counting on it yet.'

'One thing you mustn't do – show Druitt the report and give him the chance of fading out quietly. You have to go for the publicity if it's to do real damage to the Opposition. Don't start feeling charitable, you can't afford it.'

He turned away. Her hardness was almost dazzling. He felt very flat indeed. 'Let's see what Goble says for himself first!'

'Are you having Patrick at the meeting?'

'No.'

'Surely you should? Goble's answerable to him as Home Secretary after all.'

Flatness gave way to unexpectedly fierce anger. 'He's answerable to *me* first. I'll bring Patrick in when I've reached my conclusions about what's to be done.'

Long ago he had mastered injured pride at the thought she went to Welcroft's bed whenever opportunity presented itself. I know such affairs are commonplace in politics, he had told himself, the atmosphere breeds them, I only have to look round . . . . Why let it disturb me? It's not as though I want to sleep with her myself. She'd make no waves if I looked for satisfaction elsewhere. What matters is, we remain an effective team. Yet fury at her concern for Welcroft's interests could grip unexpectedly, squeezing until the poisons ran like rivers inside.

Her lips had formed a smile, intended, he knew, to be conciliatory. She was able to sense his emotions well enough. 'Sorry, I see that, of course. Anyway, the important thing will be the timing of whatever you do.'

Timing, that would be Patrick Welcroft's view of the essence of this business, he reflected. To hell with worrying about the facts; just get the timing right.

When the message came that Goble had arrived at No. 10, he played briefly with the notion of seeing him in one of the bleak upper rooms that faced the Foreign Office block. To watch his face as he read Egerton's report in the cold light from Downing Street might be rewarding. No doubt that sort of ploy was part of his investigators' dingy stock-in-trade; no bad thing for their Führer to experience the same medicine. But it would really be too odd a choice. He had him brought to the study and greeted him with a geniality calculated to relax Goble's guard, if that was possible. 'We meet too seldom.' Indicating a chair, he went on, 'Perhaps on the other hand I should be thankful for that. I seem to remember reading that one of my predecessors expressed regret at the failure of one of yours to bury his foxes. I hope that remark hasn't been regarded as strict scriptural guidance.'

'You will always be brought at least the brush, Prime Minister.'

There was something close to arrogance in his confidence. But today he could hardly be quite at ease. This summons on a Sunday evening, to a meeting for which no agenda had been slated, a meeting arranged, not through Private Secretaries, but by a call from Blackmer himself, would have caused his antennae to quiver.

A skinny, balding man with a beak of a nose and the untidy movements that went with angularity, Goble could hardly lay claim to charisma. That appearance and the donnish mannerisms made it astonishing that he had once had a successful career as a professional soldier. Overtones of Academe to such an extent, the Army would surely have found hard to swallow.

Yet not only had it done that, in the rat race to a general's baton it had made him an early winner. Exceptional wiliness must have played a part, that vital quality for a successful career in the soldiery. But once the baton was secured, Goble had changed course, seeking pastures less ruthlessly competitive. A well-cultivated range of contacts, some political, some mercantile, a few even in the universities, had enabled him to secure, first a Deputy's post in the Security Service and then, a few years later, appointment as Director-General. Since that time he had steered a careful course, neither too visible nor too remote. His pretensions were those of a soldier-intellectual, cast among brutish civilians. Soon after his arrival at No. 10 as

Prime Minister, Blackmer had noticed in the library an autographed volume of verse by Goble. It had been written in the early Sixties, when he had been serving as a lieutenant in the jungles of Borneo. The verse seemed not bad at all.

'No special problems on your side, I hope,' Blackmer said.

'Nothing I need trouble you with, Prime Minister.'

'Then let me turn to one that's been brought to *my* notice.' Taking from his desk the folder brought back from Kilndown, he placed it in Goble's dry fingers. 'Reluctant though I am to entertain the possibility, I wondered if this was a fox that had somehow been overlooked.'

Goble removed reading glasses from an inner pocket and fitted them to his face with irritating deliberation. Eroding that self-assurance would never be easy, Blackmer reflected. Ordinary mandarins could occasionally be surprised and thrown off-balance by his own mastery of technical knowledge. But Goble came from a darkened province to which he had no reliable maps. Men with lamps could be sent there from time to time; for a while the inhabitants, busy about their curious business, would come into view. But the lamps soon guttered. Then darkness rolled back, leaving the suspicion that what was really of interest had been beyond the reach of light and perhaps would always be.

Goble's eyes moved in a measured way through Egerton's reports. Occasionally his mouth puckered as at something absurd or at any rate hard to swallow. Only once did Blackmer see a muscle twitch in the jaw. That, he guessed, might have been the passage alleging he had protected Druitt as a bird of similar feather. At the end he folded his reading glasses and looked up calmly. 'Yes.'

'You're familiar with the Vienna story?'

'I am, Prime Minister.'

'And Sisson is right when he says he reported what Massenet had to tell to Bridewell – who in turn passed the details to you?'

'Yes.'

'Did you in fact decide that no action was called for?'

'I did.'

'Why was that?'

'Because I had already been put in possession of the full facts.'

'By whom?'

'By Mr Druitt himself.'

He frowned. Somehow he hadn't allowed for this possibility. 'When did he tell you?'

'Shortly before the man, Alois Reinholdt, stood trial in Vienna. Mr Druitt telephoned and said he needed some advice. When he came to my house he explained he'd heard of the forthcoming trial during one of his visits to Vienna – he has friends there. He was a little alarmed, having then just joined the Shadow Cabinet, that his name might be bandied about in the proceedings, since he'd not only visited Reinholdt's orphanage but had let Reinholdt bring a child to his bedroom in a hotel during a Pugwash meeting he'd attended. He asked me if I could discover from the Austrian police if there was any danger of his name being mentioned. I was later able to tell him there wasn't.'

'He presumably explained why the child was brought to him?'

'Yes. Apparently during the Pugwash meeting Reinholdt had discovered, from a newspaper that Mr Druitt was Member of Parliament for Hellingworth. Reinholdt had a child in his orphanage, a boy of nine, whose parents had been killed in a gas explosion in Vienna. He had no surviving relatives as far as could be discovered, but spoke of remembering being taken by his mother to stay with an elderly couple in England, in Hellingworth in fact. The child didn't know their names or the address where they lived but he was able to describe the street quite well and the approximate position in the street of their house. Reinholdt had a strong feeling that the couple could have been the parents of the dead mother and he decided to ask Mr Druitt for his help in tracing them.

'Mr Druitt agreed to see the boy in his hotel room at the end of a day's proceedings of the Pugwash meeting and Reinholdt brought him along and assisted Druitt in getting all the facts the boy could remember. Later, back in Hellingworth Mr

Druitt tried to find the elderly couple but failed. Although he identified the street, it had been bulldozed out of existence to make way for redevelopment and the register of ratepayers and the memories of one or two inhabitants he managed to trace produced no couple to match the child's recollection. When he was in Vienna about a year later, he called at the orphanage and explained to Reinholdt that he'd had no luck.'

It was a persuasive story. And it could be true. Blackmer watched Goble folding his spectacles again. 'Against that background, I don't quite understand why Mr Druitt was worried about possibly damaging publicity.'

'He explained that someone who saw the child coming out of his room was a French journalist with whom he had had a number of arguments during the conference and who he felt might harbour a grudge. That fact coupled with the sensational gossip he'd heard in Vienna about Reinholdt having arranged paedophile orgies for men who came from all over Europe made him particularly apprehensive.'

'The journalist being Massenet?'

'Yes.'

'So when Sisson's report of Massenet's story was brought to you, you considered there was nothing of importance in it?'

'That's so, Prime Minister.'

'Notwithstanding the elements that were inconsistent with Mr Druitt's account – the child crying out, the noises of sexual activity.'

'Sisson's report made no mention of those things.'

'You're certain of that?'

'Quite certain, Prime Minister.'

'How is that to be explained?'

Goble said sombrely, 'I should need to know more about the relationship Sisson and Massenet now seem to have developed before answering that. But perhaps at this point I can correct another misrepresentation in Mr Egerton's report. Sisson resigned, not over my decision regarding Mr Druitt but because I declined to promote him when Mr Bridewell, his senior officer, became ill.'

His whole demeanour repudiated any possibility that he

could be found vulnerable. Blackmer said, 'Did you explain to Sisson when he came to protest about your decision to take no action on his report that you had had a different version already from Mr Druitt?'

'I told him he must accept my word for it that I was satisfied nothing wrong had taken place in Mr Druitt's room. I couldn't be more forthcoming because of an undertaking I had given to Mr Druitt some time before. For several years he had been supplying me with valuable reports on the character of the Eastern European delegates he met at the Pugwash meetings – a number of them were of Intelligence interest. He did that against my promise that nobody else in the Security Service would be told he was maintaining this contact with me. He considered it would be damaging to his position in the Labour Party if his acting in this way became more widely known.'

With every minute that passed the Sisson allegation was losing more of its shine. Blackmer said, 'I think I should see Sisson's note of his original conversation with Massenet. Perhaps you'll be good enough to send it over to me.'

'I'm afraid that won't be possible, Prime Minister. I decided it should be destroyed in view of the fact it carried a damaging implication against Mr Druitt I knew to be untrue.'

He gritted his teeth. 'I see. Very well, send me your record of what Mr Druitt told you.'

Goble was hesitating; for the first time it seemed he might be on the run. 'Do you see some difficulty?'

With his spectacles frame Goble scratched a side of his nose. 'I was wondering about the proprieties, Prime Minister. Arising from the fact that it was a communication of a personal nature by the Leader of the Opposition.' He produced a thin smile that was almost indulgent. 'However, in all the circumstances I think he would wish you to read the note.'

The arrogance was insufferable. He seemed to think he was entitled to behave like an independent potentate. Whatever the result of the present business, he would have to be got rid of. Blackmer said icily, 'Then I expect to receive it first thing tomorrow.'

'Of course.'

'Let me get this quite clear. You believe that one must disregard what Sisson and Massenet say, that they're simply out to make trouble – right? Your personal acquaintance with Mr Druitt is such that you insist his version of the relationship with Reinholdt should be accepted.'

A touch of colour appeared in Goble's cheeks. The thrust had gone home. He said, 'My acquaintance with Mr Druitt encourages me to believe his word can be trusted. That does not apply in the case of Sisson.'

'Neither you nor I are paid to rely wholly on the word of other people, Goble. That is not of course intended as a reflection on Mr Druitt's reliability. But we need to listen whenever new facts – or what have the appearance of facts – are presented to us. I hope you agree.'

He was scarlet now. 'May I ask, Prime Minister, what you now propose to do about the matter? I feel strongly that Sisson should not be given any further hearing. His scurrilous campaign against myself . . .'

'I shall be discussing the business with the Home Secretary, who hasn't yet seen these papers. He will let you know what we decide.'

He gave Goble a frigid handshake and sent him away to lick his wounds. For a while he tried tackling files on other subjects. But the meeting had depressed him. He went upstairs to the flat. Diana was stretched out on the divan, reading. Her face had a glow. He guessed she had been working out on the exercise bicycle she had installed in the dressing room; keeping the body in shape for Welcroft's admiring explorations, he told himself grimly.

She put aside her book, eager for news. After he had told her, she laughed shortly and shook her head. 'God,' she said, 'You have to hand it to him.'

'Hand *what* to him?'

'He's so cool! He and Druitt must have sweated hard over cooking up the story of the boy's lost grandparents in Hellingworth against the day when Massenet might produce his account of what he saw and heard. Or perhaps they only got round to it after Sisson had sent up his report.'

'You don't believe Goble?'

'Do you? It's altogether too neat, too pat! Right down to his having conveniently destroyed the note of what Sisson originally reported. You surely can't buy this version?'

She was right of course – it *was* neat, to an almost unbelievable extent.

And yet . . .

· Nine ·

Rainsborough was taking an age over reading the folder. It now contained, in addition to Egerton's report, Blackmer's own note and the memorandum Goble had sent to No. 10 of Druitt's discussion with him. Barely concealing impatience, Welcroft had turned to study the wallpaper in Blackmer's room at the House of Commons. A slackening of the jowls was creeping on, Blackmer noted, and there was a spongier dimension to the chin. The joys of table and bed were at last taking their toll. He wondered if Diana had registered the changes.

Of all Diana's affairs, this had been the most unexpected. He could understand that graceful body, those smooth features, the dashing mane of hair, tempting her to a brief tasting, but not more than that. He would have supposed she would quickly dismiss the personality as hopelessly flash, along with the boxy double-breasted suits and crocodile shoes. But she had perceived in Welcroft the lineaments of someone who, with a few minor adjustments, might win ultimate power in the Party. A man for today, straddling the classes from vaguely mysterious origins, a mercantile adventurer whose ships had returned early, laden with treasure; ruthless, fluent, effective before studio cameras as much as in the House – more than any of the other younger men, he seemed to personify the elements of their victory over the old guard. Those squires and country gentlemen who had grown old and dispirited waiting in the Thatcher years for the good times to return, had had to face the fact that the future belonged to Welcroft and his kind. They must either opt for nullity or make their accomodation with him; his gifts, which included the easy relationship with the *Zeitgeist* they lacked, were too important to be ignored. He could appear literate when necessary but would never be branded intellectual. The Party Conference, the chat show, the pop interview – he adapted to each with a sure instinct. Above all he was seamlessly efficient; the bodies on the way up had not merely been buried, they no longer existed.

At last Rainsborough lifted his head. 'I don't like the sound of Sisson,' he said.

Welcroft turned to him. 'I agree he's an odd fish who obviously has a score he wants to settle with Goble. However we shouldn't on that account lightly push aside what he and Massenet claim happened in Vienna. If they're right, Druitt is clearly not the sort of man the public would want to see leading the Labour Party, or as Prime Minister.'

'You'd dismiss everything Goble says?'

'Not everything. But equally I don't shut my eyes to the fact that Goble has been close to Druitt for years and doesn't have a wife or any visible interest in the opposite sex.'

'Pagett tells me there *was* a wife,' Blackmer said. 'They divorced many years ago.'

'It would be interesting to know the reasons.'

Rainsborough had placed the palms of his hands on his knees. He was pressing down, a characteristic sign of unease. 'I don't of course know Goble as you do, Patrick. But his integrity doesn't seem to have been questioned before.'

Welcroft was looking at Blackmer now. A hint of a smile behind the eyes was saying, I am prepared to be endlessly tolerant with old Charles of course, but why in Christ's name is he here? 'I know my predecessor as Home Secretary was disposed to favour Goble. But I've never felt I could *entirely* trust him. How about you, David?'

His use of formal address at meetings like this was usually punctilious to the point of ostentation. By trotting out the Christian name now, Blackmer knew he was laying claim to a brotherhood from which the likes of Rainsborough were excluded. In Welcroft's vision of the Party, the Rainsboroughs were the Shire horses who had served their purpose long ago. It was all right to keep a few around, to provide colour, amusement and reassurance, heritage symbols for the citizenry to admire. But that was as much as he would allow.

Blackmer said, 'I don't believe I've previously regarded Goble as untrustworthy. Tiresome, yes. But not untrustworthy. I'm surprised you haven't mentioned this before.' He raised his eyebrows at Welcroft, wondering if he knew just how much he hated him. 'So bearing in mind there is absolutely no independent evidence to support Massenet's and Sisson's allegations, what do you suggest, Patrick?'

'Only that their story should somehow be got out into the open.'

'You would like us to encourage that?'

'Yes.'

Blackmer looked at Rainsborough. 'Charles?'

'Even if the allegations were true, we all know the sexual habits of a lot of politicians on both sides of the House wouldn't bear too close attention.'

'Not too many bugger little boys and girls, I hope.'

'Maybe not. What I ask myself is – would we be right to try to destroy Druitt by using this? I don't believe we should.'

He smiled at Rainsborough and was suddenly aware his own mind has been made up long ago. 'I find myself in sympathy with that. On reflection, don't you, Patrick?'

Welcroft had been holding a pen between his fingers. He applied elaborate concentration to positioning it on the desk in front of him. 'Could I just say, Prime Minister, I wasn't envisaging that you – we – should make use of the information directly. But if a newspaper were to send someone to interview Massenet, it would find itself with the makings of a good story. Assuming it found a way of running it the public could then make up its own mind on the probabilities.'

'Did you have a particular paper in mind?'

'One of Bedford's – possibly the *Clarion*. The new woman editor he's put in is said to be keen to show she has balls.'

'In full colour, I daresay,' Rainsborough said. 'A little bizarre even for the *Clarion* one would have thought.'

Welcroft ignored him. 'If you like, I could have a word with Bedford. I believe we're attending the same dinner tonight.'

Blackmer shook his head. 'No. If Massenet chooses to talk to the press off his own bat, that's something else. Druitt is always going to run that risk. But we don't prompt Massenet to talk. Nor Sisson. And we don't brief Bedford.' Welcroft's eyes were fixed on him, searching for a chink of doubt. 'I'm sorry if that strikes you as negative, Patrick.'

'No, no, I accept the decision unreservedly.'

All the same, he would not have given up hope, Blackmer told himself. Some part of post-coital languor with Diana would be allocated to discussing ways of bringing him round. He would need to watch them both for signs of that.

As they were leaving, he called Rainsborough back. 'I may be being foolish, Charles. Are you sure I'm not?'

'I hope there's still room for a little decency in politics.'

'You believe that?'

'I try to.'

He walked him to the door. Guilty he seldom felt, except, oddly, in relation to Esther and there he was guiltless. But watching Rainsborough go, he regretted he had never sought his company, only used him.

Sitting down again behind his desk, he closed his eyes. Someone knocked, opened the door, then decided withdrawal would be wise: one of the secretaries, he guessed. Soon after he had taken office, he had taught them never to ignore the signals of nonco-operation. There was a tightness to his scalp of a kind he could not recall noticing before. It felt as though his hair was being drawn and twisted into a knot at the apex of the head. The fear that always lurked at the back of his mind reached out again. He should perhaps have another check-up by Reeves. He depended on the daily evidence of his competence to be assured his judgment wasn't going. Once he suspected it was failing, there would surely be enough time to devise a strategy for retirement before prurient speculation could take hold. Long before even Diana knew the blow had finally fallen, he would have acted. And then it would be Esther and he, together, against the worst.

When another knock came at the door, he relented and demanded aspirin. After he had taken it and walked round the room, he decided his head seemed better. He drank tea, signed a batch of constituency letters, then went to the Chamber.

From the Opposition benches came those sounds that accompanied most of his entrances these days, not specific enough to be characterised as jeers or whistles, yet plainly signifying derision. Behind him, as he sat down, his own benches stayed silent, a sullen army prepared to fight for him only when driven to it by ridicule or an apprehension that otherwise a mortal blow would fall.

The debate on the environment was drifting on its predictable course. A ravaged landscape had been reached, where only carrion crows flew and anything not already extinct or at least polluted was scarcely days away from it. The Opposition front bench was well-filled; Druitt seemed able to parade his crew in force for the most unlikely business. He was there himself, handsome and Buddha-like, listening to assorted Greens cry woe to the television cameras and sometimes nodding when his own people gave tongue.

Along the Government front bench, with only a single other Minister in between, sat Whittingstall, enpurpled, living testimony to the ills of liquid lunches. As Secretary of State for this accursed empire, no doubt he would shortly be making a hash of his department's brief, if the ingredients created the remotest opportunity for that. In their box, his officials crouched, suitably whey-faced.

It was necessary to stay long enough to demonstrate he was keeping in touch, not so long that he would be caught up in Whittingstall's *bêtises*. This state of affairs was his own fault. The opportunity to send Whittingstall to the Lords had occurred a year ago. In the pressure of other manoeuvring, he had failed to seize it. Too late now in this Parliament to do anything except allow him the rope with which to hang himself, as far as possible unattended.

A government back-bencher whose name he failed to remember was called, from sound and appearance a City fancier of forestry and Sunday cattle watcher. The farmer's partnership with the soil was being mentioned, that mystical thing. The man wore an MCC tie. Blackmer listened to him with a thoughtful concentration which the cameras would observe was judicious, neither dismissive nor partisan. When it was over, he rose and escaped.

Members were drifting out towards the tea-room. He decided he would go back to No. 10, returning later for the vote. But across the Lobby, he saw Druitt, who had come out of the Chamber at almost the same time. Druitt gave a half-humorous shake of the head, directed, Blackmer guessed, at the last contribution to the debate. Observed by the more solemn of their supporters, such unspoken exchanges across the Party divide had excited displeasure in the past. He nodded back then, gripped by a sudden impulse, crossed to take Druitt by the arm. 'Perhaps we could have a word.'

They settled down in his room with cigars and tea. 'A warning,' he said.

Druitt inclined his head with that contained smile, calculated to repel the possibility of there being anything on which common ground would not be discovered. Not everyone trusted the affability. Kenneth Cridland, the Party's certain choice for the leadership if things went badly in the autumn, saw in Druitt only a smiling shit, cold as stone beneath the inexhaustible charm. But Cridland was a hater, a cherisher of enemies. Other enemies of Druitt on the far Left of his own Party sometimes told lurid stories of his service in the Army in Oman, of personally-undertaken executions of captured rebels regarded even by Omanis as remarkably enthusiastic. But the far Left had scores to settle with Druitt: in fashioning a Party into which the middle classes could be coaxed once more to tumble their guilt, he had proved a notable butcher among the ranks of the Left.

'Some days ago,' Blackmer said, 'I received a letter from someone who turned out to be an ex-member of the Security Service. He claimed he had information showing you to be guilty of serious criminal acts. I felt I had no choice but to find out what the information was, so I sent an official from the Cabinet Office to interview him. The official also talked to a

French journalist who was the real source of the allegation. It was to the effect that you'd engaged in paedophilia.'

Druitt's expression did not change. Yet the smile he had maintained throughout somehow no longer seemed appropriate to it, like a lamp left burning after daylight fills a room. He took the cigar from his mouth and said, 'And where is this supposed to have happened?'

'In Vienna, rather more than ten years ago.'

He hesitated for perhaps three seconds, not more. 'Ah, yes. This is built round my dealings with Reinholdt.'

'You remember the occasion?'

'Very well. I told Richard Goble about it when I thought my name might come out as a contact of Reinholdt, albeit for innocent reasons. I imagine the French journalist you mention is a tiresome man named Massenet who conceived a dislike for me. Why has the ex-MI5 man teamed up with him?'

'He seems to believe the Frenchman's story. But he also has a hate against Goble who he claims has been protecting you because of shared sexual tastes.'

'You've spoken to Richard Goble of course . . .'

'Yes. He gave me a note of what you told him about Reinholdt and the reason why you had the boy brought to your room. I wanted you to know that of course I fully accept that explanation. However I hardly need to add I have no control over either the ex-MI5 man or Massenet. It's possible they'll peddle their story to the press. If they do, it will not be as a result of encouragement from anybody in the Government.'

'Wouldn't the MI5 man be liable for prosecution if he talked?'

'Probably, but he lives outside the jurisdiction. I daresay the Attorney would tell me that short of sending somebody with a poison-tipped umbrella nothing could be done. And Massenet of course has no obligation to keep quiet.'

Druitt picked up a paperweight containing a miniature maple leaf. Some Canadian businessman had presented it during a trade junket. He rocked it in his hand as though he might be considering an offer for it. His calm was extraordinary, he showed neither apprehension nor anger. They sat in silence for a few moments. From the secretaries' room came faintly the sound of a telephone. Finally Druitt said with a touch of weariness in his voice, 'Who apart from yourself knows about this?'

'Norman Pagett and one of his officials. Goble as well of course. Amongst Ministers, only Patrick Welcroft and Charles Rainsborough.'

Druitt's smile made a brief, crooked return. 'I see. Well, there's no virtue in worrying. If I find the story put into circulation by anybody, I shall sue and use every weapon I've got. I shall expect Richard Goble to be made available to testify that he knew the true facts from me a long time ago.' He rose and stretched. 'I suppose I really should take a wife. A beautiful floating voter, do you recommend?' He seemed to have quite recovered. 'Of course I ought to get it in before the autumn. Have you picked your date yet, may I ask?'

'I'm still considering the entrails.'

'They should be telling you – no hope.'

'Don't be too sure.' Blackmer rose himself. 'I read some of your novel last night, by the way. It was in the Cabinet Room bookcase. One of my predecessors must have acquired it. There's something it occurred to me to ask you. Remember your two women artists?'

'Yes.'

'Despite what one of them says to a journalist towards the end, I felt some doubt about their relationship still existed. Exactly what it had been in a physical sense, I mean. The reader was perhaps expected to make his own mind up. Was that your intention?'

Druitt shrugged. 'The book changed as I went along. I'm not sure what I intended now. It's always up to the reader though, isn't it, whatever the author says.'

At the door he turned and said simply, 'Thank you. That was helpful.' Then he was gone.

· Ten ·

Louise finished her packing, went to her desk and took from a drawer the card on which Tom had written the telephone number for the house on Berkeley Square.

He answered it at once in a tone of faint impatience that told her he was either reading or writing. 'Your ex-wife,' she said. 'Is this convenient?'

'Louise!' She couldn't make out if he was pleased or not.

'I wondered if you'd be around during the next few days – in London, I mean. I have to go to Europe in connection with the book I told you about. On my way back here, I thought of stopping off in London.'

'Great! Will you stay over for a while? We could take in some shows. Is there anything you'd particularly like to see?' His tone was breezily hospitable; a hint of nostalgia would not have come amiss. But, after all, there had been nothing of nostalgia in her decision to call.

'I'm not sure how long I'll have to spare – possibly no more than an evening. Hal is expecting me back in a big hurry, there's a mountain of work on my desk. But dinner would be nice. I'll call you from Paris when I know what flight I'm getting from there. It should be the day after tomorrow.'

'So how's the book going?' he asked.

'We may have a problem. The author's had a telephone call that suggests to him the Government may not be going to use his information. He called Hal and said there had to be pressure brought to bear.'

'Is *that* what you're going to do?'

She laughed. 'Not me. Hal's decided the author needs

calming. I'm going over with tranquillisers and the draft contract for the book.'

'But there's still hope the whole thing will collapse and the story won't be surfaced . . .'

'Hope?'

'Yes.'

She frowned at the wall opposite her. 'Is there some special reason I don't know about why you want the guy in question to become leader of that government?'

'I told you – we think American interests would be best served if he does. That's all.'

'Lew Rothman doesn't think so, apparently.'

He made noises of contempt. When she laughed, he said, 'If you knew a quarter of what I know about that screwy outfit, you wouldn't be so light-hearted.'

'You're jealous – I can smell it from here. Anyway Hal's not giving up on the book. He's arranged to have lunch with Brad to put the problem to him.'

'When?' he asked sharply.

'Tomorrow. So there's nothing you can do to stop the cavalry riding in. Wasn't I wise not to tell you who the author and his source are?'

'You're a hard woman,' he said on a reflective note. He uttered a sigh of resignation. 'So we've just got to get something into Brad's soup, have we?'

Much later she thought bitterly that resignation was never Tom's style. But for the moment she only felt elation. 'Alas, poor Brad then. And I hardly knew him.'

'Editing has made you very literary,' he said grimly. 'Sparkier too.'

'Put that down to the excitement of living in this crazy town.'

'Call me from Paris as soon as you know your London flight. I'll be at Heathrow myself if I can make it, otherwise I'll send a car.'

She couldn't resist a minor probe. 'You'd say, wouldn't you, if my coming interfered with other things?'

'I'd say,' he said.

She had not seen Sisson in suit and tie before; they were perhaps being worn in honour of their dining together at the hotel. From the terrace she had watched in surprise as he stepped from a diminutive three-wheeler truck in which he had presumably driven all the way from San Donato earlier. It had been agreed they would meet at the hotel in Pisa instead of her going to San Donato after he had said he would in any case have business in Pisa during the afternoon.

The suit was of thick wool, hardly a wise choice for the time of year. She had no hope a deodorant would be at work mitigating the consequences; her recollection of the lifestyle in the Sissons' household suggested a scorning of such frivolities. Under the suit a shirt of chemical green and a heather-mixture tie were visible. His shoes were black brogues. Whether the result, topped by the usual straw hat, represented careful selection she found hard to decide. She rated him a poseur of a familiar English kind. But it was equally possible he had reached into a cupboard and simply taken what was nearest to hand.

His mood on arrival was taciturn and grim. Over drinks in her room before dinner she tried to coax him into a more sanguine state. The telephone call he had had from Egerton, finally extracted from him in detail, seemed not to justify total gloom. He was, she concluded, hyper-suspicious, abnormally ready to imagine the world was always conspiring to do him down. It was becoming harder each time they met to hide her dislike of him.

On their way down to the restaurant she said, 'I think you're too pessimistic.'

He looked at her with near contempt. '*I* know what was behind those words! You forget – I worked in that system. They're working up to a fudge!'

Their path into the restaurant was blocked by elderly American tourists waiting for a pack leader to return from organising their tables. Sisson glared at them balefully; touristic contamination had featured in his conversation at their first meeting. He went on with his gripe. 'In London I spent my life fighting against fudge and mudge . That's what British democracy has degenerated into. Hope the awkward things'll just go away! Play them long! Grasping nettles can damage your health!'

One or two of the tourists turned to gaze at him. He stared back at them then, unexpectedly, let out a cackling laugh, consoled a little by being the focus of attention.

When they were seated, she said, 'Anyway it would be against Blackmer's interests to shelve what you and Massenet have given him. You said yourself your letter would hit him at exactly the most effective moment, that with an election coming up, he would be desperately looking for a way of defeating Druitt.'

'Some factor could have cancelled out the advantage I was offering him.'

'What sort of factor?'

'Perhaps Druitt also has dirt which Blackmer knows he'd use if anything was made of the business with the child. Goble could have supplied him with some ammunition. It's not impossible.'

'Do you *know* of Goble having information damaging to Blackmer?'

'No.'

She watched him pick up his glass and lean back in his chair to brood. 'But you have something in mind . . .'

He pulled in the sides of his mouth, shrugging at the same time. If there *was* something, he didn't intend to tell her.

He had chosen to drink scotch before dinner rather than a local wine as on previous occasions. He was staying on it now. The greater part of the wine she had enlisted his help in selecting was being left to her to drink; even its choice had been made without a dialogue in histrionic Italian with the waiter. No admiring references had been made to the view of Pisa available through the window beside them. Indigenous joys were all receiving short shrift; it was not one of his days for them.

Producing, half-way through the meal, the book contract, with its promise of dollar bills little more than a signature or two away, had been her remaining hope of luring him into a better mood. But as his gaze moved intently down the paragraphs, she realised that all she had done was provide an alternative focus for discontent.

Since their first meeting, her feelings about him had turned through 180 degrees. She had begun with a certain amount of liking, seeing him as a victim, understandably gripped almost to the point of obsession by a scandal and the blighting of his career that had resulted from it. The proportion of truth to self-delusion where his own fate was involved was difficult to assess and perhaps not all that interesting. But the scandal itself seemed beyond doubt.

The anxiety to make a financial killing from the exposure had not appeared unreasonable either. He had little enough money, that was obvious; and there was the daughter being maintained at crippling expense in a private hospital. When Hal had once asked Sisson about possibly switching her to the state system, he had replied that he would never move her from a place where she was as happy as she could ever be. She had admired him then.

But distaste had grown the more she got to know him. She came to recognise the concern about Druitt, the moral indignation, the flag-waving alarm for old England, as pretexts. What he wanted more than anything was a springboard for a mortal attack on Goble for having humiliated him, cast him aside. We're buying a vendetta, she told Hal, and he had replied she was right but it was a very marketable one.

Something else finally crystallised her feelings into contempt. Behind his claimed attachment to anonymity, to the rewards of the simple life on his *podere*, he was, in fact, avid for notoriety. Acclaim in the world he professed to despise was what he wanted above all. He saw himself, heroically packaged by the book, the selfless scourge of private sin and public treachery, the great patriot, cast out but risen again. The stink of hypocrisy about him became too strong for her; on the humbug of his virtue she found she had choked.

When at last he looked up from the contract, it was to make objections to the way subsidiary rights were to be sold. He also wanted details of the likely publicity budget and a redraft of the section that dealt with his approval of her text. He was being hard-nosed but not entirely unreasonable. Mustering a conciliatory smile, she told him she'd talk to Hal.

He returned to the reason he'd called, the need to find a way to stop stalling on Blackmer's part. She hedged. 'I only said we might be able to discover how his mind was moving.'

'Using what channel to him?'

'I can't tell you.'

'Why not?'

'Because it's very delicate.'

'Look, either you can help over this or you can't. I need to *know*.' He was trying to bulldoze her. She shook her head. 'This is something Hal is handling personally. He has a contact he's talking to today. He'll let you know as soon as anything develops.'

'You could call him now.'

'There'd be no point yet.'

He wasn't troubling to conceal his annoyance. For a while she feared the meeting was headed for total disaster. But abruptly he shrugged. 'Well, tell him I feel strongly. On this sort of thing he ought to rely on my judgment. Otherwise we shall fall out.'

She wondered if there was a real threat behind that. But they had surely gone too far down the road together for it to be easy for him and Massenet to defect to another publisher.

By the time he had drunk a second Armagnac with his coffee, he was recovering. Gradually he reverted to the philosopher-scholar manner she remembered from their first working session in Massenet's apartment; reflections on the Armagnac and its origins led to a dissertation on the making of *grappa*, an addition to the catalogue of the Good Life missing in the world of telegrams and letters. At such moments, with vengefulness temporarily dormant and affectation only lightly worn, he displayed his most attractive quality, enthusiasm.

As he was placing the contract in the battered document case which seemed to accompany him everywhere, he said, 'One final thing: I want to find out what position Egerton holds in Conservative Party Headquarters in London. Listening to him on the telephone this time, I began to wonder if what he was saying really came straight from the Prime Minister or whether there's now somebody operating in the middle. Perhaps there always has been and I failed to sense it.'

She said she'd see what could be done. Together they went out to the three-wheeler truck. Sisson's walk was unsteady but not greatly worse than she had known it when he was sober. In any case, his head, she guessed, would always be strong enough to steer him clear of the ditches.

Putting on the straw hat, he said, 'Sorry if I was a bit brusque. As an American you may not fully understand my feelings. For the sake of my country, nothing is more important than making sure this thing isn't swept back under the carpet.'

He climbed into the cab of the truck. She wondered if he supposed she believed his last words, took them for more than signals as to the line he expected her to adopt when she came to write the book. If he did, she could imagine him, as he puttered through the night to San Donato, suddenly letting rip with the cackle laugh.

A sign, an intimation of the flavour that would mark the day, came early in the morning. Craning across the washbasin in the bathroom to fix the second ear stud, she felt its butterfly fastening slip between her fingers. It slid past the bars of the basin hole and disappeared, probably already bound for the sewers of Pisa; yet, on the other hand, not certainly. She picked up the telephone and called reception. Thirty minutes later, having failed to galvanise the hotel staff into producing a suitable tool with which to explore the lingering chance of the basin trap, she had to admit defeat and leave for the airport.

Frustration was still the hallmark of the morning when the flight to Paris remained throbbing on the tarmac far beyond its take-off time. Her schedule had been tight even if all went well, with less than an hour allowed to get from the airport in Paris to the restaurant recommended for lunch by Berliot, Hal Mencken's Paris agent.

Massenet had agreed to meet her there, bringing with him the tape. She arrived twenty minutes late. He was nowhere to be seen. At first, relieved to think she had beaten him to it, she relaxed with a Martini in a booth of mahogany and red velvet that seemed to promise well for a civilised discussion over the meal. But when another twenty-five minutes went by without Massenet appearing, she knew the day remained against her.

A call to his apartment produced no response. Either Massenet had misunderstood the arrangement or had flounced out of the restaurant, annoyed at not finding her here. Remembering the coolness with which he had greeted Hal's announcement that she would be writing the book, she could picture that.

After ten more minutes, she ordered as brief a lunch as the menu and the surroundings seemed to allow and took a cab to Berliot's office to keep an appointment there.

By now it was late in the afternoon. Another call to Massenet's apartment produced no response. A premonition of defeat strengthened but she shook it off. She asked Berliot to go with her to the apartment building.

It had struck her as possible that the *concierge* might have useful news. But she had not seen Massenet since the previous day when he had passed her window. Further pressed by Berliot, now more disposed to be a team player, the *concierge* recalled him having spoken of driving to Rouen during the afternoon; she supposed it might be in pursuit of material for the book he was writing about his father.

In the face of this and the possibility that he would be away overnight, she decided there was no more to be done. She called Tom at the Embassy in London to tell him she would be on the flight leaving for Heathrow at half-past six, then as a final throw, asked Berliot to try Massenet's number from time to time and to call her at Tom's if he made contact. Getting an onward flight to New York after a few hours in London no longer looked sensible. By staying overnight, she could, if Massenet was located, fly back to Paris in the morning to collect the tape then.

The first bright spot of the day was the appearance of Tom

at the foot of the aircraft steps as she disembarked at Heathrow. He looked relaxed, handsome and deceptively trustworthy. Behind him stood an Embassy car and driver. Pull of a kind familiar in postings like Manila or Saigon in the old days, she had not thought to see in action here. She guessed he wanted to impress her, and was not displeased.

He took her baggage card to hand to an airline girl. 'How was your trip?'

'Lousy. I'd rather not be reminded.'

'Right.' He dismissed it with a wave. 'Here's the plan. We go back to the house for you to change.' He paused and looked momentarily anxious. 'You *are* staying over?'

'Yes, just for tonight.'

'Fine, because I have a table at the Connaught for dinner. Afterwards, assuming you feel like it, we could try a night spot.'

She leaned her head back. 'Lead me to a bath and a long, long drink. I'm not sure about any more. I think I might fall asleep before we finish dinner. When will I get my bag?'

'It's following us – shouldn't be more than twenty minutes later.'

'You're impressing me.'

He made one of his casually grand gestures. Through her side window she saw they had already left the airport perimeter and were attempting to cross a line of traffic coming west out of London, office people presumably, on their way home. Beyond stretched a land of cosy, suburban order: houses and gardens, houses and gardens, an endless parade of them – everywhere that appearance of nothing being left unfinished, undecided, that was her memory of this country.

'How was your day?' she asked and was at once aware of an echo, like playing again an old tune. She wished she had not fallen so easily into the way of it.

'I've known better.' He grimaced briefly then looked past her at silted traffic lines with the air of indulgence which was not indulgence really but a steely resolve not to react to life's irritations quite as others did. 'The Defense Secretary flew in, he's been at the Embassy all day, en route to tell the Europeans we're thinking again about the troops' withdrawals programme. Tonight he's dining with the Prime Minister and his opposite number here.'

'Were you invited?'

'No, they know I'd let the side down.'

'What would you have said?'

'That it's madness to think we should put the withdrawals programme into reverse even if all the Europeans can be persuaded to agree – the economic facts back home are going to assert themselves as unavoidable sooner or later.'

'Doesn't the Pentagon see that?'

'Military guys never believe the laws of economics need apply to them. And they've got Lew Rothman telling the President twenty-four hours a day that it's vital to maintain a European regional force in case things go really sour in the East again.'

'Perhaps he's right.'

'Worries on that score are for the Europeans themselves. They should pick up the tab. At least Druitt acknowledges that's what ought to happen.'

'And Blackmer?'

'Blackmer likes the status quo and as long as he's Prime Minister he'll use his considerable pull with the President to argue against any change.'

They had arrived at the house on Berkeley Square. It had somehow escaped conversion into offices, unlike its neighbours. A discreetly anonymous facade in an eighteenth-century terrace on the west side, its bricks had been lightened by picking out the mortar lines in white. Above the door the fanlight was a delicate filigree. Louise saw beyond the maid who opened the door to them, a hallway of white marble that stretched to the foot of a staircase. Above where the staircase curved, hung a chandelier of a thousand drops. It was a house that reeked of class.

Transfixed in the hall as the maid took her coat, she said, 'How can they waste all this on *you*?'

'Why should you suppose it's wasted? I like it!'

'You don't need a house, an apartment would do.'

'Maria wouldn't like that,' he said, looking at the maid, who seemed to be Spanish. She laughed and shook her head in a comfortable way, playing the part of an old retainer brought over from the hacienda.

He hadn't finished showing her the downstairs rooms when her bag was delivered from the airport. She decided that before envy took a firmer hold, she would bathe and change.

The maid took her upstairs, produced a bathrobe and choice of lotions, offered to press her dress, agreed to consult someone else in the lower regions as to whether, the day being Thursday with the stores open late, a fastening for the ear stud might be obtained.

Before stepping into the bath, she parted the curtains at the window and looked out. The bathroom faced the gardens of the square. Beneath plane trees that had grown too tall, the grass was losing heart. A faintly theatrical hut stood in the middle of the gardens, with far too many gravel paths leading that way and this. But it *was* a garden and apparently open to the world at large. If Tom still attempted to jog in the mornings in defiance of the damaged leg, it no doubt provided a few useful circuits.

When a knock came at the door, she supposed it was the Spanish maid back with news of the ear stud. But it was Tom, carrying a Martini and a bowl of salted almonds. He brought them to the edge of the bath and perched on it.

She lay back, wondering how she felt about this. If he had come to inspect her, discover what the years had done to the flesh, he would see the result was not too depressing. But it was possible there was no curiosity and he was simply recalling an old custom.

'You're certainly lucky,' she said. 'Do you entertain much here?'

'The usual round.'

'You have a cook as well as the maid?'

'No, Maria gets reinforced by caterers when I have a lunch or dinner party.' He crossed to the window and pulled closer the curtains where she had been looking at the square. 'It's not so easy without you of course.'

'I suppose I had my uses.'

He came back to the bath. He glanced at her breasts, but neutrally, she thought. 'Sometimes,' she said, 'I even miss some of yours. But not too often.'

He smiled. She went on, 'Before I forget – did I tell you the name of the official Blackmer sent from his Party Head-quarters to Italy to interview Sisson?'

'You said it was Egerton, Mark Egerton.'

'Could you find out what position he holds, his seniority and so on?'

'Probably. Why do you want to know?'

'Sisson's begun to suspect he's too much of a stooge. He's afraid there could be somebody in the middle advising Blackmer to hold back on the Druitt story. It doesn't seem likely but I have to humour him if I'm to keep Hal happy.'

He scribbled a note on a pad. 'I'll call you in a day or two.'

Lying back once more when he had gone away, she saw something on the underside of a soap dish that had escaped earlier cleaning of the bathroom: a black hair, long and straight, non-pubic.

She laid it carefully along the edge of the bath for clinical scrutiny. She was sure it wasn't a man's, it was too fine. It belonged, she told herself, to the English creature, whose previously assumed appearance would have to be amended; no longer a blonde with china blue eyes, strong-thighed from the hunting field while yielding readily to other pastimes; instead a more urban, nervy creature working in – possibly owning – a gallery in Mayfair where the paintings were small and slick and very costly.

The maid appeared with the dress she had pressed, also the ear stud complete with a new fastening. The Martini must have been a powerful one; she found as she dressed she felt more relaxed and confident than she had all day. The strand of hair had become merely amusing.

On the way downstairs she paused at the curve beneath the chandelier and considered the marble hall again. Through the fanlight was a glimpse of one of the iron torch holders that hung at the side of the entrance steps. This was a place that called for a fan with an ivory handle, a hoop-skirted gown and not a dull little number from Saks.

Tom appeared from the drawing room, carrying the Martini jug. When he raised his eyebrows enquiringly, she said, 'I was trying out my fan.' She swept it shut at the foot of the stairs and held out her glass but didn't explain.

They were about to leave for the Connaught when he took a call on the telephone. He listened briefly then turned. 'For you. The name sounded like Burley or Berliot.'

She extended a hand for the receiver. 'Hal's agent in Paris. When I left him this afternoon I gave him this number.'

For a time while Berliot was giving his news, she stood motionless, reluctant to face what it must mean. Then her anger mounted and swelled. Tom was putting their glasses on a tray with his back to her. He said, 'You've been offered De Gaulle's diaries by a mysterious woman claiming she was his mistress for twenty years. Don't buy.'

She stared into his face as he turned. 'How did you find out?'

He frowned. 'What?'

'I never told you who either of them was! So, how?' She could feel herself shaking. 'But that's not the real shitty thing, is it? Letting me start on this trip without a word, making a complete fool of me. How could you let that *happen*? To *me*?'

'Louise, I'm lost. What?'

'*Lost!*' she said, '*LOST!* My God, you're lost! Don't play the innocent, Tom! I was your wife, remember? My Frenchman seems to have had a nasty accident. In fact, he doesn't exist anymore! And we certainly know who arranged *that*, don't we?'

· Eleven ·

New York tilted, fell away, was finally gone like all the others: she was back in nowhere again for a fifth successive day. Unclipping her seat belt, she considered taking from her purse a cigarette, indifferent now to prohibitions glowing overhead. Renewal of this interminable odyssey had promoted feelings of mutiny, a disposition to take her own decisions on such things.

Beside her on the Washington shuttle, Hal Mencken was reading the *New York Times*. A habit not previously noted had begun to claim her reluctant attention. Each time he switched from one column to the next, he made the paper jump with a flick of his wrists; it was as though the last item had been despatched to a mental trash can.

She was grateful that at least he was not expecting her to talk. Leaning back, she dozily eyed his head, seeking as so often in the office when she was waiting for him to finish reading some letter she had brought in, the frontier where hair and hairpiece became one. When she had met him again, after an interval of three years, to talk over the editorial post he was offering her, she had expected to see the frontal fluff still beating its retreat across his scalp. But that had gone from sight. While he had spoken grandly about her likely prospects, she had all the time been wanting to lift the new golden rug for reassurance that what lay beneath agreed with memory. The experience remained mildly upsetting. If ever I sank to sleeping with him, she thought, there would be a single compensation: I could pull it off and look.

Raising her gaze for a moment from economic gloom, he

caught her yawning and closed the paper to offer uncharacteristic sympathy. She shook her head. 'My time clock finally gave up trying over the Atlantic.'

He nodded and reinforced concern with a hand on her thigh. 'I wanted to spare you this trip. But since Lew Rothman told Brad he'd like to hear your personal account, I didn't feel we had a choice. When we get back to New York, go straight home and get some rest. There's nothing that can't wait.'

Experience had established that it was only when something was wanted from her that he was actively considerate. Today he was keen for her to make a useful impression on Rothman, if possible charm him since they were after help.

She shifted her position to break up the manual comfort. In the early days of working for him, she had supposed the constant touching whenever opportunity allowed held an ominous message, that in his mind bed and body had been written into her contract. His efforts to find her an apartment had strengthened foreboding. Even allowing for his past acquaintance with her and Tom, they had seemed to go beyond a reasonable concern for someone he was employing.

But her apprehensions proved groundless. The prospect of having to fight off a grand assault from that plump form, with its unlikely crown of curls and fingers that remained moist in deepest winter, receded, finally to vanish. It became clear that for Hal the appearance of conquest was all. He desired the world to think him relentless in his exercise of the *droit de seigneur*, that he ranged and ravished without cease. He would presumably not refuse an actual invitation to perform. But even then, she concluded, there could be a disposition towards postponement.

She had come to see some linkage with the way he ran the publishing business inherited from his father. Not that he always shirked the ultimate realities there; but it was only the cushion of the college textbook side that allowed him to shrug off the turkeys among the fiction, and brought him safely in each year to a soft landing. What kept him swaggering on in the ranks of the independents, was not so much a desire for money nor even power in the conventional sense, but his notion of *bella figura*. A deal might bring no profit, a book few sales, and he would not be cast down, provided they generated both noise and headlines. The show — the London suit, the handsome shoes, the being seen at restaurants of palpable significance — they were what mattered most of all.

'Where's the house at which we're meeting?' she asked.

'Waterside Drive. Over by Rock Creek apparently. Do you know it?'

She nodded. 'When Tom and I were living in Washington the last time, we knew some people in the German Embassy who had a house there. Whenever they had a party, the rats came up from the creek to raid the trash. The rats always knew about the parties. Perhaps they watched for the cars.'

He fingered the strap of his watch thoughtfully. 'I was offered four hundred and fifty pages on rats last month. The writer claimed it would be seen as the definitive study. I may have been wrong to turn it down. I hear they're getting bigger in Philadelphia.'

'Why won't Rothman have us go to the White House? I've never been inside. I should have liked to see it.'

'Apparently he uses this house on Waterside Drive for contacts he prefers to keep very confidential. A sort of safe house.'

His appetite for the doings and jargon of secret agencies never flagged. She was depressingly sure that what had decided him to offer her a job, notwithstanding her absence from publishing for so long, was the fact of her marriage to Tom: gilt by association. They had first met, the three of them, at a Washington party given by a Senator known to Tom. Introduced to Tom and herself by the Senator and learning of the Langley connection, Hal had insisted they join him for dinner at Maison Blanche, had later persuaded Tom to consult his own specialist about recurring trouble with the damaged leg.

As indefatigable as a society-struck widow from the Middle West foraging for the minor royals of Europe, he collected into warm acquaintance, wherever he could uncover them, the representatives of the clandestine world. His pretence that it was because they must have a book in them which might be extracted one day was not sustained for long. He found in the relationships a deeply satisfying cachet. Moreover, while believing nothing that politicians or newspapers or other publishers ever told him, he had persuaded himself that cynicism could be abandoned when it came to items from these special friends. Within the labyrinths that stretched into fascinating darkness behind them, the crystal stream of truth must run, he was sure of that.

'Why does it have to be a safe house?' she asked. 'Safe from whom? The President? The rest of the White House?'

'Maybe from some parts of it. The President may prefer that some of the things Rothman organises aren't known there.'

She reviewed in her mind what Tom had said about Rothman's influence and shook her head.

'What's worrying you about that?' Hal asked.

'Nothing. I was just wondering what your line with Rothman was going to be.'

'That with Massenet dead, unless Blackmer pulls the plug on Druitt in a big way, the book will be totally vulnerable to a defamation suit. That if the White House likes what I'm trying to do as much as Brad says it does, this is the moment to help.' Here on the plane he made himself sound pretty forceful, but she suspected it wouldn't turn out like that.

She stared out of her window, thinking of Tom's face when she confronted him with the news of Massenet's death. His refusal, steadily getting icier, to acknowledge that Langley had had anything to do with it, until the moment when she had turned her back on him to pack her bag and leave to spend the night in a hotel. He had stood silent, his expression becoming more set as she climbed into the cab, then had swung round and slammed the door of the house behind him.

She said, 'When Blackmer hears of Massenet's death he's bound to see problems for himself about going ahead. Sisson reckoned he was looking for an excuse for not doing anything anyway.'

He groaned. 'Why did Massenet have to get himself written off *now*?'

He seemed to worry at the question. She had expected him

to do so earlier, when she passed on the news from her second conversation with Bleriot before flying out of Heathrow. Bleriot had reported the French police believed the killing had been the result of a mugging that had gone wrong. Such an explanation had sounded ludicrous to her then. But Hal had let it go.

'If only we'd got the tape out of him before this happened,' he said. 'At least we'd have the record of his voice telling Blackmer's man what happened that night in Vienna. When Bleriot found himself talking to the police the other evening, was he calling Massenet's number or the *concierge*'s?'

'The *concierge*'s. He'd already got no reply from the apartment. He thought there was a chance the *concierge* might have more news. The police were with her and took over the phone.'

'So they may not have gone into the apartment. They'd have had no particular reason to search it.'

'It's possible.'

'If we could locate the tape before Massenet's relatives start sorting through his stuff . . .' He rubbed his forehead. 'I wonder if Brad could be helpful over this. He might have an idea for getting it.'

'A parachute drop on the apartment block probably,' she said.

His look made it plain he didn't think it was the moment to be facetious. She sighed. 'When are we going to call Sisson and tell him Massenet's dead?'

'Let's see what comes out of this morning's meeting first. I don't want him getting upset again if we can avoid it.'

She was slipping into a doze when Hal said, 'Did you see Tom in London?'

She decided against concealment, the risk was too great; Bleriot had known where she was. 'I had a drink with him at his house.'

'Where's that?'

'Berkeley Square.'

'He's *on* the Square?'

'Yes.'

The address had a predictable appeal for him; she could see he was impressed. With a brighter expression he recalled that when he was negotiating the purchase of the British publisher, he'd been introduced to an Earl in a gambling club on Berkeley Square. The Earl had offered to write him a thriller. She thought it had taken his mind off Massenet, but eventually he came back to the subject.

'Were you at Tom's when Bleriot called with the news that Massenet's body had been found?'

'Yes, I'd given him the number before I left Paris.'

She was sure he was going to ask if she had told Tom about Massenet and the book project, but he didn't. He simply said, as they were touching down on Washington tarmac, 'It's good you and Tom are talking again.' He looked as though he meant it. She felt a stab from her conscience at the thought of what he didn't know.

The house on Waterside Drive was in the middle of a row built fifty years ago; diplomats and people in the media had colonised it for as long as she could remember. The door of the house opened as soon as their cab stopped and Sweetwater appeared on the step. He was wearing Army uniform today. It gave him a greater air of formality than at their previous encounters in New York; there was also no sign of the pipe. After greeting Hal warmly, he said, 'Great to see you, Louise,' but his glance didn't linger. On this occasion, it seemed, she was not in line for cossetting.

Explaining that Rothman would be along shortly, he took them upstairs. The staircase opened directly on to a sitting room, so tidy and unaired she guessed it was not a house that was lived in. Beyond was a smaller room furnished as an office. On the desk, alongside yellow lawyers' notepads, sat two telephones and a tape recorder.

Sweetwater left them and went downstairs again. One of the telephones clicked and they could hear the sound of his voice from somewhere on the ground floor. It seemed that Rothman was elsewhere and was being informed that she and Hal awaited his pleasure. When he came back he poured them cups of coffee from a machine in the corner and offered observations on the weather and the morning news, mostly in Hal's direction. Settling deeper in her chair, she sampled a Defense Department handout that was the only literature on a shelf beside her.

Someone else must have been in the house because when the doorbell rang, Sweetwater stayed with them. They heard a surge of traffic noise and instructions being given to a driver before a door closed and footsteps hit the stairs. The man who strode into the office had the air of someone who had no doubt that wherever he arrived there'd be a chair, a desk, an aide or two, and a programme polished up and waiting.

Rothman appeared to be in his middle fifties, short and, in the upper half, boxily built. His white hair above heavily tanned features was cut almost as short as Sweetwater's military clip. Tom's reference to his having started in a Wall Street broker's had caused her to expect somebody smoother, more metropolitan-looking. In the flesh, aside from the absence of visible jewellery, Rothman seemed nearer to a mogul from the West Coast.

He shook hands cursorily, awarded Louise a second glance of appraisal, then sat behind the desk. The development of his shoulders and pectorals forced on the jacket of his suit a sort of *décolletage*. She wondered if he'd practised weightlifting or been a boxer in his youth. He indicated the telephones and the tape machine with a finger. 'Get rid of these, Brad.'

When they had been removed, he said, 'I understand you people have information which you want to be sure gets to the right quarter. Anything that'll help the President in tackling his problems is always welcome.'

The innuendo of total ignorance of what was to be discussed was a disconcerting start to the proceedings. Louise saw Hal shoot a baffled glance at Sweetwater, standing behind Rothman's chair. Sweetwater smiled, a little on edge. He said, 'Mr Rothman would like to be given the picture in your own words, Hal. So there's no risk we're missing any of the vital details, I suggest we go back to the first approach you had, from Massenet.'

'Massenet's the journalist?' Rothman said. When

Sweetwater nodded, he took a cigar from a leather case and pointed it briefly at Hal. 'Mr Mencken, you have the floor.'

Hal went over the beginnings, Massenet's opening letter of introduction, the synopsis, the meetings in Paris with him and Sisson, the deal that had been worked out for Louise to write the book from the material they supplied. When he was embarking on what had happened during Louise's latest trip to Europe, Rothman stopped him. 'Let's have the lady tell it.' He wasn't troubling to be warm towards Hal.

Once during Louise's account, he pulled Sweetwater down to whisper in his ear some question. His eyes did not shift from her face for more than a second. He conveyed exceptional concentration and ruthlessness in roughly equal proportions. At the end, he said, 'This Massenet guy – how was he killed?'

'He'd been knifed before his body was thrown in the Seine.'

'So it was definitely murder?'

'Yes.'

'What do the French police think happened?'

'According to our Paris Agent, there have been a lot of muggings in the district where he was dumped in the river. The police think this was one that went wrong, that he put up reisistance. All his money was missing from the body. So too was a ring the *concierge* at his apartment building remembered he always wore.'

He blew smoke reflectively. 'Maybe it was a mugging and maybe not. The money and the ring could have been taken as a blind. Somebody who knew what Massenet had been telling you and didn't want Druitt's chances of being elected Prime Minister in the UK spoiled could have done it. Have you thought of that?'

She could almost believe he knew the truth. He was thinking again while he chewed on the cigar. From Waterside Drive traffic noise seeped in to fill the silence. Rothman's gaze wandered as he thought, from her legs to her breasts and back to her legs. She rated him a womaniser of a strictly disciplined sort. If he ever decided to have his secretary on the office carpet, the urgent correspondence would have been got out of the way first and his performance wouldn't overrun into the time of the next appointment. Finally he turned to Sweetwater. 'Brad, could we get some more information out of the French police about his killing without going through other agencies?'

'I'll look into that, Lew.'

He turned back to Hal. 'Well, Mr Mencken, it seems you could have hit problems over getting this book out.' He didn't sound as though sympathy was overwhelming him.

'The lawyers are likely to tell me that unless the British Government intends to take action that exposes Druitt, I shouldn't go ahead.'

'I guess they may.'

Hal's face had tightened. 'Mr Rothman, I'd understood from Brad that in circumstances of this kind I could hope for some help from you.'

Rothman smiled. 'Well now . . . help.' He made it sound an amusingly novel suggestion. 'That's quite an order.' He held up a hand as Hal started to speak again. 'Don't misunderstand, I'm not suggesting there isn't something important here. The United States needs to see a British government elected in the fall that won't stop supporting the President's policy in Europe. What has kept the peace there for the second half of this century has been a strong American military presence. Some governments have persuaded themselves that's not needed any more. There are even people in the US Government who should know better but apparently think the same thing.

'I know the President feels that he'll have at least one reliable ally if Mr Blackmer gets re-elected in the fall. But helping that to happen by twisting his arm to use the Druitt information isn't something the President could ever agree to. But what I *can* do is discover what's happened to that information. I have to go to Europe shortly and can talk to a good friend in the British Cabinet. He'll find out for me.'

Whether this was a real brush-off or a piece of theatre which Rothman was using to conceal his actual intentions in London, to protect himself if they talked about this meeting at a later date, Louise was unable to tell. She could sense Hal was in the same difficulty. He said eventually, 'Anything you can do, Mr Rothman . . .'

'Fine. Brad will let you know.' Rothman rose abruptly to his feet and turned to Sweetwater. 'Do we have copies of my book around? These people might like one.'

It had not been a genuine question. Sweetwater had moved at once to a cabinet and extracted two paperbacks. The words on the cover read:

**Leading the World to Peace
in the 21st Century;**
The challenge facing
the United States.

Lewis J. Rothman

Rothman added his signature inside each before handing them over. He was already calling to find out if his driver was waiting outside as he headed for the stairs.

Sweetwater took out his tobacco pouch and started loading up. Before Hal could speak, he said, 'I think that went pretty well. You're going to get your book, Hal. Believe me!'

· Twelve ·

The boy's abrupt appearance on the scene was difficult to account for. Across the aisles at the back of the hall, the ranks of the stewards looked unbroken. In the main part, the seats were packed with the faithful. He must have managed to hide in a side corridor before the meeting began.

Running to the centre aisle, glancing once in triumph up at the balcony of the hall, the boy took up a position no more than a dozen feet from Blackmer on the platform. He was panting, not so much with exertion as excitement; his first volley of words came out in an uneven screech.

'Bloody Tory fascist! Out, out, OUT!'

The moment had obviously been planned earlier with the barrackers in the balcony from which most of the other interruptions had come. As the boy's voice faded the call was taken up immediately.

'OUT, OUT, OUT! OUT, OUT, OUT!'

It settled down from an initial roughness into something rhythmic, loud enough to drown shouts from elsewhere. Now and then the boy's voice, more high-pitched and frenzied than the rest, soared above, offering variants on the balcony's clamour. Caught by the lights erected for the television cameras, the spittle of his fervour glistened on his chin.

'Fascist bastard Blackmer OUT! Fascist bastard Blackmer OUT!'

To continue with the speech was out of the question until the boy and some of the ringleaders in the balcony were thrown out. Blackmer advanced from the lectern for a better view of the boy. Pale and skinny, he was perhaps as much as twenty, dressed in the uniform of his kind – trainers, frayed blue jeans that bisected the crotch, a tee-shirt with some legend across the front that his constant twisting and gesturing obscured.

The only thing left to do was to gaze down at him with an expression of noble forbearance and hope the hubbub would soon die away. But the outlook was unpromising. Although stewards were now coming to grab the boy, Blackmer could see fighting at the rear of the hall. There must have been a breach in the police ring outside, allowing some of the booing crowd that had awaited his arrival to get inside. There were far too few stewards to cope if the breach hadn't been sealed quickly.

The vanguard up in the balcony, sensing victory ahead, increased their chanting. Beside Blackmer, the chairman had ceased hammering his table for quiet. A balding Bunter figure, an emperor on party committees for sure, a lion at the nineteenth hole no doubt, here he was distinctly on the windy side. His expression, glancing up at Blackmer, combined embarassment with apprehension. He was not only chairman of the meeting but chairman of the local constituency party; some responsibility at least must rest with him for the arrangements over policing and stewards. He would be wondering how deeply the manure likely to descend from the skies tomorrow would bury him. Assuming he wasn't buried by the mob first.

Something thrown from the balcony, a coin from the sound of it, bounced on the table at which the chairman sat then down to the platform. More followed. The chairman said, 'Prime Minister, if you would prefer to break off for a few minutes until . . .'

'I never believe in running under fire.'

A suitably Churchillian response, he told himself. The chairman looked chastened, tried hammering the table again. Walking along the platform, Blackmer picked up one of the coins, held it up for the audience to see, then with a smile slowly pocketed it. From the ranks of the loyal came a ripple of applause.

But it was apparent that the uproar was not going to be contained. The central doors of the hall had been forced open and fighting was becoming general at the rear. The posse of stewards which had been advancing on the boy had been intercepted by several of his kind, also entering the hall from the side, and two more had had to be sent to seize him. Awareness that his moment of glory would soon be over, he released a supreme burst of hate. As he was dragged away, he shouted, 'You're finished, Blackmer, you bastard! You're *bloody irrelevant*!'

With an expression regretful yet charitable, Blackmer shook his head slowly at the boy, guessing that at least one of the cameras must have stayed on himself. The words echoed in his mind. Bloody irrelevant! He was trying to recall something but failing to pin it down beyond the fact of an occasion similiar to this long ago. It had not been to himself the words had been addressed, he was not convinced he had actually been present . . . yet he had heard the words clearly and seen the youth yelling then . . . *bloody irrelevant*!

As he went back to the lectern for a final attempt to make himself heard, the chairman looked up from a slip of paper that had been passed to him. 'A message from your detective, Prime Minister.'

He caught a glimpse of West in the shadows at the side of the platform. 'What is it?'

'The police outside feel you should leave. They can't be sure of re-establishing control at the front of the building and one of the side doors has been broken down. They have your car waiting in a cul-de-sac near the hall. We can reach it by a corridor which runs below us to the public library.'

He glanced again at West. He was shaking his head grimly; a uniformed policeman looking dishevelled stood beside him. 'Very well, if that's their judgment, I suppose I've no alternative.'

'I'm sure they're right.'

It was total pandemonium now. The longer he stayed, looking impotent, under the eye of the cameras, the worse it would become. Most of the audience seemed to have risen in their seats, either to defend themselves or try to escape. He owed it to supporters in the hall not to increase the risk of injury to them by continuing to provide a focus for the mob's frenzy.

Turning, he walked to the side of the platform, waving a farewell as he went, hoping that against the odds it would convey confidence not despair, contempt not submission, a promise of victory on the only battlefield that mattered, the hustings to come.

In silent anger he allowed himself to be conducted along a corridor that smelled of sweat and banana skins. Up a flight of stairs they entered the library and threaded through a gawping collection of readers. At what was presumably a staff entrance door, the same Superintendent of police was waiting whose face had caught the juice of the tomato which had landed on his sleeve when he arrived at the meeting. He looked distinctly subdued, a notable contrast with his counterpart at the gates of Kilndown.

The narrow street beyond was deserted except for the car with Evatt at the wheel and police Landrovers fore and aft. The noise that rose from the other side of the block was muffled here by the library building into something neither hostile nor friendly, a mere din. He climbed into the back of the car and looked icily back at the Superintendent. 'I hope you'll sort this out before anybody gets badly hurt.'

The Superintendent didn't risk a reply, simply put up a stiff salute. The chairman, perspiring heavily, emitted nervous expressions of regret; his wife had materialised by his shoulder, her state-occasion hat a little awry. Falteringly, they raised uncertain hands in farewell as Evatt released the brake. Then he was shot of them.

At the end of the cul-de-sac the police had erected barriers across the main street, to deny access from the direction of the hall. But there were few people about; it looked as though the mob were unaware of the escape route through the library. 'No. 10, sir?' Evatt said.

He glanced at his watch. Had the meeting run its course, he would have been delivered back with just enough time to spare for a meal before an interview arranged with a German journalist. Now there would be at least an hour to spare. He could work on boxes or look in at the House for a while. But he had no inclination for the latter; news of the abandoned meeting would have gone ahead, guaranteeing an extra dose of derision from the Opposition benches. 'Straight back,' he said.

Alongside Evatt, West sat, expressionless. Presumably he had his views on the shambles the local police had made of the security arrangements for the meeting; but to extract from him any sort of objective comment that smacked of criticism would be impossible. After more than a year as his bodyguard, West remained tribal, innoculated against even an amused sigh at the pantomime enacted on their arrival at Kilndown. Losing West in the autumn would not arouse the regret he would have when he said goodbye to Evatt.

They had entered the by-pass running south to the Edgware Road. West pointed to a lay-by where a motorcycle escort waited and Evatt pulled over. While West was confirming route details with the escort, Evatt said, 'Lively inside, sir?'

'A little.'

'I hear one of the television platforms was pushed over at the front of the hall. They took the cameraman to hospital.'

It was difficult to decide whether the reduction in the coverage would be a good or a bad thing. 'Did you hear what was wrong with him?'

'I believe it broke his leg.'

He made a note on his pocket pad to tell Cusack to enquire on his behalf next day how the cameraman was doing. 'There were a lot of yobs about,' Evatt said. 'Obviously itching for a punch-up. We could do with a few being sent down before the election.' He had faith in the virtues of the prison system. In their conversation lately, they hadn't discussed the chances of the impending election campaign. 'How do you think it's going to go, Fred?'

Evatt paused. He was plainly deciding diplomacy was called for. 'You need a fine summer, sir.'

Blackmer gazed at disheartened shrubbery still barely

turning green in gardens on the other side of the road from the lay-by. 'Is that likely?'

'My son says it's going to be hot from June onwards.'

Bird behaviour had persuaded the son, a gamekeeper in the North, they could expect a change. 'Has he been right before?'

'He's usually close. He's expecting a drought by August.'

Not much to build on, but all there seemed to be: a nation made torpid by days of golden warmth, turning to give thanks to himself for the gift of a real summer; drowsily indifferent to the renewed upward thrust of inflation, more violence on the streets, bigger prescription charges, even defeat in the World Cup (also forecast by Evatt's son), they would rally to his side, the Sunshine Prime Minister.

From hostile public meetings, he normally came away feeling a mixture of elation and concern – elation that he had outfaced the troublemakers, concern at what the media would make of the occasion. He felt no elation this time. If the cameras had caught the nastier scenes, had zoomed in on innocent citizenry, preferably aged and/or disabled, being beaten up, the results might not be all unfavourable for the Government. But there could be little consolation to himself personally because this time he had not beaten the mob, they had beaten him. He had been forced to an ignominious retreat, stealing away from danger under the eyes of the world.

He swore beneath his breath. Tomorrow promised more trouble when he paid the delayed visit to the party in Scotland. No missiles or actual physical violence perhaps, if the police took a lesson from tonight; but two days of tribal keening, endless grievances uttered in the gargling tones of Morningside or even more outlandish accents that cried out for subtitles.

Some youths were arguing in the forecourt of a pub. The face of the boy who had harangued him drifted into his mind along with that last volley of abuse. Bloody Irrelevant. . . . It was as Evatt was turning into the Finchley Road that it came back where he had registered those shouted words before.

It had been in the house in Flood Street Diana and he had taken on a short lease, the year he had entered Parliament: the time of the Vietnam war, the era of revolting youth, the great carnivals of protest; teach-ins, sit-ins, occupations everywhere.

At one of the teach-ins covered by television – drawn by the promise of Establishment figures being ridiculed as they offered their pallid wisdom – the Foreign Secretary of the day, Michael Stewart, had spoken. A forbear of his own accuser had sprung up to abuse Stewart. For a few moments he had filled the screen of the fourteen-inch black and white set on which Diana and he were watching. 'You're bloody irrelevant!' the boy had screamed. That was it, the cry he had recalled. '*Bloody irrelevant!*'

In the arrogance of comparative youth, he had smiled and thought: unpleasant for Michael, I'm glad I'm not having to put with that; but there's *something* in it all the same. Because his is the voice of a tired government that lacks understanding of this generation, of a Party run by middle-aged men and women totally baffled by the new culture. To which I, on the other hand, can relate . . .

Tonight, somebody watching the Nine O'clock News on his twenty-three-inch full-spectrum colour job, will be having those thoughts, as I am seen gazing ineffectually down through the spectacles which have failed so signally to improve my image. Blackmer, he or she will be saying, can't you see your time is up? The bell went long ago, hand over to those who really understand where we are now. Our lot, to be precise.

At No. 10 he went to the flat and removed his jacket. The tomato stain was still damp on the sleeve. Running through the options in his wardrobe, he finally settled on something not worn for a long time. Strolling with Diana one day through Harrods, he had stopped before a bottle-green smoking jacket, its lapels and cuffs ornately braided. He had tried it on and laughed at the result. Mostly as a joke, Diana had bought it for him that Christmas, adding to the package a meerschaum pipe that had turned out to be chocolate. He had eaten the pipe at once, but only given the jacket a chance a month or two later, in an interview arranged with a Japanese political commentator. The commentator had been admiring enough to ask that when his photographer came round the next day, the jacket should be worn again.

In the subsequent article had been references to an acuity of mind resembling that of Mr Sherlock Holmes. Plagued thereafter by profile writers' jokes about the Great Detective, he had not repeated the experiment with the jacket. But that had all been a long way back. Perhaps the magic would work again on the German journalist.

There was no sign of Diana about the flat. In the kitchen he found a tray, upon it a flask of soup, cold chicken and salad and a bottle of Moselle. In their bedroom his bed had been turned down and clean pyjamas laid out. Such thoughtfulness signalled only one thing. Picking at the chicken breast, he told himself that not all the side-effects of cuckoldry were bad.

Adrian Wyeth, a bundle of files in his arms, was hovering in wait when he went back down the stairs, wanting to know if the evening stint was going to be done in the Cabinet Room or the study. He told him the study.

Inside, there were already boxes of work beside his desk. He poured them both brandies and pointed to the bundle Wyeth had been carrying. 'Anything urgent?'

'Two Foreign Office minutes which I've put on top. And you'll remember we're still short of a Bishop of Bath and Wells. You felt the General Synod might back the wrong horse if you didn't let your views be known.'

On Wyeth's cheek and neck the remnants of the heat rash picked up in India had still not disappeared. 'Have you seen a doctor about that rash yet?'

'No.'

'Do so tomorrow.'

He sat down heavily behind the desk. He didn't feel like bishops tonight; or anything else in the way of work for that matter. The smoking jacket was pulling under the armpits to remind him of the weight he had put on lately. 'You're supposed to admire my jacket,' he said.

'I was thinking it had a Holmesian flavour, Prime Minister.'

From the way he said it, Wyeth was obviously unaware of the earlier stories. But he might not even have been in the Civil

Service at the time they appeared. He was smiling. He had slowly become more relaxed as the weeks went by, but he still found it hard to hit the right note. 'How did the meeting go?' he asked.

'Rather mutinous.' Blackmer frowned at his open diary. 'Why is the Cabinet Secretary coming in at nine o'clock?'

'He said he needed to take ten minutes of your time on his way home. I've telephoned Choltitz at her hotel and put your meeting with her back a quarter of an hour.'

'Who?'

'Anne-Marie Choltitz, the journalist.'

He had forgotten the name and the fact it was a woman. 'What does she sound like?'

'Good English, very quick. She said she'd quite understand if she had to wait.'

He picked up the biographical note Cusack had left for him. 'As long as she's clear that she's got only three-quarters of an hour. I don't want to be working late tonight.'

Her track record looked impressive: attendance at universities in Germany, France and the United States, feature writer work on mostly German newspapers but including a spell on the *New York Times*; a biography of Adenauer, a book on China dealing with the Gang of Four, a collection of profiles of leading politicians in France and Germany.

The hook for the interview tonight had been an expressed intention to bring out a follow-up volume to the last book, entitled *World Statesmen of the Nineties*. Only towards the end of Cusack's note was there a faintly discouraging reference. Choltitz had caused some stir in Germany, calling for better treatment of lesbians in the financial and commercial sectors. It might be significant that Cusack had not attached a photograph.

He put down the note and stared at the ceiling, still unwilling to start on the bundle Wyeth had brought but also without appetite for the supper tray upstairs. The events earlier kept returning to his thoughts. Not long ago he would have shrugged them off as no more than a temporary setback, a rent-a-mob occasion without real importance. That ability had derived from an energy that was always rallying and driving his attention on to the task ahead. Now it felt as though his will was draining from him. The surge of well-being he had known in India had evaporated all too soon.

Beside the bundle the photograph of Esther taken by Diana in the garden at Kilndown gazed at him. They had had the picture enlarged and framed because she looked so happy in it and he had decided to keep it in the study. He had not called her for several days. She relied on him, he knew, not to let a week of silence go by. Talking to her now would postpone the need to make a move in any other direction.

She sounded breathless but otherwise well when she came to the phone. 'Sorry, my hands were covered in flour. Hilda and I are making scones. We'll keep some in the freezer for you.'

They talked about the small, unthreatening things for a while: Ames had done more planting round the lake; Bron's lumps had almost disappeared; she had tried writing some verse, an interest she had had before she became ill. She laughed about the verse. The crisis the day after his return from India when she broke down while trying on the *sari*, seemed to have been totally overcome. If anything, she sounded as though it had had a cleansing effect.

'No more experiments with reducing Reeves' prescription?' he said.

'No. I know it was stupid. When are you coming down?'

'The weekend after next, probably.'

'Not before?'

'I must be at Chequers this coming one.'

'Oh, well,' she said.

He sensed her disappointment. 'Had you something in mind?'

'I wanted to try an idea on you. But it can wait.'

It seemed a good moment to ask a question he'd had stored up since his talk with Egerton. 'I wonder if you can recall whether there was a patient in the hospital while you were there, whose name was Sisson.'

'Man or woman?'

'Woman, probably younger than yourself.'

'It doesn't ring a bell. What's the Christian name?'

'I don't have that.'

There was a silence while she thought. Eventually she said, 'I'm sorry, I don't remember the name. My memory is terribly woozy for that time. There were only one or two women patients I saw much of and we used Christian names mostly. Why do you ask?'

'There was a chance it would link up with something I heard. I'll tell you sometime, it's not important. What was the idea you wanted to try on me?'

He had to press her before she came out with it. 'I'd quite like to do some work. I don't mind what sort as long as it's with people. It could be part-time to begin with. So that I could get away from the house somedays.'

He had felt himself tense. 'What had you got in mind?'

'I'd thought there might be some charity office, that sort of thing, where I could help out. If it wasn't too far away, I could cycle there.'

Taken aback, he struggled to find words that would conceal his dismay. 'Why do you make the point about getting away from the house?'

'Because that's what would make me feel more normal. I can't if I'm here all the time.'

When he didn't reply at once, she said, 'You're not against it, are you?'

'No, it's certainly an idea worth considering.' There was only one way he could think of to enable him to oppose unhurtfully. 'I *had* rather hoped that if the Government doesn't get re-elected this autumn, you'd be there to help me with the book I'm planning to write. It would be a pity if you got taken up with something else.'

'But you *will* be re-elected! They can't turn you out once they start thinking about the alternative.'

'They might.'

She wouldn't hear of it. At the end she said, 'You do understand, don't you? Being here, just pottering about, is too much like waiting to get worse. I want to be with people who don't know. Not all the time, I know that can't be. But as much as possible.'

After he had put down the receiver, he wondered if he had sounded too discouraging. Perhaps the right course was to build on this increase in her self-confidence, take some risks. But the thought of her possibly breaking down away from Hilda, among strangers, was appalling. He would have to talk to Reeves before he went to Kilndown.

Hunger was faintly stirring. He went upstairs and ate most of the supper Diana had prepared. The Nine O'clock News was about to start when the call came through that Pagett had arrived. For a moment he was tempted to stay and see what the news made of his meeting. But he was reluctant to to be reminded of the fiasco.

He met Pagett outside the study door. The phone was ringing as they went in. While he took a call about a change in the programme for Scotland, Pagett stood gazing out of the window. He was wearing his black pin-striped suit, usually a sign he had been lecturing somewhere. He was as neat as ever, not a glossy hair out of place; yet, at the base of the spine, was a little untidiness, linked fingers opening and closing ceaselessly.

He turned briskly when Blackmer put down the receiver. 'Sorry about the tiresome events at your meeting earlier.' He had heard what happened, of course; he heard everything. 'The police seem to have been badly at fault.'

'The whole thing was a shambles.' He didn't want to talk about it. 'Anyway . . . what were you going to tell me?'

'There's been a development in the matter Egerton investigated, which I thought you should be aware of. It seems Monsieur Massenet is no longer with us.'

'Disappeared?'

'Dead. Egerton noticed an obituary in today's *Independent* contributed by some English journalist who knew him. It must have happened a day or two ago.' He took a cutting from his pocket.

The obituary said Massenet had been a notable figure in French journalism up to his retirement a year ago. This was described as having been for the purpose of writing a biography of his father although other, possibly murkier, reasons for his departure from the paper then employing him were delicately implied. There were references to his having been an authority on East/West friendship organisations during the period of the Cold War and to his definitive study of the Pugwash movement. The final sentence comprised a brisk statement that he was unmarried.

Blackmer glanced back to the beginning of the obituary. 'It says his death is the subject of an investigation. Do we know what that means?'

'Egerton put an enquiry through to the Embassy in Paris. He was murdered – stabbed to death and dumped in the Seine. It's thought he was killed in the course of a robbery that went wrong. However there's also gossip that he'd lost a great deal of money on the Bourse and was trying to default on some of his debts so there could be another explanation.'

'I see.' He was aware that the news had been something of a blow. It was not that he had changed his mind about trying to use Massenet's information against Druitt; but he had unconsciously retained a hope that the story would surface anyway and work a miracle on the polls.

He walked Pagett down the stairs, homeward bound at last to the patient Dorothy in Highgate, no doubt waiting to serve something nutritious before Pagett retired to work off that carefully masked irritation with politicians on some complex carpentry. As they reached the front hall, Anne-Marie Choltitz was being admitted by the doorkeeper. She was ash-blonde, in the region of forty, with handsome features and a figure still on the right side of Aryan fullness. She was altogether more presentable than he had expected from Cusack's note. Only the wild wiry look she had chosen for her hair seemed a minus factor. If she was a lesbian campaigner, she wasn't the card-carrying kind.

In the study he settled her in one of the armchairs and brought the brandy bottle to the table between them. She produced her tape recorder from a shoulder bag. 'I believe Mr Cusack will have shown you my suggested headings for questions, Prime Minister.' Her command of English was excellent. She sat back with a notebook resting on the arm of the chair, and crossed her legs with the assurance of a woman who welcomes their being studied. He noted her red silk shirt also seemed admirably filled. At the very least, an improvement on the earlier part of the evening seemed in prospect.

The questions gave him no trouble until they got to European defence when she embarked on supplementaries that were spikier than the rest. He was conscious of answering a little indiscreetly now and then but without offering any sizeable hostages to fortune. She matched him drink for drink and laughed just enough at his jokes. Sometimes her expression conveyed a polite amusement at his occasional avoidance of truthful answers, the eyes remaining still for just long enough for the challenge to be pleasing.

Nearing the end she asked him if they could turn back to defence. 'So you are saying you will continue to oppose the view of many other European governments that United States troops withdrawal should be resumed. Why?'

'The point I have been concerned to press on my European colleagues is that the American contribution remains the key to our safety. The idea that any adequate alternative can be found in the forseeable future through Europe's own military forces is unrealistic.'

Her skirt whispered as she slowly crossed her legs. 'Your principal political opponent here, Mr Druitt, seems to agree with the other European governments. Do you really believe your views are going to prevail?'

'I can only say I believe it's vital that they do. I take comfort from that fact that the United States President takes the same line. We are greatly in his debt for his statesmanship.'

He took her smile as a pass mark for that. Only the lowest of the four buttons on the front of the red shirt was secured. He noted that each time she reached for her glass, the undercurve of a breast was revealed. 'And for his vision,' he added.

'How do you answer those critics who say your Party's defence policy is trapped in the past and reflects an out-of-date clinging to American power?'

'This is simply nonsense.'

'But they are comments which are made frequently.'

'I refute them utterly. We have a defence policy that has been very carefully conceived. It serves equally the interest of this country and of the wider world of which Europe . . .' He was on automatic pilot now, his eyes fixed on the enticing gap that was still unclosed, because she had taken the notebook on her knee to write something. When he finally stopped speaking, she looked up smiling.

'Thank you. That was most interesting.' She replaced the notebook and tape recorder in her bag and thrust her hand into the wilderness of her hair. It no longer struck him as unattractive. He could imagine the sensation as he thrust splayed fingers through it.

'Are you staying long in London?' he asked.

'Until tomorrow only. Then I fly to Washington. In two days I have an interview with the President.'

'Please give him my warm regards.'

'I understand that you're very close. That the Special Relationship is actually a reality.' She was confident enough now to be gently mocking.

'Our views on most matters connected with foreign policy and defence tend to coincide.'

'I hear there are some in Washington who would prefer you were not so close.'

'I can't believe that.' It was an agreeable lie. She laughed to show she also enjoyed it. Although her time was up, he was reluctant for her to leave. 'Would you care to see something of the house?'

He took her down to the Cabinet Room, pointed out where he sat under the portrait of Walpole, then led her through the State dining room and the reception rooms. It was difficult to tell whether she was impressed or saw the house simply as surprising in its size and amenities. He guessed her eyes were missing nothing that might be useful to her book, but she asked few questions.

Pausing by the Staffordshire figures in the White Room, she extended a finger towards the head of the Duke of Wellington and delicately stroked it. 'He had the qualities I associate most with the English.'

'I have to tell you he was born in Dublin of a family that

must have lived there at least five centuries. I don't think we can call him English.'

She was a little disconcerted. It was plain she didn't allow herself many mistakes. But she recovered swiftly. 'I believe you had an Irish grandmother, Prime Minister. And that your mother was born in Dublin.'

She was moving towards dangerous ground; yet she couldn't possibly know in what way. 'Yes. But my mother came to live in England as a very small child.'

'Is she still alive?'

'No, she died long ago.'

She let it drop. As they went into the study again, she moved close enough for him to breathe the full odour of her scent. It was slightly sharp, more direct in its message than anything Diana would wear. He checked her arm as she reached for her bag. 'A final drink before you go.'

She knew – had probably known within minutes of arrival – he was finding her desirable and that benefit could accrue from the fact. As she handed him her glass to be filled, she said, 'I would be so grateful if you could give me something new. An exclusive I could use separately from the book. It need only be a little thing.'

While he poured the drinks, she stood considering the Zoffany portrait of the Rosoman family on the wall behind his desk. He watched her covertly. More insistent than before, the excitement that gripped him in Delhi as the tiresomely provocative wife of the High Commissioner walked along the edge of the swimming pool, returned to invest his being. This time there seemed no overriding reasons to disguise its existence.

He placed their drinks on the desk and rested a hand lightly on her shoulder while he gazed at the Zoffany. 'What do you think of it?'

She appeared oblivious of the hand. 'The dog is strange.'

'In what way?'

'Its head and body don't seem right for each other.'

It *did* look wrong. 'It's certainly a little odd.'

He felt the oddity of the dog pulsing into the very tips of his fingers. Then she turned her face towards his, the lips slightly parted and he knew she had made a calculation that there could be no disadvantage to her in what might follow.

Her mouth responded at once; when she moved against him, it was as though to a remembered sanctuary. In a way he would have welcomed some token resistance so that he could take a little vengeance for the humiliation of the day, of all the other days lately.

The notion he had at first conceived of taking her upstairs to the bed so conveniently turned down by Diana became absurdly tepid: he could brook no delay. As he pressed her backwards against the desk, the flame-coloured shirt already half off her body, they reached first the chair and then, when the awkwardness it imposed became too much, sank to the carpet.

Once down to bedrock, as it were, she rallied with a competence born of long experience. No matter that her lust might be theatre, a performance contrived for the occasion; he was indifferent to the probability, could scarcely object, since artifice was the prime ingredient in so much of what he did these days. He asked only that she be imaginative and wholehearted.

It was over all too soon. Lifting his head to get his bearings again, he found his vision blurred. At some moment after their descent to the carpet, she had removed his spectacles and placed them beneath the chair where they would not be damaged by tumult. She was, above everything, efficient.

After he had replaced them on his face, he looked down at her again. Her mouth was a little swollen. Running his fingers into the wilderness of the hair, he felt moisture on the scalp and bent to kiss it. 'A little thing,' he said, 'but exclusive anyway. I fear that may not have been entirely what you had in mind however.'

She smiled equably. 'Would you like me to introduce my essay about you with it.'

'The public may not be quite ready for that.'

'The Duke of Wellington would have said it was a matter of indifference to him.'

'I lack all too many of the Duke's qualities.'

He was averse to returning to reality but this was becoming a dangerous game, had already been a risky one. Checking the whereabouts and condition of his clothing, he reached finally for the smoking jacket.

'Your jacket is very chic,' she said.

'I wore it especially for you.'

She accepted his offer to show her to a bathroom. When after ten minutes, she found her way back to the study, she looked hardly different from the elegant creature he had collected in the hall when Pagett was leaving. But in her glance now was something he had missed in these past months during which flesh had lost its savour – complicity, the wordless acknowledgement that for a while their vision would have a colouring unique to themselves, the pigment of collusion.

As he helped her with her coat, she said, 'I will send my draft text from Washington to Mr Cusack so that you can be sure I am not misquoting. It can be returned to my address in Berlin.'

'I shall try to think of something new for you to use. If I do, Cusack will include it in a separate note when he returns your text.' He extended a hand. 'Until next time then.'

The handshake was firm, almost brisk. 'Until then.' Her manner as she turned away and waited for the doorkeeper to open the door was impeccable, he thought.

Upstairs again, he looked once more at Zoffany's dog. The oddity seemed to derive chiefly from the contrast in colouring between the totally dark head and the whitish body. He found he wished to speak aloud about it, to announce the storming of the stockade behind which his senses had been imprisoned for so long and the discovery of a meaning to the dog. 'You see, Watson,' he said, '*that* is the special oddity of the dog . . .'

He smiled at his absurdity and experienced a lifting of the heart that was quite different from the moment when he had successfully startled Pagett. Henceforth, when he stared at the picture, trying to decide between courses of action which all seemed equally undesirable, the dog would carry a message that had something to do with freedom.

He had worked through the bundle Wyeth had brought and

one of the Boxes, as well as the remains of the brandy, when the telephone rang.

It was Diana. 'Are you all right?'

'Yes, why?'

'I saw your meeting on the Ten O'clock News. It looked pretty nasty.'

So she and Patrick had found a moment to switch on the set; probably it was at the foot of the bed.

'It was for a time. I wanted to hang on but the police were losing control. So I had to cut and run. Tiresome.'

'I should have been there with you.'

He could tell she was genuinely upset and anxious for him. He felt mildly touched. 'I'm glad you weren't there. Things were being thrown. I got most of a tomato as I went in the hall. There were coins later. I pocketed one.'

'They looked an absolutely foul mob in the shots taken outside.'

'They just needed control. The police blew it. I shall want to know why.'

He paused; but the temptation was not to be resisted. 'Perhaps you'll tell Patrick that I assume he'll be calling for a full report from the Chief Constable.'

When she didn't reply, he said, 'I'm sorry, isn't Patrick *there*?'

She must have turned away to speak because she came back over his last words. 'He says he's getting on to him tonight. He intends to raise hell.'

'Good.'

She said with unusual gentleness. 'David, I'd thought of perhaps coming back now. You're probably feeling . . .'

'No, no, I've been through meetings that were just as bloody, I'm not affected.'

'You're sure?'

'Absolutely. You've remembered we're leaving earlyish tomorrow?'

'Yes, of course, I'll be back by eight o'clock.'

It occurred to him it would be as well to pass on the news Pagett had brought about Massenet's death: it would save her and Patrick hatching a plot to get him to reverse his earlier decision over Druitt. Her response was predictably disappointed. He felt sure they *had* been discussing it. Possibly they had been thinking of ways of getting Massenet to show up in London and start telling his story again. She said finally, without perhaps realising what the remark revealed, 'We must find *something* to turn things round.'

He thought of the prophecy of a fine summer Evatt had passed on. 'I'm still hoping,' he said and realised that in fact he *was*, that in the past hour or two, for no reason rooted in circumstances, he had rediscovered hope.

She reverted to the meeting before ringing off. The pictures had obviously been dramatic, the appearance of the mob very threatening. He began to think the balance might come out in his favour after all; a tide of sympathy might start running through the nation, that with skill could be harnessed.

'Did you see the little creep who ran up to the platform?' he asked.

'Yes. I hope they kicked him hard afterwards. What was he shouting towards the end?'

'He said I was irrelevant, bloody irrelevant. It reminded me of something we both saw years ago.'

She continued to make noises of anger and contempt, didn't ask what the other occasion had been. He decided it wasn't worth telling her.

'Actually, when I got back, I found myself feeling *more* relevant than usual.'

She could make of that what she liked.

· Thirteen ·

The message from Welcroft reached him in mid-flight, halfway back from Scotland, and was exceptionally guarded in tone. For Welcroft to be so cryptic was unusual; discretion, even when security considerations were genuinely paramount, never came easily to him. He found restraint of any kind tiresome. As a backbencher he had polished his image with the Left of the Party by talking a lot about freedom of information. Yet, here he was, reluctant even to hint at what he was calling about.

Vaguely unsettled, Blackmer returned to his seat. Diana was gazing intently down at middle England. He asked what was engrossing her. Apparently at dinner the previous evening, her ear had been bent by a professor of geography. Over the roast chicken he had described at stupefying length the topography of medieval fields. She had managed eventually to transfer her attention to another neighbour. But a seed of his enthusism had remained in her mind; she was checking his assertion that she would be able to pick out traces on the flight south.

He joined her in staring down for a while. But the entrails of history declined to show. On this stretch of the journey, the tractors of Brussels' favourite sons had presumably obliterated them, along with tiresome hedgerows and other thwarters of subsidy.

Her perfume distracted him. He looked at her neck. Beneath the black hair, its nape was very pale, delicate and vulnerable as a young girl's. Since the encounter with Ann-Marie Choltitz, he had found himself impelled to notice Diana more.

She sat back suddenly. 'Probably all bull.'

He took out a cigar. Two days of fence-mending among the tribes had brought some improvement to their relationship, a return of a little warmth. He knew she was still feeling guilty for not having been with him to share the disaster of the public meeting. Why that had moved her so, he was still uncertain. She must have been pricked by the thought that, in the moment of his humiliation, she had been gratifying Welcroft with her ingenious *bonnes bouches*, a warmer sort of mobbing. . . . Certainly, across platforms and dinner tables north of the Border, her eyes had smiled in a way he could not recall since he had brought news he was the Party's choice for leader.

She had been on dazzling form dealing with the whingers. Her technique followed a course familiar from past occasions when his star had been in need of refurbishment. All were greeted with a warm and modest informality, leading to confidences and a bold agreement that things were not as they should be. His own awareness of that fact would be promulgated; hopes would begin to form of a new departure, possibly a major pronouncement in which the lucidity with which those to whom she was talking had articulated their grievances would be handsomely acknowledged.

Then, with their weapons piled, their gates thrown open, they were overwhelmed by sudden attack. In some unnoticed way, they found they had acknowledged the shortcomings were not his at all but the fault of others, unnamed yet recognisable; they themselves had been guilty in failing to appreciate this before. He was once more revealed for what he had always been, the Party's one great hope, post-Thatcher. To kiss the hem of his garment while the chance was offered would be both just and wise.

Not all had succumbed of course. Yet even her failures – more common among men than women – at least sowed confusion where hostility had reigned unchallenged. Misgiving she turned into receptiveness, creating for his own encounters the chance to recover ground that would otherwise have been lost. Without Diana, the visit might have yielded little profit. As it was, he felt it had stopped the rot.

'What did Patrick want?' she asked.

'He's fixed for me to go to some meeting after we land.'

'Who with?'

'He wouldn't say. Whoever we're seeing is off somewhere else later. Anyway Patrick will be waiting when we arrive.'

She was curious. 'I wonder what it's about.'

'He said it wasn't a crisis so I suppose we can rule out the end of the world. And if there'd been an accident with major casualties he'd have mentioned that. I just don't know. But he's got No. 10 to postpone my business this afternoon. I suggest you take the car back there.'

She frowned. 'He's usually pretty cool.'

Cool: yes, but a gambler's cool, with calm deliberation being followed by an audacious move, risking everything. Cool, lean and hungry; hungry in all the ways.

'But I *have* wondered about his judgment lately,' she said.

It was the first time she had voiced real misgivings about Welcroft.

'What makes you say that?'

'Little things.'

He would have liked to learn more but decided against pressing her. Perhaps Welcroft had canvassed some ploy over Massenet's information she had rated as rash. Or she had viewed it as amounting to disloyalty to himself; but he avoided hoping that had weighed with her – the end of the Welcroft bull market had still to be established beyond doubt. Experience over Diana's earlier lovers had taught him not to take too much notice of a single blip in the index. An independent chartist might discover an encouraging pattern when looking back now, but that sort of analysis required an absence of emotion. To himself, the past course of his marriage was not a subject for unblinking recall and dispassionate study. Too often, it laid a hand on his throat.

Welcroft's official car was standing beside his own as the plane taxied in. A little ahead of the usual brace of airport officials, Welcroft waited to be the first greeter. Cool, lean and hungry; and, for all the thickening of the jowls, handsome still. Passing him en route to where Evatt was holding open the door of Blackmer's car, Diana said for the benefit of the assembled minions, 'Hello, Patrick, how's Lorna? I must give her a ring about lunch soon.' Welcroft's expression was lively rather than troubled. Whatever his news was, it must fall short of the poleaxing category. 'Where are we going?' Blackmer asked when they were seated. Welcroft closed the glass partition behind his driver. 'Not far – a hotel in Egham you probably know. There's been a development in the Druitt business. On your visits to the States, has the President ever introduced an old buddy named Lew Rothman?'

'I don't remember him. What does he do?'

'He's running something called the Contingency Research Staff in the White House, a sort of foreign policy think tank.'

He supposed the Foreign Office knew about it, but for Machiavellian reasons of their own, officials had chosen not to refer to its existence in their briefings for his visits. 'I know Lew quite well,' Welcroft continued. 'We met at Harvard Business School originally. He went on to Liesching and Karr, the Wall Street brokers, where he was very successful. They sent him to London to run their European operations at the time of Big Bang. That's how we met up again. Lorna and I had him and his first wife to stay in the house on Corfu one summer.

'Over here Lew came to the conclusion he didn't want to stay in broking all his life. He rode out the downturn in business at the end of the Eighties but he told me at the time he was going into politics as soon as possible. There were always diplomatic people and visiting American politicians being entertained in the house he had on the East side of Regents Park. He began to contribute the odd article to the *Journal for International Relations*. I remember one he showed me on the invasion of Grenada.'

'What was his line on that?'

'Surgical prophylaxis is a necessary instrument for maintaining peace.'

'The Sawbones school of diplomacy,' Blackmer said to the hedgerows, surviving better here in Surrey than when he and Diana had been looking down for medieval fields. 'I hope his contingency planning makes occasional allowance for other methods.' Rothman sounded like a soul-mate for Kenneth

Cridland. If satellite intelligence came up with an old SS-20 lying about a railway yard at Minsk, they'd probably both want a pre-emptive strike.

It was discomfiting that Welcroft claimed close acquaintance with someone in the White House who could be described as an old buddy of the President's and might well be influential in foreign affairs. He thought he had met and could name all the President's cronies who mattered. 'How long has he been in the White House?'

'Since this President was elected. Their friendship goes back to when the President was a State Governor. When the President started his campaign in the last election, Lew threw up his job to join him as a foreign policy adviser. I suppose he may have hoped to become Secretary of State but didn't have quite enough pull.'

'And is this who we're going to meet?'

'Yes.'

'But what has Rothman to do with the Druitt affair?'

'He telephoned me early this morning, having just landed at Heathrow from Washington. He takes off again for Germany this evening. He said we should get together either for lunch today or when he's on his way back to America towards the end of the week. He explained that he'd recently learned we were facing a tricky problem over which the President thought he could be helpful. He wouldn't mention a name, but it was clear he knew about the Druitt enquiry.'

He stared. 'You're absolutely sure of this?'

'Absolutely. I guessed you'd want to hear at first hand what he had to say. Initially I plumped for a meeting on his way back, but I was told when I rang your office that you would be very tied up then. It seemed best to catch him today, since your Private Secretary said he could rearrange your appointments this afternoon.'

'Why couldn't we have met at No. 10?'

'Lew said it was important not to be seen calling on you.'

'You got no clue to what he meant by "help"?'

'No. Whatever it is, he says he's discussed it with the President.'

He lay back and closed his eyes. His thought and feelings were in conflict. To discover, through some report from the President, that the decision he had taken over the story from Sisson and Massenet had been wrong, would be profoundly disagreeable. On the other hand, he couldn't suppress the hope that a weapon to win him the election might after all be placed in his hand. Perhaps this was the President riding to the rescue. If so, it would be chalked up as a favour, carrying as these things always did, a price. The bill, when presented, would almost certainly arrive in circumstances of maximum political awdwardness. But that disadvantage would have to be accepted.

Welcroft said, 'There's something that could be relevant in the political column of today's *Mail*. It claims Westminster is seething with rumours of a security scandal.'

He opened his eyes again. 'Is it?'

'Not that I've noticed.'

'So what's behind the item?'

'My Press Officer's picked up nothing to explain it. *My* guess is that it's all the same thing. A bottle with a genie of the size of Druitt in it isn't going to stay corked forever.'

Rainsborough would say there were a lot of bottles with interesting contents and we should be careful not to create a temperature in which all corks became unstable. He wished he could have had Rainsborough as Home Secretary. Common sense and decency were qualities he'd given insufficient weight to when appointments needed to be made. Rainsborough had been his Duke of Omnium. He should have realised that long ago.

They had turned into the grounds of the hotel. As if on cue, the sun broke through a salient of cloud. Ahead a rosy-bricked facade glowed behind rows of sculptured topiary. No doubt an agreeable spot to pitch camp for a few hours on the way to Germany, and of course convenient for Heathrow. Yet he was surprised Rothman had not chosen to be nearer to his Embassy in case of messages from Washington, or even to pass a little time with the Ambassador. He voiced the thought.

'I meant to add,' Welcroft said, 'Lew explained his trip was entirely *sub rosa*. He doesn't want the Embassy to know he's passing through.'

'Why is that?'

'Apparently he's on special White House business. Anyway I agreed we wouldn't mention our meeting to the Ambassador.'

Welcroft's detective, a more relaxed creature than West, was waiting for them in the entrance of the hotel, having been sent ahead to check the security arrangements for the lunch. Somebody in a formal suit, presumably the hotel manager, was beside him. Then, as the car stopped, another figure with cropped white hair appeared from the doorway behind and advanced.

Rothman's powerful neck and shoulders made his feet in highly polished black shoes seem diminutive in relation to his upper structure. He was stocky and a vigorous mover. The general effect was of great physical strength beside which the sobriety of his dark blue suit and matching tie seemed somehow inappropriate.

He greeted Welcroft with jesting sounds, then thrust a hand towards Blackmer. 'Prime Minister, I appreciate your making the time to meet with me. The President sends his warm regards.'

'I hope he's well.'

Rothman was already turning to lead the way in. Over his shoulder he said, 'He's fine.' He gave the impression he didn't think deference need figure too prominently on the agenda.

The suite where they were to lunch had windows opening on to the lawns in front of the hotel. On a table beneath the windows a buffet had been laid; another table in the centre of the room had places set for them. Two waiters stood around, one beside a trolley of drinks. From somewhere outside came the scent of wisteria.

Over the drinks they talked generalities. Rothman spoke of his time running the London office of Liesching and Karr. He made the memories sound agreeably varied and mostly luxurious: Goodwood, golf at Sunningdale, staying on for breakfast by the fireside at Annabel's, if the journey north to

Regents Park suddenly seemed too demanding. Even the apparently habitual jogging round the Inner Circle of the park got favourable mention. He said he'd never forgotten the flavour of Welsh lamb.

He could have been genuinely nostalgic about the memories, but in all his remarks and anecdotes there was the hint of a stopwatch, he was blatantly programming himself. Either he didn't know it showed or didn't care if it did.

Asked about his trip to Germany, he was uninformative, saying it was partly private, partly White House business; he hoped to meet with several Ministers in Bonn before he left. He drank one vodka Martini, then switched to Perrier. Blackmer's glass was still half-full when he began to move them to the buffet.

It seemed reasonable to match his briskness. 'I understand you have something to tell me, Mr Rothman.'

Rothman delayed replying until the waiters had closed the door behind them. 'It's a story I picked up from a source in the New York publishing world. A book has been on offer from a guy who was once an official in your security set-up. The book will be partly an exposé of the unreliability of the head of the set-up. But I understand it also fingers the leader of your Labour Party as using child prostitutes. The guy is apparently going to claim he warned you about this. There's some sort of evidence on that to go into the book.' He held up two bottles, red and white wine, for Blackmer's inspection. 'Which will you drink, sir?'

He read the labels carefully, chose the white. Whatever else, he was not going to let Rothman see how unpleasantly the news had hit him.

'Naturally,' Rothman said when they were all seated, 'while we don't want to pry into British affairs, in view of Druitt's position we're interested to know if there's anything in this story. If you're having difficulty in resolving the facts, I'm here to say we may be able to help.'

It was plainly necessary to appear appreciative, whatever his feelings. 'Well, thank you. It happens I did receive an allegation against Mr Druitt, based on information provided by a French journalist named Massenet who had been at a conference with him some years ago. I decided after a careful review of the facts with Patrick that there was no case for action on my part.'

'You mean there wasn't a legal case? Or not enough material to enable you to move in other ways?'

'Politically any move would have been very difficult on the information I received. And unwarranted.' He glanced towards Welcroft and went on looking at him until he had forced a nod of assent. 'However, if you have more information I should be glad to look at it.'

Rothman poured more wine into their glasses. 'When I told the President about the allegations that are going to be made in the book I said you might be having difficulty in deciding whether they were soundly based. I needn't tell you he wanted everything done that might help you. It happens that the guy from your security outfit plans to name in the book the person who is supposed to have provided Druitt with child prostitutes, an Austrian who went to live in Mexico a while back after serving a prison sentence in Vienna.'

'Alois Reinholdt.'

'Yes. Our Immigration people have close links with their opposite numbers in Mexico. With their help Reinholdt has been traced to where he's now living.'

Blackmer forked warily at cold salmon. 'Do I understand you're offering us the opportunity to talk to Reinholdt?'

'Yes. Not necessarily in Mexico. We can bring him quietly over the border into the States for a day.'

He felt a mixture of annoyance and unease. But to decline the chance to discover what Reinholdt could disclose was out of the question. 'The offer is much appreciated, Lew. I accept.'

'Fine. As soon as I get back to Washington from Germany I'll let Patrick know what we can fix up. I think you'd be wise to get on to this now – I understand the arrangments for the book are pretty far advanced.'

'How far?'

'My impression is they could go to print in a month or so.'

Anger with the trick Sisson had played made the food in his

mouth taste like sawdust. But for the moment he had to stay cool. They moved on to talk of different things. Another fly cast over Rothman about his German trip found him a little more communicative. 'One of the things the President wants me to do is take a hard look at the Agency's Head of Station there. He's been sending some pretty dumb stuff back to his Headquarters about speeding up the withdrawal of our forces to avoid political difficulties. He seems to have gone soft. I guess he may need de-Europeanising.' He made it sound like a root canal job.

'The President's still firm on freezing the withdrawal programme at the present force strength?' Blackmer said.

'Absolutely. Some of the people Langley employs don't seem able to get into their heads what our policy now is.'

The waters seemed interesting enough for further fishing. 'The President doesn't feel well served by the CIA at the moment?'

They had moved on to cheese and biscuits. Rothman scooped up Brie with celery, looking contemptuous. 'There's a culture there that's got to be changed. One of the things the President asked me to do when I joined him in the White House was to go out to Langley and take a cool look at the Agency. Of course it began as an Ivy League affair – the old Yale elitist arrogance is still around – they always think they know best what's right for America. I wasn't impressed.' He reached for a box of cigars and handed it round. They were clearly getting into a subject close to his heart. 'Right now those guys are trying to put across a lot of crap about the inevitability of decline in American power in the next century. In my book that isn't what intelligence agencies are hired to do.'

Welcroft said, 'Elites that have passed their sell-by dates can be a problem.'

Rothman was clipping his cigar. He wasn't bothering even to nod. It was plain he didn't expect to hear real sense talked in this fancy Jacobean room looking out on a garden that was all fussy reminders of the past. What he was probably thinking was that the United States risked disappearing down the same tube as the Brits if those Ivy League bastards weren't brought to heel.

Blackmer said, 'The Agency's senior man here, Busch, has always seemed pretty balanced whenever I've met him.'

Rothman made a gesture of disgust. 'I know Tom Busch. He illustrates the point I'm making. Of course he's a Whiff, like his father before him who was big in OSS and probably brought him into the Agency. I've heard Tom Busch argue that the President should be thinking about how to educate the American public into accepting the erosion of power before it hits them in the face. Talk like that comes close to what I'd call un-American.'

Blackmer glanced at his watch. Even assuming a clear run, it would be three-thirty before he was back in No. 10. He rose. 'You'll forgive us, I hope, but I think I must leave. Thank you again for the offer to make Reinholdt available for interview in the States. A man in our Cabinet Office named Egerton will be standing by to carry out the interview.' He smiled warmly as he shook hands with Rothman, but he guessed the other knew he'd not found him exactly captivating.

In the car he said, 'Not a graduate of Yale, I gather.'

'University of Oklahoma.'

'What's the meaning of the word he called Busch – a Whiff?'

'A Whiff is a Yale man – a Whiffenpoof. Yale men sing the Whiffenpoof Song when they get together.'

He smiled. 'Whiffs of the World, Unite! Oklahoma Lew is out to get you! Which reminds me – how are we going to get this bastard Sisson? There has to be some way of bringing him to heel. He presumably signed away his right to publish anything when he left Whitehall.'

'He's out of the jurisdiction now.'

'Out of the jurisdiction wouldn't stop the rest of the world from getting tough with its' Sissons. The Israelis would probably send a helicopter and winch Sisson out of his Tuscan bolt-hole on a meat-hook. Are we so wet we can't do *anything*?'

Welcroft was taking a while to crush his cigar butt. Finally he said, 'I understand your feelings, David. But have you thought there could be sound reasons for not hitting him? Suppose Reinholdt convinces us that Druitt *has* been using child prostitutes, you're bound to want to take action. To screw Sisson at the same time for having brought the facts to your attention would be impossible.'

True of course. And there was another reason, a personal reason unknown to Welcroft, for avoiding making an enemy of Sisson. Blackmer stared morosely out of his side window. They were halted in a traffic jam on the approaches to Staines. A woman with ginger hair drawn back to a meagre bun was walking on the pavement alongside them. Beneath an ethnic-looking skirt she wore black stockings in a knit hardly less bulky than that of her cardigan. She had a heavily-filled briefcase under one arm. Glancing casually in the direction of the car, she fixed her gaze on him and he knew he had been recognised. She was trying to decide whether to step over and give him a piece of her mind. At a guess she was a zealot in some caring profession.

He began to lower his window to let her have her say. But then the car moved as a gap opened ahead; the woman was left behind, one hand raised in protest. Once more it had looked as though he preferred to run. This mustn't go on, he told himself, this appearance of declining to face a challenge. But the woman had disappeared. And anyway, there would have been hardly any other voters and no photographers around to note the democratic exchange of views.

He said, 'Rothman's status in the White House strikes me as an unhealthy sign. Presumably he's got the President doing things that the State Department and the CIA doesn't know about. That can't be right.' But, he reflected, who am I to throw stones? In dealing with Sisson's approach, I wasn't much better. Had I consulted Goble at the beginning, at least I'd have been better prepared for the possibility Sisson was playing a double game.

Pushing the thought away he said, 'I can't think why we haven't had a glimmer of this from the Embassy in Washington. I must talk to Roger Lang about it.'

'I'll make a point of keeping in closer touch with Lew,' Welcroft said.

Of course: that would fit in with his hope of escaping from the Home Ofice to take over Foreign Affairs from Lang, if they got back next time.

Much later, he remembered asking Welcroft, as the car turned into Downing Street, what he supposed the rest of Rothman's business in Germany was and realised he had been close to something crucial. But it would have been impossible to have guessed.

He went straight up to the flat to wash and change. Diana was on the telephone in the drawing room. It became apparent as he listened that she was negotiating her attendance at the opening of a Girl Guides' jamboree. 'Sounds healthy,' he said when she put the phone down.

'I'm not staying overnight. My canvas days are over.'

'Don't tell me *you* were a Guide.'

'I was a Brownie.'

He shook his head: out of thirty years of marriage, still something new. 'What happened?'

'I didn't progress. I don't remember why. Some crime against the Brownie code, I suppose. However they don't seem to have it on record.'

'A black-balled Brownie,' he said, trying to imagine her in the uniform, already developing those remarkable legs, the walk that never failed to cause the eye to pause, the mind reflect.

He told her about Rothman's offer. She was more cautious about expressing hope for the outcome than Welcroft had been, but her eyes had brightened.

'Of course,' he said, 'even if Reinholdt does come up with the real goods, we could be in great difficulty about using the stuff.'

'Don't look on the black side so much.' She seemed to check herself then. 'But I do understand.'

As he left the flat to go downstairs, she said, 'You were pretty good up in Scotland, David. Your old form really.'

He raised an eyebrow, but she was being serious. 'For a time I felt you were willing yourself to lose in the autumn. But you've changed.'

So he hadn't been wrong. His morale *was* on the turn.

· Fourteen ·

Fumbling for his diary to note in it the name and telephone number Pagett had read him, Egerton brought out with it the final demands for payment of electricity and telephone accounts. They fluttered to the carpet beside his chair. Gathering them up, he wondered if Pagett had noticed them. But when he looked up again, he saw that Pagett's attention was momentarily absorbed in brushing cigarette ash from his waistcoat. That was perhaps fortunate. Otherwise he could have been the recipient of some politely acid comment – 'Not financially overstretched, Egerton, I hope?', or even, 'Your private affairs are of course your own business, however you realise, I trust, that indebtedness beyond a certain point can raise questions regarding your Positive Vetting status . . .' But that alarming radar of Pagett's had been temporarily switched off. He stuffed the demands back in his pocket and waited.

Needles of rain were scoring the windows of Pagett's office and the sky had an ominously bruised look. Pagett looked up at last. He said, 'I think that's all you need. They're checking on flights for you.'

'Sweetwater – he's an ordinary official on Rothman's staff, is he?'

Pagett referred to a sheet of paper in front of him. 'I doubt it. He's a Colonel – Colonel Brad Sweetwater. Rothman says that all he'll be waiting to hear from you are the details of your flight to Albuquerque. He'll meet you at the airport there and take you to see this creature. Then it's up to you to get the real facts out of *him*. I rely on you to make a good fist of this. You've made an excellent impression on the PM so far.'

He felt bucked and emboldened to question Pagett further. 'Is the PM well? I saw him being interviewed on television last night. He looked very tired, almost drained.'

'Did he? I missed that.' Another cigarette was being lit, the match shaken then disposed of, each movement a display of neat precision, a frame within which to order thought. 'That's a pity – I'd thought he seemed happier with things during the past week. However he may be fearing his Ides of March have arrived. I understand there was a call from Chequers yesterday to say that the tree he'd planted there – the one every Prime Minister is invited to put in – had been pronounced dead. They've suggested he puts in another before he calls an election.'

'Hasn't anybody else's tree ever died?'

'Probably. But he may regard this as a sign that the lioness has whelped.' Pagett sat back and crossed his legs. 'He can be quite superstitious you know.'

Mixed in with the rain, Egerton could now see a little sleet. So dramatic change in the weather would no doubt be helping to orchestrate Blackmer's moods. What with the polls, the constant baying of the press, the growls of dissatisfaction inside his own Party, the pressure at the moment must be relentless. He said, 'If it *is* his Ides of March, who is going to be Brutus?'

Pagett smiled. 'In politics, Egerton, when the lioness whelps, everyone is Brutus. Always remember that.'

Back in his own room, he called Gail to tell her the news of his trip. 'Where to this time?' she asked.

'America – Albuquerque.'

'Injun country!' she said. 'Don't get scalped.'

'They'll have to be quick about it – Pagett wants me back inside three days. Or the PM does.'

'He can't manage without you now. They'll *have* to promote you!'

He laughed. She sounded relaxed about his going, even carefree. But he could never shake off the thought that the old craving might return when he was away from her. 'You'll be all right?'

'Don't worry. With the new show at the gallery I shan't have time to breathe tomorrow.'

He replaced the receiver and sat for a moment, then took out the final demand notices again. Further delay over them was becoming impossible. He had to do something already planned but repeatedly postponed. Leaving the Cabinet Office he went to the Underground in Parliament Square and took a train to the City.

At Monument he stepped out into a world once familiar on a daily basis but not revisited or even thought about in recent times. He had a momentary misgiving that Mr Wimbush, Gentleman's Tailor, might have changed his spots when he arrived at Ship Tavern Passage. A new shop had appeared beside the entrance and other intimations of novelty were visible beyond. But Mr Wimbush had held fast. Still on the staircase leading up to his rooms, the patterned linoleum, vaguely oriental where the design could still be made out; still at the stair head, the flower-shaped pendant light, one petal broken off; still on the dado facing him, the dragged brown paint over yellow, producing a grain never known to wood. Best of all, the glass case on the mantleshelf of the cutting room beyond, displaying the paper patterns of a modified design of morning coat made in 1919 for Horatio Bottomley with, alongside, a sepia photograph of Bottomley himself in the very creation.

Mr Wimbush seemed little more changed than his rooms, perhaps a deeper sprinkling of cigarette ash on the waistcoat, a more handsome ballpoint behind the ear. His pause for recognition was impressively short. 'Mr Egerton!' It was the mildest of reproofs for absence.

Requested to consult his ledger, he went away with a springy step. When he returned to announce the amount to Egerton's credit from the quarterly standing order that had remained uncancelled through all adversities, directness was the only course available.

'Could I trouble you for a cheque for that?'

'You'd like the *money*?'

'Yes.'

He went away again, came back with the cheque. Egerton said, folding it in his notecase, 'A little financial difficulty.'

'I quite understand, Mr Egerton.'

'Thank you.' They shook hands. He found he very much wanted Mr Wimbush to believe he would be back.

Downstairs again, he strolled into Leadenhall Market. Real things, reassuringly commonplace, were still being sold in open-fronted shops. At a greengrocer's a man was stacking oranges in a pyramid. He paused, not so much to watch, but for memory to offer anything else it cared to. A voice spoke his name. Turning, he confronted memory actualised, but from a time he had no wish to return to.

Beresford was tidier than in their days at Oxford, the flowing blond hair cut to a conventional length, designer stubble dismissed in favour of the smoothness that had been waiting all along to take over. He had come up a year later than Egerton and to a different college but they had played squash together. Beresford had followed him into the City, handsomely lured by Massiters and Grote on their annual cream round of the dreaming spires. Oddly their paths had seldom crossed; in the days before Egerton left for New York, they had met only twice, bag-carrying for their respective gladiators in take-over struggles.

'I heard you were in New York,' Beresford said. 'I'd no idea you were back again.'

He was wearing a sharper suit than Mr Wimbush would have advised, its cuffs double and curiously curved, also a shirt of salmon and green stripes, the collar cut away in the style favoured by Antrim when he headed the Crimes Bureau.

Beresford was saying, 'If you haven't already eaten, how about a sandwich? I'd suggest lunch but I'm rather pushed these days.'

He resisted the temptation to make excuses. To slink away would be wimpish, a cowardly avoidance of giving an account of the years between. They went to a wine bar which looked new, on the other side of the Market, a flashy affair with spotlit sherry barrels and unlikely grapes spilling down the sides of panniers.

'You *are* still with Hogarths, aren't you?' Beresford said.

'No, I decided merchant banking wasn't my scene.'

'What did you switch to – broking?'

'I left the City altogether. I work in the Cabinet Office now.'

'You're a civil servant?'

'Fairly civil.'

Beresford said, 'Quite a switch.' His eyes were searching Egerton's face for an explanation that might add up.

Trying to steer him off the subject, Egerton asked for his news. Beresford talked of his work in the amused, dismissive way that had always been his style. He made it sound almost ordinary. But he was describing a world they both knew was nothing like the one they'd entered less than ten years ago. It was an altogether Bigger Dipper now, one that never slowed, with random ejection seats to sharpen up the dozy as the buzzards hovered overhead. But the rewards had grown bigger too – the Campden Grove house knocked off for a mere £270K, courtesy of a triple mortgage before the Treasury had slammed the door, the GTI soon growing into a BMW, the chalet at Verbier in February . . .

'And the pay?'

'The pay is something I'd rather not think about at the moment.'

A girl was collecting empty glasses from around them. Beresford smiled at her. 'Lydia, do you know Mark Egerton? He's abandoned the City and its boring ways. He governs us.'

She managed a tired smile. In her movements was that special slovenliness of a Sloane driven to toil by want or boredom. When Beresford made a joke and patted her rump, she showed him her tongue between her teeth. As she went away, he said, 'Seriously, you're not staying in the Civil Service for ever?'

'I'm not sure.'

'Why don't you come back to the City? Massiters are still recruiting quite hard. There might be a slot. Would you like me to make an enquiry?'

He was being patronised by a man he'd once classified as a Philistine, someone he supposed he would never be tempted to cultivate or envy. The idea of going back with Beresford's helping hand was more than he could happily stomach. Yet not to consider it would be a stupid vanity, divorced from common sense.

'Let me think about it.' He wasn't sure he meant that. He wasn't sure of anything.

There was no mistaking Sweetwater at the flight exit in Albuquerque. Although not in uniform, wearing a check shirt and jeans and with a briar pipe clamped between his jaws, he had an air of brisk authority, reinforced by sunglasses of an intimidating kind that were presumably Army issue. The hand he held out in greeting closed with a grasp that crunched Egerton's fingers. He added 'Sir' to Egerton's name when he pronounced it, but only as an afterthought.

Sunlight, ferocious in its purity, engulfed them as they emerged at the front of the terminal building. In the distance a range of mountains had a cut-out quality in the clear air as though belonging to a stage set. Sweetwater raised a hand and a chocolate-coloured Lincoln nosed towards them. The driver got out and offered a similar handshake to Sweetwater's. He was also in shirt and jeans. Sweetwater introduced him as Melvin. 'Albuquerque's Melvin's home town,' he said. 'Those of us from Texas try not to hold it against him too much.' There was some running gag that Sweetwater found funnier than Melvin did. Climbing into the back of the Lincoln with Sweetwater, Egerton had a fleeting glimpse of a green soft-top beginning to crawl up the entrance ramp about a hundred yards behind the Lincoln.

Soon after leaving the airport, they entered a freeway, heading north it seemed. Melvin was gunning the car through any gaps the traffic allowed. 'How far are we going?' Egerton asked.

Sweetwater embarked on relighting the briar pipe. 'The guy's waiting at a motel about thirty miles on. We brought him over the border last night.'

'Does he know what I've come to ask him about?'

'We gave him the name. He's thinking about it.'

They were entering open country, its flatness relieved by sage and low evergreens. Sweetwater waved a spent match towards a river bed. 'The Rio Grande. This is the route the Spaniards took when they came north out of Mexico.' But soon they were swinging away from the river on to a road towards mountains that was mysteriously signed Cuba. With less vegetation visible now, the plain became like the skin of an ancient elephant, with occasional deeper fissures between the folds. Melvin had slackened speed since leaving traffic behind and now glanced over his shoulder. 'You might not believe it, but this plain is covered in sea shells. Maybe the start of things was around here. It's where they also found a way of ending them too.' He pointed ahead. 'Los Alamos is over there. How's that for symmetry?' He grinned. He was quite different from Sweetwater, laid-back, ready to be amused.

They had been driving for another ten minutes or so when Sweetwater leaned forward to touch Melvin's shoulder. 'How long has that car been behind us?' His expression had become urgent.

Melvin was shaking his head. 'Don't worry, it's State Police. He's hoping we'll go over the limit. I saw him turn out of a gulley a few miles back.'

'I want to take a look.'

Melvin slackened speed. Gradually the car behind began to close on them. The colour display on the roof became visible. Apparently reassured, Sweetwater leaned back again. They passed through a valley and reached a road fork where the landscape opened out again. Scrubby fields stretched on both sides. Round a bend, Melvin pulled off the tarmac alongside a motel sign. Swinging the Lincoln behind a clump of cotton-woods, so that its nose pointed towards the road, he killed the engine.

Neither Melvin nor Sweetwater made any move to get out of the car. They appeared to be following an agreed drill, their eyes fixed on the bend in the road. Almost at once the State Police car appeared and went by. After a few moments more, a second car came into view. It was a green soft-top, identical with the one Egerton had noticed at the airport. A man was at the wheel with a girl beside him; the girl had a Coke can to her mouth. They didn't glance in the direction of the cottonwoods or the motel. Silence returned. After a minute or so, Sweetwater said 'Right' and opened his door.

The motel was built in the adobe style, its single storey walls of terracotta cement rounded at the edges. At intervals along a veranda that gave access to the apartments stood tubs of wilting geraniums. There was a general air of seediness shading into neglect. As the three of them paused by the car, Melvin said, 'I'd say that's a damned hard sell.' Following his eyes to the roof of the building, Egerton saw a sign, peeling and lopsided because of a broken support. It said, "Welcome to Shangri-La."

A man appeared at the door of an apartment and nodded in their direction. They made their way on to the veranda and through the open door behind the man. From an armchair at the other end of the room they'd entered, a short, heavy figure rose. 'Mr Reinholdt,' Sweetwater said, 'this is our friend from the UK.'

He was if anything more unattractive than he had appeared in the newspaper photograph Massenet had produced. The face was fatter and the mouth looser; the plastic frames that had replaced wire in the spectacles did nothing to soften the curiously staring expression of the prominent eyes. When he sat down again he rested a plump, white hand on the chair arm. Occasionally in the conversation afterwards, the finger curled and uncurled along its edge in accompaniment to his thoughts.

Sweetwater and Melvin sat in chairs alongside Egerton's. The man who had been on the veranda brought beer then disappeared. As Egerton placed a tape recorder in front of him, Reinholdt shook his head. 'I will answer questions but that's all. No tape.' He spoke quite good English. Sweetwater was shaking his head at Egerton in mild apology. So it was to be a laborious notebook job. Egerton uncapped his pen. 'Mr Reinholdt, I understand you know this concerns your acquaintance with one of our politicians in the UK.'

'Mr Druitt – yes.'

'You met him some years ago when you were the director of an orphanage in Vienna . . .'

'Yes.'

'How did the contact arise?'

'I believe he telephoned me at the orphanage and said he had been recommended to do so by a mutual friend.'

'Who was the friend?'

Reinholdt shook his head again, smiling. He was conveying the message that although a boundary was once more being overstepped, he was prepared to treat the impertinence in a fairly tolerant way. 'He is no-one you would have heard of, I think. Let us leave it that it was a mutual friend.'

'Very well. Then what did Mr Druitt say was his reason for telephoning?'

'He was interested in meeting one of the boys in my care – a particular boy.'

'Why?'

'The mutual friend had told him he would find the boy interesting. A pleasant experience.'

'A sexual experience?'

'Of course.'

'You provided this service as a regular thing from among the boys in your care?'

'Only from those who were willing and showed a talent. There was no pressure on the others.'

'So you took the boy Mr Druitt had asked for to his hotel one evening?'

'Not on that occasion. He came to the orphanage and met the boy there. It was on a later visit to Vienna that he asked me to bring one to his room in a hotel during a conference he was attending. He had asked for a different, younger boy who could co-operate in different ways.'

'Sexual ways?'

'Yes.'

'You were present and watched it happening?'

'Yes. I believe I took part. The boy was very . . . skilful for his age.' Reinholdt made a little gesture of emphasis with his hand.

'Did Mr Druitt pay you for arranging this?'

'I would have insisted that he gave money to the boy. I always required that.'

'Had this boy spoken to you of a memory of visiting England at some time before he came to the orphanage, and did you or he ask Mr Druitt to make enquiries about this?'

'Nothing of that kind took place.'

'You're quite sure?'

'Quite sure.'

'Was that the last time you had dealings with Mr Druitt?'

'Yes. As you will no doubt know, I was arrested not long afterwards.' He looked down at the fingers curled on the arm of the chair, his head on one side like a bird's. 'Hypocrisy had its great triumph at my expense. They thought it could be used to bring down the Government.'

Egerton raised his eyebrows. 'Who were "they"?'

'The opposition parties.'

'Why do you speak of hypocrisy?'

'Because what I was doing would never have been attacked in earlier civilisations. Sexual practices of this kind have always been accepted by sensible people as having a place in society.' There was hauteur now in his manner, an evident conviction that only fools would disagree with him. 'I took great care that the boys were never exploited. Some of them were very grateful to me for the friendships and security I found for them. There will always be a need for what I was doing. To pretend otherwise is the hypocrisy.'

There seemed little more to be said. Egerton flicked over the pages of his notebook. 'Would you be willing to testify in a legal document to what you've just told me?'

Reinholdt didn't even bother to shake his head this time, but simply gazed impatiently past Egerton at the wall behind. 'I made it clear that I would answer questions but nothing more. I will not become involved again in what belongs to the past.' He glanced at Sweetwater who in turn looked towards Egerton. 'That was the deal, Mr Egerton.' It was obvious there had been an agreement with Reinholdt before he had come here.

Reinholdt was rising to make clear he considered there was no more to be said. A little tension showed in his face but on the whole he had been at ease throughout the interview.

Shaking hands with each of them in turn, he produced his wet, loose-lipped smile to show how pleased he was with himself.

On the veranda outside, Sweetwater said, 'I guess that's what you needed. I'm glad we could help. I'll say goodbye now. Melvin'll take you back to Albuquerque. I have to get this guy back over the border now. Otherwise our Mexican friends are not going to be pleased. Hope you have a good flight back to London.' He stood watching, clear grey eyes slightly narrowed until Melvin and Egerton reached the Lincoln, then went back into the room. There was a purposefulness about all his movements, an enviable air of conviction. He was a warrior free from doubt, a dragon-slayer come down from a time when everything in life was much more straightforward. He needed dragons and knew all the ways of dealing with them. That was what he was for.

Melvin swung the Lincoln back on to the road. After a while he said, 'Alois is not a guy I take to. Still he seems to have given you the goods. That's what matters.'

Across the sage bush flats, the range of mountains seen from the airport had come into view. At one end of the range a column of cloud was appearing, curiously solid and rising vertically from the ridge. Melvin said, 'See that over the Sandias? Watch it build as we get nearer to Albuquerque.'

'What is it?'

'A thunderhead. You get them in these parts on days like this, but usually later in the summer. There'll be a storm before long, probably just a baby but you never know. When you're born in those foothills you learn to watch out.'

Egerton was aware of being gripped by an unease as he watched the thunderhead. He could not pin its origin on any single event. There had been something wrong with the whole day, but what sort of thing? He had the sense that there were questions to be put to Melvin before it was too late. But they remained unformulated in his mind as they turned into the airport.

Lightning was beginning in earnest, a skyful of jagged light that seemed to belong to some unseen war behind the mountains. Heavy rain was also falling and the temperature had dropped with astonishing rapidity. But the take-off of the St Louis flight where he would pick up a London plane had not been postponed. He shook hands with Melvin. 'Thank you.' He only wanted to get away now.

Melvin grinned aimiably. 'Guess you may have problems handling that stuff back in London. But you'll find a way I suppose. The British usually do. Experience counts.' He could have been a believer in the infinite resource and cunning of the Old World but he was probably just trying to be polite.

There were two hours to wait when he got to St Louis. Pagett had asked for early news and he decided to call him. When he was put through, Pagett said quickly, 'Don't go into detail. Tell me which of the stories he backed.'

'The Frenchman's.'

'Any support at all for the other version?'

'None.'

'Was he convincing?'

'He added a fair amount of detail. There was more than one contact apparently. The purpose each time was what the Frenchman guessed it was.'

Pagett said briskly, 'So all in all, you were satisfied you got the truth?' When Egerton didn't respond at once, he went on, 'Anything wrong?'

'I can't say I found anything ... *wrong* – although he wouldn't agree to making a formal statement or even to disclose his address. I suppose I just don't like the situation. I rate him unpleasant and unscrupulous. I don't feel it would be right to rely on this sort of evidence. Particularly if it was going to lead to somebody's career being destroyed.'

There was a silence at the other end of the line. Then Pagett said, 'Forunately this is not something on which you or I have to take the final decision. Ministers are paid to do that.'

Egerton could imagine him tapping away the usual half-inch of ash before replacing the cigarette very carefully between his lips. 'Meanwhile,' Pagett said, signing off, 'I'll expect your report on my desk tomorrow.'

· Fifteen ·

As Louise unlocked the door, the occupant of the apartment above was coming down the stairs with dog and pooperscoop. He would just have returned from whatever he did during the day; on a hunch she had classified it in her mind as to do with computer systems. Now the dog would be walked to the Ukrainian church, never further. Variety would be provided by return along the sidewalk opposite. There was a bag in his back pocket for the used scoop.

She rated him well into his twenties, yet the face was so smooth it was difficult to believe he shaved. His tee-shirt and jeans were like a second skin. She found him unreal, his neatness a little eerie.

She reached out to stroke the cocker's head. The man gave a tight smile, pausing as briefly as possible, consistent with her fingers not being left in space. Getting him to utter a greeting was a challenge to which she still aspired. But, although tonight his ears were unmuffed, he belonged to a Walkman world. Reality was to be touched at only the minimum of points necessary in order to get through the day. Anything ventured beyond could invite disturbance, involvement, threat.

Inside her own apartment, she settled for purposefulness, went straight to take a shower, afterwards put on a robe and made a cream cheese salad before resorting to a bottle of any kind. When finally she sat with glass and plate on the divan, she had to accept she must now discover her reaction to the letter from Tom.

She had procrastinated throughout the afternoon. The

length of the attachment to the letter and its need of translation had played into her hands, although she had deciphered its main thrust. But the principal excuse had been the other things calling for attention in the office; a conference with sales, lost galleys only located after an hour's search behind cupboards, the appearance of Hal in her room wishing to discuss his migraines. Deliberate delaying tactics had hardly been called for. But here no credible diversion obtained.

There had been a touch of nostalgia in the way the letter reached her hand, a reminder of errands once carried out for Tom in places where his own movements were being too closely watched. This time the frisson of danger had been missing; yet there was still an agreeable sense of clandestine intrigue.

A call had come through on her office extension from someone announcing himself as Jordan Kingsley, a friend of Tom's. 'The Company?' she had asked and found herself reproved by silence at the other end before he agreed. Surely not a gaffe in these days, she thought. But perhaps the jargon was viewed as passé now by someone who sounded pretty young.

Kingsley had gone on to say he had been visiting London and was in New York for a few hours. Tom had asked him to deliver a letter to her personally but not at the office. She had agreed to meet him in Central Park, choosing a point conveniently close to where she was lunching an author, passed on by Hal as still bankable but emotionally on crutches, and therefore in need of a woman's touch.

Jordan Kingsley was at her side without her being aware of his approach. He was not as young as he had sounded on the telephone, but well under thirty, a rangy figure with light blue eyes and deep tan and a profile that could not be denied a handsome rating. His way of smiling indicated he wouldn't be taken aback by a gasp of admiration.

'You're exactly as Tom described,' he said.

'Yes?'

'I knew you at once.'

'Let's hear the text.'

He laughed. 'It was *very* complimentary.'

From an inside pocket he had taken out the letter, remarking, 'Tom said you'd understand he couldn't risk the enclosure to the post.'

She read no more than was necessary to know what it was about, preferring not to have his eyes watching her reactions in case he knew something of the background. Putting it in her purse, she said, 'It looks pretty long. I'll read it later otherwise I'll be late for my lunch appointment.' She stood. 'Thank you for bringing it. Are you on your way back to Langley?'

'Yes, I work with Ray Brooks. I gather from Tom you know him pretty well.'

'Pretty well,' she said. 'I hope your life premiums are up to date.'

He laughed again: something similar had obviously been said before. 'He's desk-bound these days. I've heard the stories of course. But that was before I joined.'

They had strolled together to the edge of the Park where she had refused his offer to find her a cab, saying she would walk to the lunch. After they parted, it occurred to her that, for all his assurance, he had been uncertain how to handle her. She wasn't a professional target or licensed game or in the family any more. She was a woman with a warning sign round her neck which said: Divorced but Still in Touch.

Taking the letter from her purse, she read.

> Dear Louise,
>   Since I wasn't able to convince you that what
> happened to M. hadn't been the result of anything
> you told me, I decided to call George K., who's
> now in the Paris Embassy, and ask him to discover
> all he could through his channels. The attachment
> was provided by a friend of George's. Please
> destroy it. According to an update I have just got,
> the main suspect disappeared from M.'s
> apartment two days after the murder. However
> it's thought he may be in the Lyons area and the
> police expect an arrest quite soon.

Please call me after you've read this. The things
I wanted to say in London got buried in the fall-
out from the call from Hal's Paris agent. They're
important – to both of us, I hope.

My love,
Tom

A postscript which obviously assumed she was reading it all
with Kingsley still around struck a lighter note; he didn't want
her to get the notion he was becoming mawkish. 'Handsome,
don't you think? But much too callow for you. T.'

The attachment to the letter was a photocopy of a French
police report, in language occasionally difficult to translate, on
the subject of Massenet's death. It consisted mostly of a
summary of the interrogation of a Vietnamese national named
Nguyen Nhac, described as a waiter. Nguyen Nhac had been
pulled in for questioning about drugs trading. Presumably to
improve his prospects, he'd volunteered information about
Massenet's killing.

Nguyen Nhac claimed that it had been Massenet's
Vietnamese servant, Truong Chin, who had killed him, out of
jealousy. Three years before, he and Nguyen Nhac had
escaped together to Hong Kong and subsequently gone under
the wire of the holding camp there. Truong Chin had managed
to get himself picked up by Massenet, then working there as a
journalist, and Massenet had somehow arranged for him to
accompany him back to Paris. Nguyen Nhac got himself to
Paris at a later date and they met up again. Truong Chin had
boasted how well off he was as Massenet's houseboy.

Recently however, Massenet had become attracted to a
male performer at a transvestite club where Nguyen Nhac
worked, with the result that Truong Chin had become very
jealous. The night of Massenet's death, he had followed
Massenet to the club and made a scene, resulting in his being
thrown out. Apparently he had then waited outside, followed
Massenet when he left and killed him. Afterwards he had
returned to the club's kitchen entrance and told Nguyen Nhac
to find the dancer for him, since he intended him to suffer the

same fate. The dancer had prudently made himself scarce and had never returned to the club. The report ended with the note that Truong Chin and the dancer were now both being sought.

Louise closed her eyes, trying to decide what she now thought. That her immediate suspicion in London of what lay behind Massenet's death might have been hasty, she had begun to recognise even in the cab that had taken her from Tom's to a hotel. But once her accusation had been formulated, she could not acknowledge that it might be flawed. In a sense, her mood when she arrived at the house on Berkeley Square had willed some sort of crisis. Too near to being hopeful, she had been more ready to embrace disillusion. To believe that Tom had been so careless or ruthless (her anger wished to choose both) as to deny her even forewarning of Massenet's removal from the scene, offered escape from feelings which had begun to make her vulnerable again. Disenchantment, the familiar of these last few years, was too reliable a companion to be cast aside in an evening.

Once back in New York, however, she had found the scenario she had constructed round Massenet's death less credible. True, a Ray Brooks could well have proposed taking Massenet out, if a strong wish to see Druitt protected had been voiced at the right level in Langley. But she could scarcely believe such a scheme would have been allowed to get started. Or if it had been, Tom would surely have known and taken care to tell her what to expect. Surely. . . . But misgiving had returned and her heart had gone cold again.

Here was a fresh appeal to reason. Likelihood pointed to the story Tom had now sent as the true explanation for what had happened. And yet . . . the houseboy wasn't in custody, the dancer had conveniently disappeared as well, everything turned on the reliability of someone who might have a score to settle with Truong Chin and had certainly been in need of obliging the Paris police with whatever they wanted to hear. It was quite a satisfying tale that Nguyen Nhac had told. But that was the hallmark of a good cover story.

The street buzzer sounded and she went to answer it. At first the voice, competing with background crackle, was unidentifiable; she asked for the name to be repeated. When it was, she groaned beneath her breath. Sweetwater was below.

He had flown into La Guardia an hour or so ago, she gathered. Calling the office, he had found both she and Hal had left for the day, Hal on a journey up-state. When her apartment number yielded no response, he had not accepted defeat. Instead he had postponed an onward journey to Washington and headed for the East Village in the hope she would have returned in the meantime. He plainly thought she'd be touched.

'I have news,' he said. 'Good news. I thought maybe I could tell you over that dinner we planned.'

Her wits struggled towards evasive measures. 'Brad, I'd have liked that very much. The trouble is I've a typescript here on which I must give a decision first thing tomorrow. I'm going to be reading most of the night.'

'We could be back at your place in a couple of hours.'

'I can't spare even that time. I've just eaten and I'm starting on the thing now.'

Traffic noises filtered through his silence. This conversation while he hovered on the sidewalk was absurd, she couldn't leave it like that. She made herself more welcoming. 'I'd like to see you though, to hear the news. Why not come up for a quick drink?'

In the interval before he arrived at her door, she took a typescript from her case, added another to bulk it out and stacked the result threateningly on the coffee table. There was no time to dress again, only to wrap the robe with care to exclude all possible signals of wantonness.

He was back in civilian clothing this time, the Aquascutum raincoat draped in soldierly folds over one arm, the pipe bowl nestling between thumb and forefinger. He had had another of his witchfinder haircuts since their meeting in Washington. But, that apart, he looked as usual, more than presentable – well-made, graceful, the cleancut sword-of-honour man. America needed its Sweetwaters, she had tried telling herself; and if America needed them, so did she. She had to remember that.

While she got him his scotch, he offered civilities about the room, nodded regretfully at the typescript pile when she focused his attention on it, but seemed less disappointed at the way things had turned out than she'd expected. Frustration was being balanced by a buoyancy to his morale that was unusual even for him.

'So tell me the news,' she said. Since the meeting with Lew Rothman in the house on Rock Creek Drive, there'd been total silence from Washington. When Sisson had telephoned, enquiring about developments, she had fortunately been out of the office. Hal had avoided speaking to him, getting his secretary to say all was going well, there'd be good news very soon. The next day, Hal had called Sweetwater and received an uninformative reply that also seemed to be on the brusque side. She had detected in Hal further signs of disenchantment with his old buddy. He was ready to write off the project and had begun to compensate with a new castle in the air; a German prince of impeccable credentials was offering the low down on incest in Royal Houses, through an agent in Rio.

Sweetwater said, 'The news is you'll get your book.'

'They're definitely moving against Druitt in London?'

'If Blackmer doesn't organise some action in the next week or so, the President is going to want to know why.'

'What's made the difference?'

'We managed to locate Reinholdt in Mexico. The Brits have got from him the full story of how he took the boy to the hotel and why. Plus a hell of a lot more.'

'So Blackmer's already got this?'

'He will have it in a day or so. He sent over the guy you told me about, Egerton, to meet Reinholdt. I guess he'll be writing a report about now.'

She leaned towards him, hoping to look appealing without quite selling the pass. 'Isn't there some way you could arrange for me to talk to Reinholdt as well? It would make a lot of difference to the book.'

He was shaking his head slowly, wearing his guardian-of-the-holies look. 'Sorry. This was set up on Lew's instructions specifically for the Brits. A lot of people in Mexico had to be fixed. We promised Reinholdt he'd be left alone afterwards, as well.'

Wheedling was not going to produce a different answer, she decided. Even if she let him spend the rest of the night with her, she suspected he would relent very little. And she wasn't going to pay that price.

While he lingered over his drink, she dealt with queries on the incidence of nights when typescripts didn't have priority and whether she was wearing the same perfume as when he had first met her; in return she asked how things were with Helen, waiting patiently in Maryland for his return. By the time his glass was empty, she felt he was beginning to admit a possibility he'd never sleep with her, that some fatal flaw, like lesbianism, was standing in the way.

He went at last. Glancing at the phone as she closed the door behind him, she was aware of her fingers tingling and realised that while he had been with her, in some mysterious way she had come to a decision about Tom.

The phone in the Berkeley Square house was answered by the Spanish maid, sounding very tired. There had been a dinner party, she had just finished clearing up and was about to leave. Mr Busch had said he needed to look in at the Embassy and wasn't back yet. She agreed to leave him a message.

An hour went by. Although she had asked for Tom to call her as soon as he came in, the phone remained obstinately silent. She began to feel less well-disposed towards him. Taking the typescript with her into bed, she turned a page or two without enthusiasm then fell asleep.

Dredged from limbo by the ringing tone, after an interval she was unable to gauge but which seemed substantial, she went to pick up the receiver. 'I hope you weren't asleep,' Tom said.

She was hardly enough awake to know whether she was glad or irritated to hear his voice. 'You,' she said. Her mouth felt like a sandpit.

'I only got your message five minutes ago.'

Taking the phone with her, she went back between the

sheets. The clock on the radio beside her registered one thirty-five. It would be dawn in London. 'Haven't you been to bed at all?'

'No, I got involved at the Embassy in what looked as though it might turn into a crisis. I've just walked back. How are you?'

'Comatose. How are you?'

'I'm all right.' But he was tense, she could tell.

'I met your messenger yesterday.'

'Jordan?'

'I didn't know you'd gone over to recruiting beach boys.'

'Don't be fooled. Jordan has a good brain.'

'He'll need it, working with Ray Brooks. Otherwise he may not get away with just a leg turned into meatloaf.'

'You got my letter anyway,' he said doggedly. 'So you know now what *really* happened.'

'I know what it said in the police report you sent.'

'Well?'

'The two things don't necessarily go together.'

He was silent. She felt a little contrite. 'All right, perhaps that's what *did* happen.'

'Be reasonable, Louise, there's no perhaps about it! I'd have told you of anything that could affect what you were doing over the book.'

'They could have ordered you not to tell me.'

'Why should they have done that? Do you think I'd have accepted it if they had? You're getting too cynical.'

'I had a good teacher.'

She hadn't intended to sound this belligerent, but being woken from a deep sleep had rattled her. 'What I'm saying is, the police report doesn't have to be the truth, they could have swallowed a cover story. I don't say you'd have agreed to keep anything like that from me. Others could have decided that it would be less embarrassing all round if they didn't tell you what was going to be done.' As he started to interrupt, she went on, 'Alright, I jumped to conclusions too easily in London. I was on edge. It wasn't your fault either. I'm sorry. I'm also sorry it ruined the evening, the dinner you'd arranged. It was bad luck the call from Paris came through when it did.'

'You're really meaning all this?'

'Yes.'

'Then you'll agree to try again?'

'Try what?'

'Come here on another trip. You can find an excuse – the company Hal bought must need looking at again.'

'Hal plans to do that himself. He also wants to take in Ascot and hopes you'll get him into the Royal Enclosure. I told him that was the sort of thing you could arrange easily.'

She enjoyed the noises at the other end and laughed. But then he said, 'All right, if you can't work a trip through Hal, come anyway, I'll send you the ticket.'

'Free?'

'Absolutely.'

She felt she was allowing herself to be persuaded too easily. It was, after all, a trip into jeopardy. She had rebuilt her house after it had fallen in and it kept her relatively safe and dry. She didn't want to risk another collapse.

'Come on,' Tom was saying. 'What have you got to lose?'

'There's something we've got to get clear first. Is this for old times' sake? Or something more? Because I have the impression you're already into something more. I'm not interested in being a subsection of that.' When he made sounds of mystification, she went on, 'I guessed when you came here you were having an affair. Fine, it's not my business. I just don't have any interest in being run alongside that.'

'I'm not having an affair.'

'You have been, I know you too well.'

She could sense he was genuinely taken aback. He said eventually, 'I might have been near to it. But she decided what I did would get in the way.'

'She doesn't approve of your work?'

'There are problems about that.'

She almost laughed: candle-lit evenings going sour because the English Rose had turned into a Congressional Committee with a liberal majority! She felt almost defensive on his behalf. 'What sort of things does she imagine her own team have been getting up to since the British stopped wearing skins?'

She knew she ought to leave it at that. But the desire to bring to life the owner of the long black hair in the bathroom of the house on the Berkeley Square was too strong. 'Tell me her name.'

He sighed heavily. 'Antonia Strachan. She's a widow, in her thirties, and very nice. Can we leave it now?'

She would have to go, to discover if there really was a chance for them again. But of course the risks weren't equal, nowhere near being so. If it didn't turn out right, work and other distractions would soon cushion disappointment for Tom. There would always be Antonia Strachans drifting past, vacant craft waiting to be boarded. For her the waters lapping at the door held no such invitations, only floating debris and the slow wink of crocodiles as they cruised Manhattan's shallows.

'There's something that could get in the way,' she said. 'I may soon be working against the clock on the book. Brad called here with news.'

'He visits now, does he?' he said nastily.

'Brad says the top man on your side of the water is getting more evidence that corroborates the original story. It's from the horse's mouth. He won't have any choice but to act on it.'

'Yeah?' He sounded almost disinterested.

'Don't you want to know more?'

'We can talk about it when you come.'

Afterwards she thought: he knew about the interview Egerton had with Reinholdt. How, she couldn't imagine at the moment. But he knew all right.

· Sixteen ·

Welcroft said, 'Reinholdt's account fits what Massenet told Egerton like a glove.'

Blackmer flicked over the pages of the file. 'True.' He sighed and sat back, frowning.

'Something wrong?'

'I suppose not. Egerton, you'll notice, isn't entirely happy. I gather from Pagett he expressed deep unease at the prospect of action being taken on the basis of Reinholdt's testimony. He regards him as slippery. *And* he won't give an affidavit.'

Welcroft tried unsuccessfully to conceal impatience. 'Egerton doesn't like him. Neither do I, from what we know of his record. But that's no reason for rejecting his evidence in this instance. He could have absolutely no reason for making up his story. We haven't paid him anything or made any promises to encourage that. Egerton's no doubt bright enough for his years. But he still has to learn what the police know – that the truth often has to be dug from very unsavoury places.'

They were seated in Blackmer's study at No. 10, Welcroft, Rainsborough and himself. He had hoped to give some part of the afternoon to a final round-up with Roger Lang and others about his trip to the Far East. But it would have to be left to the plane now.

'Suppose you gave the facts to Len Halsey on Privy Councillor terms?' Rainsborough said. 'After all, if this is going to blow up, as their Deputy Leader he'd have to take over until they held one of their leadership elections. Doesn't he need to know?'

Blackmer shook his head. 'The only thing that would

happen is that notwithstanding my telling him not to, he'd go off and warn Druitt he had the choice of either fighting it as a pre-election smear or doing a Stonehouse more efficiently than Stonehouse did. Druitt would of course fight, relying on us having no reputable evidence. Which is pretty well the case. I don't want him forewarned if we *are* going to let this surface.'

Rainsborough took out a handkerchief with an air of despairing resignation; he had arrived complaining of a summer cold. It being Friday, he would have hoped to escape to the country by now. 'I daresay you're right.' He blew his nose noisily. 'Bloody fool. I'd thought he had more sense than to get himself involved in anything like this.'

Welcroft averted his eyes from him. 'In the absence of any better course I suggest we reconsider using Kevin Bedford. Given the sort of money his papers can throw around when they're after a story, the end result couldn't fail to be useful. Druitt's private life from day one would be gone through with a fine comb.'

'You'd let him in on all that Egerton has dredged up?' Rainsborough asked.

'Why not?' He had the bit between his teeth now. 'His people might even manage to find where Reinholdt's living in Mexico and change his mind about going public. But even if they didn't it wouldn't matter too much, as long as they got out a story to the effect that Druitt was known to enjoy the sort of sexual relief of which the Great British Public does not approve. He'd be finished.'

He chopped the table in front of him with the side of his hand, signalling retribution. One day when, freed from the grim treadmill of the Home Office, he could range more widely on punishments to fit the crime and the need for a return to moral standards that had made the British People Great, he would be the darling of the Party Conference.

Kevin Bedford: Blackmer had known Welcroft would come back to proposing they use Bedford, that cadaverous creature with his sunken eyes and a complexion that seemed more drained of colour whenever he came to call. He always had the aura of being unaired; the frequent trips to the yacht in the

Mediterranean, avidly reported by the gossip writers on the newspapers of his rivals, gave no added tinge to his skin. No doubt he spent most of his time below deck. There, in the communications room, said to be far in advance of anything Whitehall had, the ceaseless manoeuvring to acquire yet further slices of the media business presumably continued without interruption.

'He'd be risking the biggest libel action of the century,' Blackmer said.

'It'd be up to him to be sure he had enough ammunition to defend it successfully. Anyway, it wouldn't be our worry. And this is a moment when he may feel the need to be particularly obliging. He wants approval for another satellite TV channel.'

Blackmer turned to Rainsborough. 'What do you say, Charles?'

He was still holding the handkerchief at the ready. 'You know my feelings about Bedford. His newspapers and TV channel revolt me, his business ethics are a disgrace.'

He was displaying his most tiresome side — self-indulgence masquerading as gruff honesty as a way of avoiding an issue. Too often he behaved as though sounding off at the bar of his club, instead of as a Minister tackling hard choices. Blackmer could feel irritation with Rainsborough on the increase again. 'It's no good wishing Bedford away. He exists. We can't ignore his power.'

Standing up, Blackmer went to the drinks tray and poured himself a brandy. On the way back to his chair he paused in front of the Zoffany to take more time to think. It seemed a very long while since Ann-Marie Choltitz had pointed out the oddness of the dog. He wondered how her interview at the White House had gone. He must ask the President sometime if he'd found his exchange with her rewarding.

He looked round at Welcroft. 'If we did let Bedford in on this, who do you envisage speaking to him?'

'I could do so, since you're going to be away in the Far East for a while. We can't afford to lose too much time.'

'What would you tell him?'

'Reinholdt's story, absolutely straight, plus what Massenet

told Egerton as well. I'd add his people would also find it useful to see Sisson and ask . . .'

He shook his head as he sat down again. 'I would want Sisson left out of this entirely. If I can't have his guts for the trick he's been trying to play on me, I can at least spoil his chances of presenting himself to the world as our saviour. When Bedford gets in with his exposé, the publishers in New York may well lose interest in him. Also, I should want no mention of how we heard the Massenet story, no mention of my sending Egerton to see him. If that aspect's revived by anybody, I shall decide how to handle it at the time. So far as Bedford's concerned, he's just getting a lead he may wish to follow up.'

'So you'd like me to go ahead?'

The tips of his fingers tingled; he almost agreed. But misgiving whispered, held him poised on the brink. He pursed his lips, wanting still more time to think. In the silence while they waited for him to speak, Rainsborough, reaching too late for his handkerchief, sneezed violently across the desk, then turned away.

'I'll let you know,' he said. 'Diana and I are spending the night at Kilndown before we take off for China. Where will you be this evening, Patrick, if I want to call you?'

'I'll be at Frobisher Street until tomorrow morning.'

'Right. That's as far as we can take it now. I'll think it over. Thank you both.'

When they had gone, he sat for a while, doing nothing. The tightness in the scalp was back, he seemed to have it every few days now. Stretching out a hand towards the pen tray in front of him, he watched the fingers as they dipped to pick up the nearest of the pens. For a moment it seemed as though the hand had jerked towards the side of the tray. But the fingers gripped the pen and came back with it, more or less as they'd been told to. So there was surely no need to worry.

At Kilndown, it was Esther who opened the door as they drove up. She looked well, tanned from the sun of the past few days. She was waiting, he knew, to hear what he would say about her idea of working. After they'd had a drink with Diana and Hilda, he said, 'Let's walk down to the pool before dinner.'

The evening was still quite light. Above them as they crossed the lawn, swifts swept the sky, rising higher and higher, looking for the place where they could switch to automatic pilot.

They sat on the stone bench and watched Bron exploring the pool's edge. 'You look fine today,' he said. Walking down from the house, she had moved with hardly a hint of impaired control; a stranger would have supposed she was just a little clumsy.

'About your work idea,' he said. 'I agree absolutely. I called Reeves, and he said the same. He'd just like to see you again before you start.'

'When will he come?'

'As soon as I'm back from the Far East. Then we can talk to him together. Unless he suggests holding off for a while, you could start doing something straight away. I've been exploring that. There's a woman in Sedgeworth who runs the local Age Concern outfit. She'd be very bucked to have your help two days a week.'

'Not more?'

'Maybe later. Her name is Croom, Jane Croom. She can pick you up here and also bring you back. She sounds nice, she's the widow of someone who used to be on the constituency committee down here.'

'You haven't told her anything?'

'No. But it might be sensible. We'll ask Reeves.'

Reaching down, she plucked from the pool's edge a late bloom of crowfoot. 'I don't want her to know. I hate it when others know. Please support me on this when Reeves comes. I want no more people to know from now on. Let me explain any difficulties I have some other way.'

Over the years he had had to find the way to deal with his own difficulties, to blunt or turn aside the dangerous question. Oddly enough, no awkward moments had arisen until 1974. That was the year when his performances in the House were beginning to be talked about and the *Sunday Times* had decided to include him in a feature about backbenchers who might be Party leaders one day. It was to be a major story in the Colour Magazine, the first time he had had important coverage nationally.

He could still remember the euphoria with which he had learned he was one of the choices for the feature and had welcomed the reporter into his study at Flood Street. Offering a humdrum résumé of early existence, expecting to move on quickly to his aspirations for the country's future, he had been surprised by the reporter's continued questioning about childhood. He had obliged with an anecdote or two about his father, knowing that subsequent burrowing into his father's career as an estate agent in the West Country would yield no dangerous collateral clues. 'And your mother,' the reporter had said. 'You say she had been a schoolmistress before her marriage to your father and died when you were very young. How did she die?'

How did she die? Foolishly, he'd not allowed for such persistence. Compelled to extemporise, he spoke of a serious heart condition developing over the years, of her being sent to a hospital abroad for treatment which had been unsuccessful and of her dying there. He had closed down on further questions, saying it was a painful memory he preferred not to recall.

And so it had appeared in print, partly in question and answer form, the reporter having sensed the drama of the moment but not the true reason for it. Reading his inventions later, he had flinched and had a momentary feeling of apprehension. But the lie had after all been harmless enough, irrelevant to the political philosophy that formed the substance of the feature.

Other profiles had occasionally built on the detail of that first interview, expanding imaginatively on it, in one instance to suggest he had been present at the bedside when his mother's death occurred and this event could account for a melancholy streak in his character. So the legend had taken root, become so integral a part of the record that at times he could almost believe it was true and that he had rewritten the past. On a radio phone-in programme soon after being made a junior Health Minister, he had smoothly acknowledged the excellent memory of a caller concerned about heart disease research, who had reminded him he had a personal reason to be interested. 'Yes,' he had said, 'it's a subject that naturally has concerned me deeply.'

Leaning closer, he took the hand that didn't hold the flower and pressed it between both of his, not caring if he hurt her because that was unimportant compared with the assertion of their oneness. She put her head on his shoulder. 'Thinking about it here, with nothing much to do, is no joke. No joke at all. You understand?'

'I understand.'

No other bond, not marriage, not parenthood, could be like this, he told himself. He had the image of blood springing from their joined palms, the wound finally shared.

'How long will you be away this time?' Esther asked.

'Nine days.'

'When will you come down for a long spell?'

'August, I promise. And if I lose the election, much more. We'll be doing a book together.'

'You mustn't lose. I want you to win – although that means not seeing you more. You have to win because you're the right person to be Prime Minister and because when you're successful *I'm* stronger, I feel it.'

She had drawn back, was smoothing each petal of the crowfoot in a repeated sequence as she spoke. She might have been testing co-ordination. It was possible to read an underlying purpose in all her actions. Possible and foolish; but he would go on doing it.

Back at the house, she went to change shoes wet from dew. In the drawing room, Diana looked up from a book on Korea Wyeth had collected at Hatchards during the afternoon. 'Is she happy about it?'

'Reasonably. A little apprehensive about what Reeves might say.'

'I suppose the woman in Sedgeworth will have to be told.'

'She doesn't want her to be.'

'If she's intelligent or has heard about other cases, she'll probably guess. You're then dependent on her being discreet. Have you thought about that?'

'Everything suggests Madam Croom is *very* discreet. She has my photograph on her piano apparently. In a silver frame.'

Not long ago she wouldn't have smiled, would simply have turned away. Instead, she said, 'It would be sensible if I got to know her, wouldn't it?'

'Probably.' He glanced at the clock. 'I ought to ring Patrick.'

He had told her in the car of the proposal to involve Bedford. She had wrinkled her nose but had held back from arguing for or against. Since their *rapprochement*, he had sensed she was unsure how soon she could resume the role of frank adviser.

'If I say go ahead, the result will be sewage, tabloid sewage. What can't be established will be insinuated or fabricated, if his lawyers think Bedford can get away with it. The prospect appals me. But it may be the only way of getting the result we need.'

'Does Druitt deserve any better? You gave him the benefit of the doubt once. He accepted it and let you think that was right, that he was whiter than white. Have you forgotten?'

There was something in that.

Hilda came in to tell them dinner was ready and that Esther was already downstairs. Putting his empty glass on the drinks tray after she'd gone, he said, 'Esther spoke about the election. Do you think she would take it badly if I lost, had to give up?'

'Probably. She lives through you, you must know that. She desperately wants you to succeed all the time. So do I of course.'

The expression in her eyes was challenging, ironical as well. Pressed to define it, he would have said it consisted of barbed affection. She was absolutely back on his side now, he knew. That would remain true as long as he fulfilled the role to which their compact had committed them both long ago, and never stopped fighting to win. To want more from a political marriage, even one that had begun with love, was perhaps being greedy.

At the door he turned back, deciding to speak to Welcroft straight away. When his voice came on the line he said, 'Patrick, I promised to call you . . .'

Even now he paused, still wanting to temporise. '. . . about your media chum.'

Welcroft laughed shortly. 'Piranha fish I exclude from chummery, David.' He had his pride, he didn't want to be thought a crony of Bedford's. But he belonged to the same species all the same.

'Have you decided?' Welcroft asked.

'Yes,' he said. 'Brief him.'

· Seventeen ·

Reinholdt eased his bulk into the driving seat of the Volkswagen and looked again at the letter which had been pushed under the door of his apartment. The meeting place it specified was a square unknown to him but whoever had typed the note – Sweetwater or perhaps one of his subordinates – had obligingly drawn a route map for him on the reverse. He spread it on the seat beside him and swung out into the early morning traffic.

Smog was once more forming over Mexico City. Soon it would mask most of the mountains and cast a pall that would last all day. That a place so far south and which he had never imagined as much industrialised could be afflicted like this, had surprised him. When, without telling anyone of his decision, he had sold the apartment that had been provided for him in Merida, the town he had first thought he would settle in – for no better reason than an old interest in Mayan civilisation – the capital was the only alternative that had attracted him. He had come prepared for a spell of altitude breathlessness but supposing there would always be a sharp light and an honest sun. Now he was already plagued with respiratory troubles and the beggars gave him almost equal irritation.

But he still felt no real regret that he had chosen for his resettlement this country so far away from Austria, so unlike in every way the Europe he had once supposed would always be his home. His memories of Vienna were all bitter. It had imprisoned him and treated him as a pariah. Yet none of his accusers could deny the conscientiousness with which he had cared for the children, could claim in their own lives to have created opportunities of at least a tolerable adulthood for so many others.

Most of the route took him along wide avenues but he now entered a series of narrow streets frequently choked with cars and trucks. A black saloon that had appeared ahead of him for a while halted abruptly; for once there seemed to be no obstruction ahead. There was a long pause and he sounded his horn. A boy of about twelve, dark-skinned and smiling, appeared beside him. Expecting the usual appeal for money he shook his head, but instead the boy was handing him a note.

He read, with the horns of other vehicles behind him now clamouring for movement, the handwritten words. *Alois, small change of plan – the square doesn't strike me as satisfactory after all. Follow the car immediately in front of you, it will lead to a safer place where we can talk and I can hand over the money London have sent for you. Brad.*

Looking up, he saw the saloon begin to move, and followed. At the end of the street, it turned left into an avenue with apartment blocks screened by gardens. Towards the end of the avenue, taking a driveway running at the side of one of the blocks, it swung into an underground parking area, and finally stopped at the far wall of the bays. Someone he didn't recognise as having appeared with Sweetwater during the expedition to New Mexico got out and waved to him to do likewise.

There were two figures to the side of him, standing in the shadow of a concrete pillar, and he guessed the taller must be Sweetwater. The other was already advancing, one hand outstretched – a man swarthy enough to be a local. The man said, 'Buenos Dias,' in a friendly voice. In almost the same moment came the noise of the shutter being dropped at the entrance to the parking area.

Reinholdt sensed then that he was in great danger. He had time to wonder briefly if there might be anyone in the other bays who would respond to a cry for help. But it was too late for that. The driver of the saloon had moved behind him and was twisting his wrists upwards against his spine, while the swarthy man produced a cord which he slipped about

Reinholdt's neck. He was conscious the cord was being adjusted with care, something like delicacy. When it was tightened, pain exploded through mouth, nose, ears and eye sockets. But as he felt consciousness slipping away, the cord was eased again.

When he could focus his vision again, he saw that the taller figure had moved in front of him. But this wasn't Sweetwater, it was someone much more familiar, although last seen nearly ten years back, an American in a pale grey suit, with hair that grew very thick above his ears. The man said, 'Alois, they tell me you've been very naughty! That you've been talking about our business together, which you promised you'd never do. Fouling things up in a big, big way. Do you remember what I said would happen if you ever did that?'

· Eighteen ·

Afterwards, looking back, Blackmer thought of the flawless dawn in which they returned as having been the nearest thing to glad, confident morning.

The trip had gone better than anyone had foreseen. Even without Cusack, left behind in London at the last moment, nursing a tooth abcess, the media coverage had been exceptional. Two trade agreements for brandishing in the Commons were in the bag, a third was in reach, provided Pagett, delaying for another day in Kuala Lumpur, ironed out a last-minute snag. His interview on Chinese television had gone out in prime time. During the walkabout in Canberra, nobody had called him a Pommy bastard once, at least on camera.

Gazing through her window as they taxied in, Diana said, 'Did you *order* half the Cabinet to come and touch forelocks?'

A quick count among the figures struggling across the tarmac against the breeze showed it wasn't too much of an exaggeration. 'Charles called me yesterday to say that he thought it worth putting on a show.'

She raised her eyebrows. 'He must be improving on top since they shrank his prostate.'

'He's always been sharper than you've allowed. Never underestimate people who operate largely by instinct. Give me the Rainsboroughs of the Party every time over the lot with their hair jobs and personal license plates.'

He hadn't intended a barb; but somewhere at the back of the carriage house of Welcroft's Northumbrian pile must be the Rolls that bore his initials. Discretion had obliged him to abandon it when he entered the Cabinet. That must have been quite a blow.

Diana said, 'Since Charles has arranged a show, I'm going to do something about *my* hair.' She slid past him to the aisle.

Standing up to stretch, he looked round for the Foreign Secretary. Lang was seated two rows behind, once more at work on the Foreign Service cost controls review, to which he had reverted throughout the trip when other diversions palled.

None had absorbed more enthusiastically the great nostrums of the Eighties. Lang had built a career out of denying that any economy in public expenditure had reached a logical end; only when function faltered did he feel he'd reached the real canker. The Foreign Office had failed to sap his zeal. At Party Conferences, the faithful knew that Ambassadors' wives in golden beds or bathing in asses' milk could no longer feel safe. Roger would have them out.

Blackmer leaned over. 'Since we're back in good time, I'll be taking my Questions in the House after all. That means leaving the airport press conference pretty soon. Perhaps you'll hang on for as long as Cusack thinks it's worthwhile. He's coming aboard in a minute or two.'

He looked through Lang's porthole. 'I hope the colleagues aren't too mutinous at being paraded. Can you see the Home Secretary out there?'

'He may not be down from Northumberland yet. Last night would have been his daughter's twenty-first birthday party.'

Of course. He recalled now Diana declining the invitation because it clashed with the trip; not that he would have gone anyway. He heard a voice say, 'I hope the gondolas arrived in time.' Judith Lang had appeared beside him. Presumably she had been in one of the toilets, reapplying the disastrous jampuff hat, worn for take-off nine days ago but fortunately not revealed to the lesser breeds.

'Gondolas?'

She nodded. 'They were being flown in from Italy. The party was to have a Venetian theme, making use of the river in the grounds. According to Lorna, there was going to be a Rialto Bridge, complete with musicians in medieval costume.'

'Rock around the clock with Vivaldi,' he said.

She laughed excessively. 'Patrick and Lorna adore a good party. I hope there were no disasters.'

She was hoping for a little malice from him, but he wasn't to be caught. 'I'm sorry Diana and I missed it.'

'I expect it was quite a thrash. I wonder if Patrick arranged for the local constabulary to keep their breathalysers locked up for the night.' She laughed again, full of spleen.

He knew exactly what her thoughts were, that she was aching to say: Prime Minister, you know Patrick's a frightful *arriviste*, far too much new money for his own good. What he fails to understand is that the Party will never want to rally round anyone who likes to flaunt the stuff, however busy and smooth-faced he makes himself. Roger would never do that sort of thing, I wouldn't let him anyway. Nor would he be so tactless as to sleep with your wife, however available she might make herself. All things considered, wouldn't it be best to let it be known that after Kenneth Cridland bows out, you'd rather Roger were your successor?

He tossed her a crumb while waiting for Diana to return. 'I wonder if he kept the press away. Conspicuous consumption is not what we want talked about in the run-up to the election.'

'No indeed.'

'Are you and Roger getting in a holiday beforehand?'

'We hope to.'

'Where?'

She was more than ready for that. 'Wales. We still have our ugly old house on the sea near Fishguard. Roger wants to be accessible for the Office. And of course the grandchildren adore it. Shall you go to Switzerland again?'

'Probably.'

He realised relations with Diana had until recently been so remote, they had failed to discuss the subject. All he had done himself was agree with Cridland he could take the first half of August.

She had put her hand on his arm. 'You must get a good break, David, you're looking tired.' She was pushing hard now; he wondered if Lang realised what a liability she was turning into.

Cusack had appeared on board in the company of a gaggle of airport greeters. They talked for a few moments about the arrangements for the press conference, while Judith brushed dandruff from Lang's collar. At the end, Cusack fished a note from his document case and handed it over. 'I thought you'd like to glance at the Gallup poll results due out this afternoon. As you'll see, there's a significant improvement, three percentage points better than last time. And on the personal vote, you're now level pegging with the Leader of the Opposition.'

Diana reappeared, as immaculate and clear-eyed as though the past days on the move, the interminable glad-handing in searing heat, had never happened. She wore no ridiculous hat to hide the hair, silky black as the midnights he had known it against his cheek. When Cusack repeated the poll details for her, she allowed him his first smile for months.

Cusack said, 'One other thing: the *Independent* are carrying a shortened version of the Choltitz profile of you, Prime Minister. It reads very well indeed.'

'What did you *do* to that woman to make her so friendly?' Diana asked.

'I wore my smoking jacket. She said it was very chic.'

One of her eyebrows lifted. She knew something had happened, might even have guessed what; but if so, she would rate the political dividend as fair return.

Cusack said, 'If you could pause about ten seconds for the cameras at the top of the steps . . . I promised them they'd get that.'

'Right.' His adrenalin was answering the call, a lava flowing into every part of him. He took Diana's hand. ' 'Ere we go, 'ere we go,' and she was still laughing as they stepped forward into England's milder sun and those waiting lenses, so merciless, yet so indispensable.

The early part of the afternoon went even better. He had never been more effective at Question Time. From the moment he entered the Chamber to an approving growl from his backbenchers – that same inconstant infantry which had sulked on the edge of mutiny barely a month back – the House had sensed he felt invincible. They were there to be ravished and he had obliged, shown them he was the master of everything put to him, even the latest City Scandal, of which the DTI had, of course, supplied not a whisper before he left on the tour. He had also managed to slip a knife between Druitt's ribs, through an arranged question on defence. Afterwards he had watched him flushed and angry, listening to the discord on his benches, the shouts of a rabble he must have supposed he had tamed for good.

When he left the Chamber again, he was sure the barren times were over and he was back on top. For moments like this, he had sweated through his Commons' apprenticeship, the dreary mornings in Committee rooms, the chores of a junior spokesman fielding the dull stuff while the stars proposed and disposed and grabbed the headlines. In the tea room, the sketch writers brooding on their pieces would sigh and acknowledge that no more could they make him their target for tonight.

Back in his room, still trying to catch up with the day, he glanced at the diary. A marathon session with the Chancellor and the Governor of the Bank on the City scare had meant a briefing over hurried sandwiches for his Questions; he had still had no time to look at business that had awaited his return.

Welcroft was due in a moment or two, presumably to elaborate on the cryptic message passed through the Ambassador in Seoul that there was good news from the piranha fish. He had had to spend irritable minutes searching his mind before he remembered their telephone conversation about Bedford on the eve of his trip. Afterwards he must make a routine call on the Monarch, pencilled in weeks ago when he had expected to be back a day earlier. From the Palace he would need to return to the House for a couple of hours. Last of all, at nine o'clock, the name of the head of the CIA station, Tom Busch, appeared with an apologetic note from Grice, alongside, saying he apparently had an urgent personal message from his Director to deliver.

Welcroft looked a little hollow-eyed but as pleased with himself as ever. 'Party go well?' Blackmer asked.

'The young seemed to think so. They were still at it at seven-thirty this morning.'

'No Bacchanalian scenes likely to feature in the tabloids, I trust.'

'No press got in. I had security guards round the perimeter as well. How was your trip?'

'Useful, if a little depressing at times. After two days in Korea, I decided the message to the nation probably ought to be: I've Seen the Future and it Works – Too Hard for Your Comfort. However that might not be the ideal quote to be read by the electorate on the beaches.' He lit a cigar. 'So what was behind the message delivered rather archly by the Ambassador in Seoul?'

'Bedford has made progress. Or rather his people have.'

'Which paper is he using?'

'The *Clarion*.'

He sighed. 'Ms Fitton. Is it true she breast-feeds during her morning news conferences?'

'I hadn't heard that.'

'Cusack claims it's happened. What has she produced?'

'They've apparently found a witness in Vienna. Fitton's had several reporters working there, as well as some digging into Druitt's back history in this country. There's also her Paris correspondent, who's in contact with Massenet's heirs in the hope he left something useful in his papers. The home team are after a girl Druitt was engaged to for a few months after coming down from university. The reason for the break-up has never been explained in anything published about Druitt.' Welcroft was looking down at notes scribbled on the back of an envelope. 'However the real break came in Vienna. A hairdresser there who was in the orphanage at the right time remembers one of the other boys describing how he'd earned handsome pocket money when he was taken by Reinholdt to a hotel one night to be buggered by an English politician.'

'Does he name the boy?'

'Apparently he can't remember that or what happened to him afterwards.'

'How did Fitton's reporters come across this hairdresser?'

'They put out enquiries in the local homosexual community.'

'I see.' Blackmer sighed. 'And ten years later it all comes conveniently back to him! Well, well! Anything else?'

Welcroft took a photograph from the envelope. 'Only this. Fitton's thought is to publish it as an ordinary news photograph and without comment a day or two before they break the main story.'

It showed Druitt emerging from what might have been a council building or village hall. Alongside him, gazing boldly into the camera as though it was there for him as well as Druitt, was a youth, handsome in a certain way. Blackmer raised his eyebrows. 'Is this genuine?'

'I fancy the boy may not have actually been with him.'

'He'd been manoeuvred there?'

'I didn't feel inclined to ask Bedford that.'

He tossed the photograph back over the desk. 'Ms Fitton's appetite for Green Bag seems well up to her paper's past standards.'

Welcroft frowned. 'I'm sorry . . . Green Bag?'

'Yes. Haven't you ever heard of that, Patrick? You should read more history, it's instructive. When George the Fourth wanted to get rid of Queen Caroline, he sent a team to Italy to collect evidence that she'd been acting scandalously there. It brought back depositions by Italians who were willing to swear to various things they'd witnessed. Unfortunately for the King, when the evidence was presented, the public decided it was all a put-up job. The bag in which the depositions went to the House of Lords from the King's lawyers was green, so Green Bag became the general term for tainted evidence.'

'We don't *know* the hairdresser has fabricated his story.'

'Given what Fitton's brief to her reporters will have been, it strikes me as the almost certain explanation for this remarkable coup. If the hairdresser had come up with the other boy's name or a line on his whereabouts, I might have been a little less suspicious.'

Welcroft put the photograph away. He had seen the ground was marshy, calling for more cautious movement than he had expected. 'If Bedford and Fitton convince themselves the evidence is sound enough to go ahead on, that will be their problem, not ours.'

'It'll be mine if the public's verdict is that I'm at the back of this, playing George the Fourth to Druitt's Caroline. When are they thinking of breaking the story?'

'Fitton's waiting to see what the enquiries in Paris and here finally come up with.'

The clock showed four-thirty. Blackmer said, 'Anything more to tell me?'

'No, except that during your absence there've been strong rumours floating round the House of there being a scandal in the wind. I understand Druitt has begun to figure as a possible candidate.'

Useless to speculate where the rumours had come from. Enquiries by Fitton's reporters were as likely an explanation as any. Welcroft was pausing at the door, with what was presumably intended to be read as an encouraging smile. 'Incidentally I hope you noticed when you came into the House that the Party is in much better heart. The backbenchers have at last appreciated what they owe to you in turning the situation round. Perhaps I could say how delighted I am, David.'

He was playing his cards more carefully now Diana was no longer an advocate at court. He knew that the appearance of unflagging loyalty from here on was vital if he was to retain his place in the pecking order. Should there be bodies to be buried as a result of the Druitt affair – or any other business for that matter – his would be the strongest arm, the readiest spade; no-one would dig a better pit.

From childhood, when the first of two bad things had happened, he had never been free of superstition. Eating supper with Diana back at No. 10, before going to his study to deal with Busch, he looked up when she spoke of the magpie she had seen in the garden earlier. Knowing him, she had added the mate must have been out of sight in the shrubbery.

The unease had been floating about his mind beforehand, probably a symptom of fatigue after the long flight. But he fastened on the magpie, saw it with his inward eye, and wished it had not seemed alone.

That there were maxims and auguries it was dangerous to ignore, he had discovered when he was eight. Leaning from a bedroom window, he and Esther had watched Patricia practising a dance step alone on the lawn below and had sung a nonsense song to irritate her. Those who sang before breakfast, she had called up, cried before supper. Esther had stopped singing but he had gone on because he was a boy, not to be frightened by an elder sister.

That afternoon Patricia had died, drowned in the lake where she had gone swimming with the children next door. He had realised at once it was because he had disobeyed the rule. He never spoke of his guilt, not even to Esther, hoping that since she was younger she hadn't understood the significance of the happening. But it stayed with him and he awaited punishment.

Not until he was well embarked on adolescence did he finally accept he could not have had any part in Patricia's death. He proved that ladders across his path had no power, while still preferring their absence. But he never sang in his morning shower.

Diana was peeling a peach. 'How was the Monarch?'

'Tiresome. There was a distinct lack of interest in our triumphal progress elsewhere. The visit to the North while we were away seems to have been the trouble. I was asked a number of questions. When was I last there? What were my expectations for the unemployment figures? Why weren't more companies being coaxed to set up in the area? Even, had I happened to be shown the designs of an appalling new Inland Revenue building that's apparently gone up, when they were approved? The message was that we weren't throwing enough money at things, or showing any taste over what we *did* spend. I hope no pubescent Royals likely to report back were at the party Patrick and Lorna gave their daughter last night. Otherwise a further pursing of the lips is likely.'

She placed the peach in his mouth. 'You could suggest a trimming of the Civil List as a contribution to the money problem. Did you part on reasonable terms?'

'I had the impression that if an end-of-term report was being written, "Could Do Better" would feature somewhere.'

'Damned sauce,' she said.

Deciding against coffee, he went down to the study, to tackle some boxes before Busch arrived. But almost at once he was interrupted by a call from Roger Lang. 'You asked me the other day,' Lang said, 'what the Embassy in Washington knew about Lew Rothman. I've just been telegraphed the text of a story in today's *Washington Post* that may interest you.' He read it out. The gist was that Rothman had announced his resignation from the President's staff with immediate effect. He was quoted as telling reporters how grateful he was to the President for freeing him to fight allegations of financial misconduct, which were totally baseless and malicious. The allegations weren't spelled out.

'What have the Embassy to say about it?'

'For a day or two it seems there've been stories going the rounds, that the Justice Department has been supplied with damaging information about his business dealings while working in the White House. The Ambassador's assessment is that the skids are being manoeuvred under him by some powerful forces and nobody in the Administration is going to be sorry it's happened.'

He sat thinking for a while when Lang's call was over. For some reason it had awakened the unease he had felt earlier in the day. Now it was accompanied by a physical discomfort, coldness in his cheeks that almost amounted to a lack of sensation. He swivelled his chair and sat gazing at the Zoffany picture, tensing the muscles in his jaw in an effort to loosen up the cheeks. But the numbness was becoming more pronounced. Agitation took possession of his bowels. He decided to call Reeves.

Reeves answered the phone himself. Now that he had his

on the line, pride made him dissemble for a while. He spoke of the arrangements for the weekend when Reeves was coming to Kilndown to see Esther. 'By the way,' he finally went on, 'a couple of symptoms of my own since we're speaking . . .' He described them, laughed apologetically, waited.

'When are you taking your holiday?' Reeves asked.

At once he felt a fool. 'I hadn't thought about it.'

'I'll look at you when I come down on Saturday. But I doubt if you need worry much. Unless, that is, you don't intend to take a complete break this year. But you do, don't you?'

He grunted.

'I think you should do it soon.'

Already as he replaced the receiver, the cheeks seemed to be becoming more mobile. Not for the first time he felt anger and disgust that he had surrendered to weakness. He should have waited until the weekend. Someone unmanned so easily had no right to be sitting in this chair. He fetched himself a large brandy, then another.

He felt only fatigue by the time Busch was shown in. A tall, good-looking man, he carried himself well despite the handicap of a limp. He had a disarming air of relaxation that Blackmer guessed had been carefully cultivated over the years to mask a mind that was missing nothing of importance in his surroundings. Blackmer sat him down, offered a cigar, enquired after the health of his Director. 'I hope it's good news you're bringing from him.'

But, as he went back to his own chair, something seemed already to be warning that it wasn't good news at all.

· Nineteen ·

From either side of the bridge, two tree-lined roads stretched beside the margins of a canal, their sidewalks flanked by handsome houses. Through the branches of the trees, the stuccoed facades of the houses glimmered enticingly. Most had front gardens, softly shadowed except where the afternoon sun still reached in to make the flower beds glow. The contrast with the hustle and petrol fug in the street behind struck Louise as remarkable; it was as though the canal's stillness had seeped beyond its banks, imposing an aura on the whole neighbourhood.

'I thought we might walk a little down here,' Tom said.

She looked at him in surprise. It had seemed he had drawn her on to the bridge, after leaving the restaurant, simply to pause and gaze at the scene. His car was parked on the other side of the Edgware Road, away from the canal.

He pointed. 'Beyond the next bridge, the canal widens and there's an island. They call the area Little Venice. That's pushing it. But it has charm.'

She remained puzzled. Walking had never been one of his voluntary recreations. Throughout their marriage, apart from sessions of violent exercise curtailed abruptly by the leg injury in Vietnam, he had jibbed at even the shortest of strolls that held no special purpose. She had learned that anything of the kind was likely to be keyed to professional interest, a reconnaisance or the clearing of a drop. She hoped business could be ruled out on this occasion. But there was more to the suggestion than inspecting an urban pond with fanciful pretensions.

Her shoes were beginning to pinch from walking about Mayfair streets in the morning. Also it was warmer than she had expected when she dressed for breakfast. But to appear unwilling and perhaps disturb the harmony that had taken over their relations in place of the prickliness of the previous two days would be silly. 'Right,' she said.

The earlier debacle had been of Tom's making, the result of gambling with uncharacteristic rashness on the weather. Within minutes of her flight landing at Heathrow, he had announced they were off to the Cotswolds for a couple of days. The Embassy had been told he would not be available for anything short of a nuclear alert. While away, they were not going to talk about Sweetwater or Rothman or any of that stuff. Quite soon, perhaps on their way back to London, there would be a happening which would leave him free to explain everything that had been going on in that area. Meanwhile they would have Time Out.

He had reserved rooms in an inn he had liked the look of on a previous trip. The inn was in a village still miraculously overlooked by tourists; it had a garden of old roses. There was also a Norman church he wanted her to see.

From the moment of crossing into Gloucestershire, it had rained. At first, peering optimistically through the screen wipers, he had laughed it off, remarking on the encouraging rapidity of cloud movement. She nodded hopefully, but the sodden sheep, huddled together on windswept pasture beyond the stone walls of the lanes, looked less sanguine. The stone, he told her, is greyer in the northern part of the wolds, compared with the south. Her response had lacked enthusiasm, had perhaps been a little sour. The rot had set in there.

More coolly, he had recalled that his proposal had been for her to come for Wimbledon, when there had been unbroken skies throughout. This was July and the British never trusted July. Morosely she had settled back in her seat, trying to take comfort from his recollection of the log fire in the lounge of the inn which, he was certain, would now be roasting the chintz fronts of gigantic armchairs.

The logs in the lounge fireplace were unlit and even dusty. It turned out that the chimney was under reconstruction. There was also evident trouble with the central heating, as the girl in the large cardigan behind the reception counter acknowledged with a tightly rationed smile. Lying in a narrow English bed that night, rubbing feet together against the chill, she almost blamed Tom for, as well as everything else, inconsiderateness in reserving separate rooms; at least she would have had the chance of warming her feet on his back.

The following day had proved no better. Through curtains of rain billowing across their path, they had gone to the local market town, in search of a remedy for her reawakened sinusitis, calling later for lunch at a pub where the loudest voices in the bar had been American, those of airmen from some nearby base discussing their unit's imminent departure home. In the afternoon, by now as edgy as she was herself, he had stubbornly walked her to the Norman church, enduring at the heart of muddy meadows. When she had asked him to explain its existence so far from the village, he had provided a grim, astonishingly knowledgeable account of the consequences of the Black Death for rural communities. So he'd turned into an *intellectual* Head of Station, she thought bitterly.

There was something about the church, however. She knew at once what had spoken to him and realised her own response belonged to feelings shared before their parting and now extinguished by it. Standing in the centre of the nave, she was aware, as she stroked the roughness of a pillar of something to which she felt *connected*, something that was both human and inanimate. Then the faint exaltation of the moment passed she was once more conscious of moisture seeping through the soles of her shoes and of the likelihood that back at the inn it would not seem appreciably warmer than here.

By evening, Tom had recognised defeat. Bringing drinks from the bar to where she sat, doggedly turning the pages of *Horse and Hound*, he had put them down abruptly and canvassed immediate return to Berkeley Square. Driving back at midnight, they had laughed for the first time and agreed it had been as bad as the honeymoon in Massachusetts.

The change of plan worked. Next morning in London the weather showed it was not implacable; before she had finished dressing, the sky was rinsed, a lemon sun was drying the raindrops on her bedroom window. They had breakfasted late then drifted lazily through shops and galleries. In the Burlington Arcade Tom had bought her two cardigans and a tie for himself. When he had proposed lunch at the restaurant on the Edgware Road, she had thought it was a spur-of-the-moment decision. But there had been a hidden purpose, she now decided, connected to their walking down this quiet road.

Against the far bank of the canal were moored barges with curtained windows and brightly decorated sides. A few had gardens along their strips of tow-path. A man was manoeuvring a cooking stove aboard one of the barges. There seemed to be a settled, urban community in them.

She handed Tom a chocolate scooped up from the plate that had been brought with their coffee. 'Do you know anybody who lives round here?'

'A couple in the Embassy have an apartment nearby, although it doesn't actually look out on the canal. And there's a woman I mentioned to you once.'

'Ah,' she said. 'Would that be Antonia Strachan, pronounced Strawn?'

'Yes.'

'So it's hallowed ground.'

He looked ahead in a weary way.

'Tell me about her.'

'She works for the Government here.'

'What else?'

'Her husband was a test pilot who died years ago in a crash.'

'Go on.'

'She's in her thirties, plays a good game of tennis, is taking lessons in bookbinding. Is that enough?'

'A bookbinder!' she said. 'That's sexy! And you've slept with her of course . . .'

'No.' With the excessive tidiness she always found infuriating, he went to drop the silver paper from his chocolate into a trash basket. When he came back he said, 'It didn't get to that stage.' He was embarrassed, she noticed.

They were approaching the other bridge to which he had earlier pointed. He led her to look over the other side. The scene was pleasant but hardly sensational, a triangular piece of murky water where it seemed that two canals had been arranged to meet. There were more barges, one of which had been converted into a cafe; in the middle of the triangle, patrolled by a flotilla of ducks, was a willow-hung island.

'Very pretty,' she said. 'On the telephone you mentioned that she didn't like what you did. Was *that* why she wouldn't sleep with you?'

He looked irritated. 'It was much more complicated than that. But it's true she has a hang-up about the Agency.' He was silent for a while, watching the ducks. Eventually he went on, 'I found she'd bought the liberal view of what we are, and I couldn't really shake her on that. You and I know there's another side to the story but nobody wants to hear that side now. The Agency *has* to go down in the history books as having been an Invisible Government. There *had* to have been people on white chargers riding in to expose it all. Fashion and expediency wrote the script. What sells newspapers and books and helps politicians to make their reputations will always have the edge on truth, the whole truth. The truth of what Presidents said they needed, had to have – the truth of what the American people in their hearts wanted – that had to be buried.'

She said, 'I remember when you and everybody else thought being the President's Men was just fine and to hell with everything else. You should have known it would all end in tears. You and the history books will just have to accept the downside now.'

She could have added that Ramon Eckersley Brooks' ideas from time to time of what Presidents wanted – or ought to want – had been pretty unwholesome. But to have said so would have been to give the liberals, and Antonia Strachan along with them, more than they deserved. She let her own scrap of silver paper drop into the water. 'To hell with history anyway. My father thought Henry Ford got that about right.'

He grunted, consulted his watch and straightened. 'We ought to go back to the car. There's a radio transmission we need to catch.'

'We?'

'You'll be interested.'

In the car he tuned to what seemed to be a transmission from Parliament. She stared at him in disbelief. 'Is this the happening?'

He grinned. 'I hope so.'

When Blackmer rose, the House became still at once. 'With permission, Mr Speaker, I shall make a statement.'

He lifted his head a fraction. He had pocketed the hated spectacles so that the moon-faced look they produced under the Chamber's television lights would be dispelled. 'Many members, perhaps all, will be aware of a tide of rumour and allegation that has regrettably entered this House in recent weeks. While there has been some variation in the substance of the stories, the target has become identical in all instances. It is the reputation of my Right Honourable friend, the Leader of the Opposition.

'We are of course no strangers to rumour, nor do we take it too sensitively, I hope. None of us, on entering politics, expects, or would ask, to be spared a ruthless scrutiny of our fitness to be Members of this House. The public has a right to know what manner of men and women we are and whether it can safely entrust the country's affairs to our hands. We accept we shall not be afforded the degree of privacy the ordinary citizen claims for himself, that our deeds must always be subject to probing and question. We have to learn to live with robust criticism, even malicious misinterpretation of our actions – the cynical innuendoes that, in Swift's words, can be used to "wink a reputation down". But when false or distorted facts are used to impute wrong-doing of the most serious kind in one carrying the responsibilities of my Right Honourable friend, I judge it incumbent on the holder of my present office to speak out.'

He glanced down at Druitt. He sat with legs stretched out, head a little cocked, as though he was inspecting the shine on his toecaps. There was a wisp of a smile on his lips.

'I shall not oblige the sensation-hunters or the determinedly malevolent by giving further publicity to what is alleged to have forfeited my Right Honourable friend's right to hold a position of trust. I have of course looked into it. I first became aware of the matter through a former official who decided he must pass on to me what seemed to him, in possession as he was of what proved to be incomplete information, a very grave allegation. I decided that only a careful enquiry could clear the matter up. It was a painful duty for me but I am glad to say that my Right Honourable friend, with whom I naturally discussed it, fully accepted it as such.

'My enquiry established what I had never had cause to doubt, that there was nothing in the events to which the allegation related – they took place several years ago – reflecting any discredit on my Right Honourable friend.

'Regrettably, the circulation of rumours which began during the enquiry has if anything increased since it was satisfactorily completed. There has been press interest – which of course has been entirely legitimate, in view of the seriousness of some of the wilder allegations – and this has opened up the possibility of wider publicity, all based on false assumptions. I have concluded that the air can only be cleared by my testifying to my complete confidence in the Leader of the Opposition in relation to the matters in question.'

On the benches opposite, he could see a variety of expressions. Some showed relief, others were giving open approval to his words. But most were more ambiguous, suggesting a mixture of thoughts. No less swiftly than those on his own side, the listeners were moving on, before his statement had even ended, calculating its effect on the audience outside the Chamber, drawing up the new balance sheet for the autumn.

He turned a little towards the camera that would frame him best. 'I now invite Members on all sides to join me in treating further attempts to pursue this issue with the contempt they deserve. There may be a few who still think to make

ishonourable profit by circulating a patchwork of fact and
ction, accompanied by pious words as to the purity of their
motives. Should they do so, let us make plain our total
condemnation.'

He waited for a few growls of assent before his wind-up.
The honour of the whole House called for this statement. I
need hardly add that it will in no way deflect those on this side
of the Chamber from the task of ensuring the nation is aware
of the folly that would be attendant on placing confidence in
the Party opposite. But in doing that, my friends and I will
never seek advantage from squalid slanders that are an affront
to each and everyone of us in this place.'

He sat down and listened to the growls steadily building to
an approving chorus on the benches behind. When Druitt rose
for his acknowledgement, his tone was muted. He could draw
sympathy from the occasion, but little more. No grand
gestures were open to him: generosity had been bespoken.

He let his eyes roam along his own Front Bench. For the
most part, the faces had chosen solemnity as the safest bet. The
cameras would be on the hunt for signs of relish; the scene had
to be played as an occasion of The House At Its Best. The
Chancellor and Lang were keeping their eyes fixed on Druitt as
he spoke. Beyond them, Whitingstall, puce from another
liquid lunch, was whispering to Welcroft, no doubt trying
vainly to catch up with the story. Rainsborough sat with arms
folded, gazing into a corner of the Chamber beyond the
television lamps. His face, in profile and upturned, had a
classical quality. He might be having noble thoughts; but more
likely he was imagining pheasants in those shadows, waiting
plumply for The Day.

He looked back at Welcroft. He had begun to tap a finger
against his cheek, paying little attention to Whitingstall's
whispers. At a guess, he was raging inside. When Druitt sat
down, Welcroft rose at once and left the Chamber.

Later, crossing the Lobby to go to his room, he saw Druitt
chatting to a few of his backbenchers. He waited for the
conversation to finish, then drew him aside. 'I hope that'll be
the end of it.'

'I wish I could share your optimism. I understand th
Clarion are still planning to run some sort of story.'

'Then you'll have your writ ready.'

'Of course.'

'The Clarion may have second thoughts,' Blackmer said.
'Your damages would be enormous.'

Druitt wasn't listening. 'What would you have replied had
told you at our meeting this morning that I preferred n
statement?'

'None at all?'

'Yes.'

'Did you contemplate saying that?'

'It was in my mind when you showed me your draft tex
Then after we'd gone through the rumours, I dismissed i
Perhaps unwisely.'

'The atmosphere was getting poisonous. Since I knew wha
the true facts were, surely it was right to clear the air?'

Druitt produced a wry smile. 'You still won't tell me wher
you got your independent information?'

'I'm afraid I can't.'

Druitt seemed on the point of continuing; but he decide
against it. As he turned away, he said, 'I fancy congratulation
are probably appropriate.' He already suspected the balanc
sheet would not turn out in his favour.

At No. 10, when he returned later for his dinner, Diana wa
in the hall, talking with Cusack. She took his arm as they wen
upstairs. 'I never thought of you as a gambler until today.'

'You felt it was a gamble?'

'Yes.'

'Some would say I hadn't any choice in view of what
knew.'

'Cusack has been checking media reaction. The coverage i
going to be very, very favourable.'

'I think we have to wait and see how the other side play it
Druitt could still be cast as a hero the Right Wing press hav
been trying to destroy.' When she shook her head, he said
'Anyway, in three months time it'll all be forgotten.'

'You're wrong. People will remember you did somethin;

they thought decent, that seemed moral. They may not remember exactly what it was. But that won't matter. There'll be an image, a confidence in you that'll remain in their minds.'

In the study after they'd eaten, he took a call from Esther. She talked about Reeves' arrival on Saturday; she was still worried that, while he might agree working with Jane Croom would be a good idea, he'd insist on Croom being told the facts of her condition.

Afterwards she said, 'We watched your speech to the House on the box. It was marvellous. I was proud of you.'

Her admiration pricked. She sometimes disconcerted him with her pleasure in his successes; it was another aspect of guilt, he supposed. Her accolades only sharpened the sense of his advantage over her. 'It was politics,' he said. 'Mostly politics anyway.'

'Don't pretend you were being a hypocrite when you aren't. You were being honourable. I wish father and mother could have heard you. Mother most of all.'

He reflected on how seldom they spoke of mother nowadays, despite her shadow on their lives. Over the years, his need to conceal the truth about her death in public had left its mark on their private exchanges in a way he had not foreseen. At the beginning, when their father, returning hollow-eyed and drained from three days at the hospital in Dublin, had told them she was gone, they had supposed that the pain of losing her was the single consequence they faced. Both were still at school then. They had been aware of something a little mysterious about the death but had settled for believing their father's vague reference to a nervous illness held no deeper meaning for them. 'One day,' he said, 'we'll talk about it more. What I know she'd want me to say now is – promise always to stay close to each other, for her memory and also for the comfort you'll find it brings. Promise you'll never forget that.' Not until a week after Esther's seventeenth birthday had he told them everything.

Afterwards, they had held the truth away from the world, as their terrible secret. He had recognised the importance of keeping it tight most clearly at the time he had embarked on a political career. There had to be no whisper of the curse he'd inherited if ambition was not be hobbled; otherwise he would be seen by the Party managers – shaking their heads in compassionate but unyielding regret – as not worth the trouble of bringing on, useful as Lobby fodder for as long as he lasted, but in other respects an unsound bet.

A manager now himself, however the leader of them all, he could face the thought of disclosure more robustly. A bald revelation of what was in his genes, the fifty-fifty chance of the trick fate could play on him at any time, would still hardly be welcome but could nevertheless be handled. Public sympathy might even add to his support in the country. The fact that he was still in full possession of his powers, able to dominate House and Cabinet alike, would be demonstrable. The uneasy might have to be reassured by references to check-ups by Reeves and a statement that he would of course tender his resignation if advised to do so by doctors. But nothing else would be needed. No-one could argue his health, actual or prospective, was an unacceptable risk.

'So I *know* you'll be the winner in the autumn now,' Esther said. 'They won't let you go. They *can't*.'

He laughed, but felt warmed all the same. Watching a TV repeat of his performance later, listening to the verdict of commentators on his performance, he told himself that he deserved one cheer anyway; possibly even two.

That night he slept with Diana. They had not shared a bed for fourteen months. At first it was she who made love to him, in the old, absorbed way. When he finally took her, he was momentarily distracted by a thought, an image of himself that amused. He smiled against her hair. This was a Return, a coming again, the leader back from the wilderness, to enter his kingdom

Tom switched off the radio and swung the car out into Edgware Road. 'So you knew all that was coming?' Louise said.

'I hadn't too much idea of the line he would take. I just knew he had no choice than to make a statement favourable to Druitt.'

'How did you know?'

'A few days ago I had a message from Langley – from the Director, actually – telling me to ask for an urgent personal interview with Blackmer to hand over some information. In essence I was to tell him we'd heard there was a story going round of Druitt engaging in sexual abuse with a child ten years ago and that we wished him to know we had conclusive evidence it never happened.'

'Conclusive evidence?'

'Yes.'

'How could that possibly be?'

'Because the man you wouldn't name when we spoke on the phone, the guy who took the boy to Druitt's room in the hotel, was our agent at that time.'

She stared at him speechless. He went on. 'Before you jump to any wrong conclusions like you did over Massenet's death, I have to say I knew none of this because it was all buried in the records at Langley.'

'So when was it unburied?'

'A week or two back, the Director decided the extent of Lew Rothman's influence over the President and the wild things he was using his White House unit for were becoming too alarming to ignore any longer. One of the things he ordered was round the clock surveillance of your friend Brad Sweetwater. Which resulted in the team behind him following Brad into Mexico where he picked up an unknown fat guy, took him to a motel over the border in New Mexico, collected someone off a plane at Albuquerque to meet the fat guy, whom he then returned to Mexico City.'

'This could have been the meeting he set up for Blackmer's official, Egerton.'

'It was. The team had to establish the identity of the fat guy of course. When they did and his name, Alois Reinholdt, was passed over the records, it produced an interesting result. Alois Reinholdt, when Director of an orphanage in Vienna, had been run by our Station there and had produced valuable, extremely reliable information on the sexual interests of some public figures in Austria and elsewhere.'

'Including Druitt . . .'

'Yes. Langley looked back through the file, and sure enough, Reinholdt had reported contact with Druitt. He'd described taking a boy to Druitt's room in a hotel because there had seemed to be a chance Druitt could discover whether as the boy thought he had some English relatives. Reinholdt was an odd mixture apparently, and took some of his responsibilities in the orphanage in a very conscientious way. Anyway, that was the reason the boy was taken to Druitt, and Reinholdt had told his handler afterwards he was sure Druitt had no sexual interest in children and there was no point in targeting him.'

Louise felt that her brain was beginning to stall. 'But if that's what he reported at the time, why should he have produced a different version of what took place for Sweetwater and Egerton?'

'You don't really have to ask that, do you?'

'Sweetwater paid him to produce the new version?'

'Of course. That's what Lew Rothman wanted Egerton to be told.'

Tom was slowing the car. She looked ahead and saw a girl with red hair poised on the edge of the sidewalk. Beside her, unleashed, was a Weimaraner; the dog wore a handsome blue collar that gleamed with metal studs. Tom waved them across the street and sat watching the red-head's undulations appreciatively. She could remember a time when he'd told her he couldn't stand redheads. He said without looking back to her, but perhaps a shade anxiously, 'You do understand, don't you, that I couldn't tell you any of this before because I just didn't know?'

She ignored that and said instead, 'How can you and Langley be sure that what you've told Blackmer is the real truth? Reinholdt sounds totally unreliable to me.'

'There's a bit more to the story. After Reinholdt had served a prison sentence in Austria, it was decided that although he'd be no further use as an agent, he ought to be resettled and given a suitable pay-off. He chose to go to a town called Merida in Mexico, where we bought him an apartment. He got bored with Merida and without telling any of our people sold the apartment and disappeared. Discovering him again under Sweetwater's wing made it important to find out what he'd been up to and in particular what he might have revealed to Sweetwater about past operations. So his original handler in Vienna was sent down to Mexico City and a confrontation set up. After a little persuasion he talked. We reckon we know everything he ever let slip to Sweetwater. Incidentally, he was paid 1000 dollars for telling Egerton the phoney story about Druitt.'

Louise sighed. 'Has it been money that's been behind everything Rothman was doing as well?'

'Not entirely. It's true he was taking pay-offs from defense contractors in return for influence in favour of the retention of some weapons programmes. And the documents Justice have also show he was on the take from German provisioning corporations, which supply American forces in Europe and stand to lose heavily if the force reduction programme as originally scheduled goes ahead unmodified. But he's a genuine hawk about keeping large forces in Europe – his Pax Americana idea. He just took the view it would be wasteful not to cream off a little personal profit from the policies he's been persuading the President should be adopted.'

The car had turned into Berkeley Square and Tom stopped outside his house. She said, 'I imagine I don't need to ask who arranged for Justice to get its information.'

He leaned across her and opened her door as though he hadn't heard. 'Maria will let you in. I'll be back when I've parked the car.'

She was drinking tea and trying to ignore the plate of cakes the maid had brought in when he reappeared. 'How much of all that can I tell Hal?' she asked.

'None. It's for your ears alone. But bearing in mind your position in all this, I got Langley to agree to warn him informally last night that we'd heard he was thinking of buying a book about a British politician and he might like to hold back because the Prime Minister here was probably going to make a statement that would completely undermine it. He'll be flattered to have had the tip-off. See how I think of you?'

She decided he was looking too pleased with himself. 'Langley may hope it's fixed Rothman with the stuff it's passed to Justice. But it doesn't follow. The President could still go on buying his ideas on foreign policy and the rest.'

He looked grim. 'It would be madness, but it could happen. *Anything* can happen in a place like Washington. It's a wonder we ever get sensible decisions with a constitution like the one we're saddled with.'

He was mounting the hobby horse he'd trotted out before. To get him off it, she said, 'Now tell me why we walked along that canal today.'

He picked up a cake, then put it back on the plate. 'I wanted your reaction. Assuming I finish at Langley at the end of this posting, I'd thought I might take an apartment along one of those roads. What do you think?'

'You could do worse I suppose. *If* you're still thinking of settling here.'

'I'm not. I've realised I shall always want a place back in the States. But I'd like to spend time here as well.'

'You could afford that?'

'Just.'

'Lucky you,' she said lightly. 'Maybe I should tell my lawyer you seem to be seriously rich after all.'

'Don't joke about it.'

'Who said I was joking?'

'What I do in the end depends on you. On how you feel. I want this decision to concern us both. You must know that by now.'

She wished she hadn't raised the business of the walk. She had led him towards pressing for a decision she had sensed looming but which she wasn't ready to make. She began, 'I don't think this is the time . . .'

He wasn't to be deflected. 'If you felt we could work something out together, one way would be for you to keep the apartment in New York – or for us to get a bigger one – for as long as you wanted to go on working with Hal. The apartment here we could use for visits to begin with. Or maybe Hal could be talked into your working some of the time in the British company he's bought. Later on we might sell the apartment in New York for something further south, and split the time more equally with London.' He threw a hand over the back of his chair. 'Just ideas.' He was trying unsuccessfully to be casual as well as serious.

'Why do you have to have two places?'

'I find Europe pulls when I'm away from it. There's plenty I don't like about this country. It's damp and it's cramped and I can't stand the way people go on accepting things that make them so unequal. But here I also feel *connected* in a way I never do at home. I see life in more dimensions and I don't want to lose that sense. Do you understand me?'

'I think so.' But whether the same ambiguities of attachment could ever become compelling for her, she doubted. That could work against a new relationship between them.

He went on as though he had sensed her doubts. 'I wouldn't press you into any of it if you thought it would make you unhappy. What's important to me now is that things should work again for us. As they did before.'

'As far as that's concerned,' she said, 'I don't imagine it really matters where, or how much here and how much there. The question is – what do we feel? Do you know what *you* feel – truly?' She had to meet it head on now. 'Do you believe you love me? Or do you reckon we've been through all that?'

'I *know* I love you. I knew it when I saw you again in New York.'

She stared at him for a few seconds then laughed, but not unkindly, only to hide her feelings. She'd expected him to acknowlege what she had already sensed. Yet, when he did, it was somehow more than she had forseen.

'How about you?' he asked.

'I'm not sure. I can't help being fond of you. But that's perhaps because of what we had once. I don't know whether it would amount to love again. I sometimes think I threw that option away for good when we broke up. I find I can be jealous about what you do and who you're with. But that's different. What I *do* know is that I don't want to make a decision now. I've become very allergic to risk and I think that's what we add up to.'

She went to take a bath. When they met again for drinks before dinner, Tom was tense. He was trying not to show he was disappointed. Despite the fact his work could be stretched to last for as long as he wanted, despite a social round to which the same would apply presumably, as long as he stayed at the Embassy, despite diversions like Antonia Strachan, he hadn't learned to master loneliness as well as she had done. He would never be at ease unless he was living with someone who shared his background and at least some of his convictions.

For all the pain she'd blamed him for when they separated, she still admired those convictions, respected him for what he'd aspired to be. He had seen himself, without vanity, as belonging to an elite with a mission. Like his father before him, he had believed his education and background qualified him best to act for what Dick Helms had said long ago was a provincial nation when it came to dealing with others. His kind had done exactly that for nearly fifty years. In the process they had also done the things some preferred not to be aware of or even think about but which were inseparable from the exercise of power confronting other power. There had been plenty of lost battles, and shattered illusions. There had been too many mistakes as well for the confidence with which he had begun to survive intact. But with the learning process he had become a nicer person.

As they were finishing dinner a telephone call summoned him back to the Embassy to deal with fall-out in Washington from Blackmer's speech. When he returned and they were drinking nightcaps, she sensed he was wondering whether to revert to his earlier proposals. To head him off, she said, 'There's something about Blackmer you wouldn't tell me when we talked before – a particular reason aside from ordinary political ones why you thought it would be better if he weren't re-elected Prime Minister. What was it?'

He swirled the drink in his glass for a while. 'Not everybody agrees it matters. For the time being anyway. It's just something about him personally.'

He was reluctant to go on, but under pressure finally began 'About nine months ago, one of the medics at Langley who studies the tapes of TV appearances of politicians for signs of health problems looming, announced there might be worrying developments on the way with Blackmer. I wasn't told then what he had in mind, but I was asked to find out what Blackmer's parents died of and at what age.

'In the case of his father, it was easy to get the answer. He'd been a figure in real estate business in the West Country and died of bowel cancer at the age of seventy-two. Tracing the mother proved much more difficult. The biographical details Blackmer had given to the press in interviews described her as having been a schoolmistress who'd died young of a heart condition. There was no record of her death in this country. As a long shot, because of a hint in an obituary for the father that she had come from Southern Ireland, we looked into the possibility she'd died there. That proved right. She'd gone to Dublin in 1955, entered a mental hospital and died a year later at the age of thirty-eight. The death certificate made no mention of heart disease. But it backed up the medic's suspicions from watching Blackmer in a studio discussion. She died from Huntington's disease, more often referred to as Huntington's chorea. In case you don't know, it's an inherited, relentlessly progressive disease, characterised by the chorea, and leading to dementia. There's no cure for it. In the end it's totally disabling. The children of a parent with Huntington's disease have a fifty per cent chance of developing it. Some aspects, like the chorea, can be controlled for a while with drugs. But from our angle, the crucial thing is the capacity of the disease to affect judgment in a big way, the mental disintegration. That can't be stopped once it starts. In someone with Blackmer's powers and responsibilities, that could be extremely dangerous unless he was being tightly monitored.'

'Are you saying he's already developed the disease?'

'There's still an argument going on about that at Langley. Some of the other medics believe there are alternative explanations for what made the first medic suspicious. It seems to me that's stretching coincidence too far.'

'Has anything been noticed about his judgment?'

'It doesn't seem to be affected yet. But nobody can be sure of that. It seems unlikely that he's warned his Cabinet of what could be happening to him, since he's gone to considerable lengths to lay a false trail to how his mother died. There's also an unresolved mystery about a sister who's never seen in public. It makes me wonder whether she's already developed the disease and is being kept away from people because they'd draw the right conclusions. Although nobody in Langley thinks there's anything that can or should be done yet, my belief is that American interests would be best served if Blackmer didn't get another five years in office. Not while he still has a button to press and other things to loose off.'

She put down her glass and went to look out of the window, trying to imagine herself in Blackmer's place. The window gave on to the terrace at the rear of the house. The light had almost gone but the colour of the geraniums in the stone urns was still detectable. 'You don't really have to worry about the next five years do you? Surely his statement to Parliament today destroys the one weapon with which he could have beaten Druitt in the election?'

She was conscious he was brooding, and turned. He said, 'I thought so to begin with. But I've started to wonder.'

'About what?'

'About which of them will be the real beneficiary of the statement. Blackmer's very shrewd. He will have thought hard beforehand about its likely effects. We shall have to wait and see.'

He didn't as she had expected, go back to their earlier conversation. When she announced she was going to bed, he kissed her on the cheek with a hint of resignation and said he was going too.

In her room she lay staring at the ceiling. She needed to review the day, discover what it had meant to her, but her thoughts would adapt to no ordered pattern. She had been happy, most of the time. That must mean *something*. There had been a moment when, coming out of the Burlington Arcade and briefly dazzled by sunlight caught in the windows of a passing bus, she had seemed weightless, free of all the baggage the years had loaded on her since she had started on a separate existence again. A trick of light and movement of course: not to be trusted. And trying to reach conclusions about how she felt, when under the influence of a new place didn't seem sensible either.

But stretching to switch off the bedside lamp she realised there was, after all, no point in postponing her decision. She might as well jump in the dark. The risk was going to change or look different however long she waited.

Tom was already in bed. He was wearing glasses to read a batch of press cuttings; it was the first time she had known he had any. When she commented on the fact, he whipped them off; it was almost as though he had been discovered in some undesirable activity. She rated his physical vanity as still thriving. But it was not without reason.

Sitting on the bed, she said, 'I came to say I've made a decision.'

He looked tense.

'Perhaps we *could* try again. I'd want to stay working in New York for a while yet. But if you're keen on an apartment by that canal, I wouldn't mind your planning on it. Maybe Hal could be persuaded to give me a spell in London later.'

He nodded silently.

'The only thing is – I can't make any promises. Will you settle for not knowing what I really feel about you? Because I don't know myself. Only that I'm fond. God knows why, but I am. And you may find things duller than you expected. I hope you're ready for that.'

'I'm ready for anything, if you are.'

He put his arms about her and they kissed. It was not exciting, neither of them meant it to be, but it was significant; a pact-sealer, she told herself.

Getting into bed beside him, she thought, for the first time, in a generous way about Antonia Strachan. 'As I recall, I don't have a problem with you at this,' she said. But she knew he'd failed to catch the echo and she didn't bother to remind him.

· Twenty ·

The waiter gave a celebratory flick of the wrist as he finished filling their glasses. It was a sort of affirmation, Egerton reflected, that London's *accidie* had not yet numbed him, Italy still possessed his soul. His air conveyed both intimacy and detachment; it also hinted that they were more *sympatico* than the other punters he was serving. Possibly he'd tagged them as tourists, in love and likely to over-tip.

Egerton toyed with asking him where he came from in Italy. It would add a flavour to the evening if it turned out to be Tuscany, that he had perhaps even waited on tables in the square at San Gimignano, as the birds wheeled round the watch towers. But he was already turning away, summoned by the woman in a white pyjama suit at the table alongside.

Gail had been watching the sextet at the table. He waited until her gaze came back then raised his glass. He hoped she would not be looking beneath the surface of the moment, for why he had brought her to this restaurant, where the cover charge alone caused the breath to rasp in his throat. In the morning he had justified it with a vague reference to a windfall from a London Weighting increase. She had received the news with slightly widened eyes, but didn't ask questions.

Her foot pressed his under the table, telling him to listen to the conversation of the sextet. Holidays were being discussed, the impending departures to a better class of sun, the remoter beaches, the villas in the *villages perchés*, the islands God had kept unpackaged. The woman in the pyjama suit had a house in Bargemon. He pictured it, bougainvillaea-hung, set into the hillside, its walls bone-white in the midday glare. On the terrace the lizards dozed and darted, attentive to the splashing from the pool below. There were rats in the pool house, he learned; but they were being attended to.

He smiled at Gail, aware a melancholy loomed and needed to be resisted. Before indebtedness became importunate, plucking his sleeve at every turn, the spectacle of money about its pleasures had left him indifferent. Now envy was his familiar, inciting him to scorn and bitterness. He had begun to hate money in all its forms, but mirror money most of all. Here, mirror money would be paying for practically everything tonight. After the ceremony of meeting the bill with plastic gold, cars of incorporeal ownership would carry mirror money people home from this restaurant to houses and apartments owned by similar jugglers' tricks that substituted illusion for reality. But being without the tricks oneself meant another kind of fraud, a stifling of impulse until it came to seem like vice.

'Where are you?' Gail asked.

The truth was too disreputable to tell her; he said he wished they were eating the dinner in San Gimignano.

She reached across to touch his hand. 'Is there a chance of your having to see Sisson again? Perhaps I could come with you after all.'

'I doubt it.' He had told her the whole story after the Prime Minister had made his Commons statement in support of Druitt. 'I can't believe I'd be welcome, anyway. He must be livid his ploy didn't come off.'

'Have you any idea yet what it was that convinced the Prime Minister the story was untrue?'

'No. When Blackmer called me in to say what he was going to do, he said he was sorry he couldn't tell me but his source was very delicate. Pagett's been equally tight-lipped.'

'Blackmer must have had mixed feelings when he got up to make a statement that would let his opponent off the hook.'

'But the way he handled it was very astute. It did him more good than it did Druitt – look at the opinion polls now. He's a clever politician.'

She sat back with an expression that was half-amused, half-resigned. 'God, I hate politicians!'

'If you'd met him, you wouldn't hate Blackmer. He has a rather vulnerable quality, and I can't make out why. One starts feeling sympathetic for no reason. I also remember something Pagett said to me in a fit of frankness – that Blackmer had a dangerous weakness as a politician, because he wasn't a shit. He explained he wasn't implying he couldn't be ruthless, but that at his level there was no room for mercy towards opponents, and Blackmer had a definite reluctance to put the boot in. According to Pagett, that's a serious problem in a Party Leader.'

'That makes me hate politicians even more.'

While they were drinking coffee, Gail said suddenly, 'You're not going to go back to the City, are you?'

He was taken aback that she'd guessed. 'Do you mind?'

'Not if it's what you really want. But what decided it – falling for Blackmer's charm?'

'I'm still not sure. Perhaps I have been affected, working directly for him and Pagett. I just have a feeling that dreary though Government service can be, with the chances of making any decent money nil, at least I've the opportunity of being involved in something that's occasionally worthwhile. Politicians sometimes actually want to do the right thing for people as a whole. Making that possible while fouling up their bad ideas, isn't the worst recipe for a career?' He grinned then shrugged: maybe he was only trying to convince himself it wasn't because he wouldn't face the challenge elsewhere. 'So what do *you* think?'

She played with her coffee spoon. Perhaps she was thinking again of how she felt about politicians. Or wondering if it would ever be possible to scale that wall of debt on what Government paid at his level. But finally she said, 'I think you're right.'

Paying the bill, he folded the currency inside so that Gail wouldn't know the worst. He asked the waiter, as they rose, where he came from. It turned out to be Potenza; he had never been to Tuscany. He spoke politely of hoping to see them again, but the tip had probably been a considerable disappointment.

Outside it was still light. The air had become oppressive; above the shops at the end of Old Compton Street lightning flashed, a pale version of the display he had seen over the Sandia mountains with Melvin. They strolled through Soho's summer stew, stopping before windows to gaze at goods they had no wish to buy, simply out of an unspoken pact to make the evening linger.

In Beak Street Egerton paused at the open door of a restaurant, its plaster facade tricked out with fibreglass beams. The name in Tudor lettering above the entrance was new to him yet he had a sense of familiarity. He took her hand. 'Do you remember what was here before?'

She shook her head.

'It was Dido's, the night club. We came the evening it opened. Dido was a negress, terribly handsome. You must remember.'

'I think I don't want to.' She was already looking away towards Regent Street.

He said gently, 'I realised that evening I couldn't bear losing sight of you ever again.'

She squeezed his fingers but pulled him on. In Piccadilly, when he thought the subject dropped, she abruptly returned to it. 'Was it *really* then you felt that about me?'

'Yes.'

'I can't think why you should have done. I must have been impossible, for everybody. I suppose I had a vague sense of what you were feeling. Half of me wanted you, half didn't care at all. Life had become totally unreal. It seemed that at any moment I might just fly off into space, disappear. The only question was, would it be before or after the next fix.'

She plucked a leaf from the hedge running along Green Park. 'When you and Jamie were talking to some others, I found myself with a man who said he was Dido's agent when she used to be a singer in Chicago. While he was telling me about it, I suddenly began to shake, more than ever before. I left him still talking and went off to the loo. The workmen hadn't finished in there and none of the cubicles had door latches. I had to hold the door closed with my bottom while I fixed. When I saw you afterwards, your look seemed to say you'd watched it all happening. Afterwards whenever we were together, I always had the sensation of your watching at certain times, waiting to see if I needed to fix. I hated you for that. In between I loved you.'

She reached up and kissed him. 'Anyway, that's all in the past. Even if *you* don't believe it is.'

They decided to take a bus before the rain set in. Waiting at the stop, he gazed across the Park, trying to pick out shapes in the dusk beyond the ghosts of deckchairs abandoned for the night.

He wondered how she had guessed he was never quite free from the fear that heroin would come back and claim her again.

Later, back in the flat, she put her arms about him and closed her eyes. 'Don't tell me why we went out tonight. Just let me think we've started to be rich.'

They kissed. When he started undressing her, she pulled him into the bedroom. By the time the phone rang, they were talking about the way things were going to be better. He reached across the bed and lifted the receiver. His secretary in the Cabinet Office was calling from her home. Before she'd left for the evening, Sisson had tried to get Egerton on the special number with which he'd been provided. He had sounded pretty wild and she thought it might be wise to call him back tonight.

Sighing, he sat on the edge of the bed and dialled. He had hardly given his name before Sisson started in. 'I want you here, Egerton!'

'I'm sorry?'

'Get on a plane tomorrow – we have to talk!' He certainly sounded as though he had worked himself into a state. Egerton said, cautiously, 'I doubt if there would really be much point now . . .'

'On the contrary, there'd be more point than ever.'

'But in view of the Prime Minister's statement in the House of Commons . . .'

'I'm not talking about that! If he prefers to have a political fix over Druitt and Goble, that's up to him! This is different. There won't be that sort of fix now. No chance!' He was full of venom.

'Are you saying you have information for the Prime Minister on a quite different subject?'

'That's exactly what I'm saying, Egerton! Can't you understand plain English?' He was almost raving; in the background, Aileen could be heard trying to calm him. For the first time it struck Egerton that he had become unbalanced. Temporising, he said, 'I'll of course let the Prime Minister know what you say.'

Sisson said, 'You do that! Tell him my message is – I'm looking at something very interesting from Dublin. Did you get that? From Dublin!'

Then the line went dead.

· Twenty-One ·

Seated again at his desk after seeing Walden out, Blackmer was conscious of the noise of scratching behind the walnut bureau. Somehow the cat had slipped in from the corridor. Twice in the past week, it had chosen his study to advertise a failing bladder or, possibly, to convey some more complex message. Beside the bureau the odour still lingered. Retirement from its No. 10 duties might need to be considered. He would have to speak to the housekeeper.

He went over to the bureau but discovered there was, after all, no fresh dampness or smell, merely a scored patch on the carpet where claws had been at work. The cat sat gazing at him; it seemed it had simply been trying to expunge the traces of past misdemeanours.

Gathering the cat up, he held it against his shoulder until it purred and decided against complaint. Going to the door, to drop it outside, he found Pagett about to knock and apologising that he was early for their appointment. 'No matter.' He turned back to his desk. 'My Svengali has finished delivering his advice on how the world should see me. You find me reborn. Or about to be.'

'I saw him downstairs. A striking new hairstyle.'

'I was considering it while he talked. It has an impressive sculptural quality, particularly where it rolls forward onto the forehead. I wanted to lift the roll to discover if it stayed in one piece.'

He removed his spectacles and looked again at their frame. He had told Walden this morning that he didn't intend to wear them any more. Walden, more industrious to please these days, had spoken of arranging for other shapes to be sent in for consideration tomorrow; there had been a hint of injured pride in his manner.

Replacing the spectacles on his face, he became aware that the fuzz at the edge of the ears had begun to grow again. It would need to be got rid of before tonight's dinner at the Guildhall. He pushed his cigarette box towards Pagett. 'I may turn out to be the last Prime Minister not to command a telegenic rating of alpha. Have you thought of that, Norman? Ugly politicians, regardless of competence, will be seen as too much of a liability on the box. The first requirement is going to be looks, the second voice, the third a gift for acting sincerity in all circumstances. Scouts from the parties will haunt RADA, searching for talent to be optioned before it's signed up by anyone else.'

When Pagett had lit his cigarette, he said, 'I asked you over because I wanted you to know I've decided to call the election for 19 October. I hope you can see no objection.'

'None.'

'Good. That's for your personal information at the moment. The announcement will probably be at the end of next week. Shall you be having a bet on the outcome?'

'My father gambled five hundred guineas that the Second World War would be over inside nine months. Frequent repetition of the story by my mother inoculated me against all betting at an early age.'

It was hard to imagine Pagett with a gambling man as a father, yet it must be true: Pagett never lied, only resorted to contriving that misconstruction would be the easiest option when it suited his purposes best. He shook his head. 'You should break out! Walden's finger on the nation's pulse has convinced him I shall be five points ahead in the first half of October. Hopeful though I now am, that may be a little optimistic. Walden's one concern, I gather, is that I don't yet come over as squeaky-Green as the Leader of the Opposition. I shall have to work on that.'

Pagett produced one of his immensely polite and non-committal nods; to provoke him into indiscretion was always an uphill task. Blackmer glanced down at his diary. There was nothing remotely inviting in the day ahead: lunch with a Party fund-raiser to please Charles Rainsborough, followed by twenty minutes with a Third World bishop known for exceptional halitosis; later on, Patrick Welcroft, probably bringing more alibis for the mess he'd made of the prison building programme; finally, the glittering tedium of a Guild-hall dinner. Now that he'd decided on the date for the election, he couldn't wait to get out into the country and start campaigning.

He sat back, still with an itch to tease Pagett. 'I've never asked, Norman, if you thought I got the statement to the House on the Druitt business about right.'

Pagett was hesitating a little. 'I was . . . interested that you were so unequivocal.'

'Shouldn't I have been?'

'It was only that you had no more than Busch's assurance to go on . . .'

'In other words he might have been misleading me?'

'You mentioned once having picked up a hint that the Agency might not be averse to the Leader of the Opposition succeeding in the next election.'

Blackmer smiled. 'Are you being rather subtle, Norman?'

'Not really. But I suppose it *could* turn out that what Reinholdt told Egerton was the truth, not a fiction made up at Sweetwater's behest. That would mean the Agency have a hold over Druitt, which they may hope to exploit one day. I wondered how you felt able to exclude the possibility so firmly on Busch's word.'

He clasped hands behind his head. 'I rejected it by no process of reasoning of which you'd approve, I'm afraid. I decided Busch was to be trusted in that moment. Of course he could have been misleading me on the instructions of his master. No doubt he's lied for his country as convincingly as the next man, when the interests of the United States called for it. But I fell back on instinct. There comes a moment when one has to say – this is what I believe. History may prove me wrong. But history seldom deals in truth anyway – not in the form it usually reaches us. More and more I find myself accepting that certainty is damnably elusive. Meredith was absolutely right when he said that dusty answers were all that being hot for certainties ever produced.'

He had mildly hoped to provoke Pagett, but he was in one of his more maddening moods. He simply gave a neutral nod of the head and changed the subject somewhat. 'You may be amused to know that your statement seems to have been largely responsible for Egerton deciding to remain in the Civil Service.'

He smiled again. 'I wonder if he'd still be of the same mind if he knew how much calculation went into it.'

'Egerton might still feel, as I did, that political advantage was not foremost in your mind.'

He had not expected that. In the years they had known each other, Pagett had never disclosed a personal view of himself. He would not have sorrowed overmuch if it had been unsympathetic; but he would not have liked it either. He said, 'Do you suppose Egerton will really settle down?'

'His standards may prove occasionally difficult to accommodate. Egerton belongs to a generation which is more demanding than its predecessors. On balance that will be good for the system. When they think Ministers are wrong, they won't stay silent.'

'I've not found your generation exactly tongue-tied.'

'There's a difference. When I entered the Service, I remember Alex Cadogan's opinion of MPs being quoted – that they were self-seeking, irresponsible, mendacious. I was young enough to be rather shocked that a PUS, even in the Foreign Office, could have such contempt for the politicians we were paid to serve. Later I realised he was quite right, of course. The answer, however, seemed to be to apply one's energies to supporting the exceptions every Parliament somehow throws up who genuinely want to do good. I suspect, however, I may not have fought their occasional stupidities as much as I should have done. That sort of acquiescent approach will not do for Egerton and his kind.'

'Are you going to keep him in order while I'm in this chair?'

'Fortunately I shall have Fender back to do that. He telephoned earlier to say he expects to be fit enough to return in September. He is of course a rebel at heart himself. But rebels can be the best people to discipline other rebels.' Pagett smiled enigmatically, pocketed his cigarette case and withdrew to his lair.

Somehow he struggled through lunch with the fund-raiser and the talk with the Third World bishop without showing boredom. He was coming to the end of the meeting with Welcroft when Diana put her head round the door. She had been staying at Kilndown for a couple of nights. 'Sorry to interrupt, but Esther received another letter from Sisson. I thought I'd better bring it straight in.' She placed the sealed inner envelope in front of him.

The letter was peremptory, to say the least.

> Prime Minister,
> Since you have ignored both my advice and more recently my request for you to send Egerton again, I am forced to write this letter. Its message is very simple. In seven days time, a copy of the enclosure will be sent, with a suitable explanatory note, to every major newspaper editor in London, unless in the meantime Egerton or some other confidential messenger has delivered to me one hundred thousand pounds in cash. Do not disregard this warning – I shall not give another.
>   J. Everard Sisson

He unclipped an attachment to the letter. It was the death certificate of his mother issued in Dublin.

Staring at the certificate, he had the sensation of at last being confronted by a challenge that had awaited him almost all his life, yet had somehow never been really expected – not even after the earlier message which Egerton had passed and which he had decided was bluff. Already a scenario was beginning to unroll in his mind, beginning with articles by those paragons of virtue, the leader writers on the heavies . . . 'While only the stoniest heart can be indifferent to the tragedy . . . the deceit over the years cannot be ignored. . . . Is someone who, by repeated deception, conceals his vulnerability to a cruel disease known to have effects on judgment fit, in that word's deepest meaning, to hold the highest office of State?'

Other comment would be less elevated in tone. A juicy piece could be written about the steps taken with Reeves' help to prevent Esther's identity becoming known while she was in hospital. And sooner or later somebody would dig out Bishop Butler on the dangers of insanity in rulers. Once the campaign got under way, he would be finished, utterly.

He was conscious of Welcroft watching him. He pushed the letter and the death certificate across the table to him. 'Patrick, the time seems to have arrived when you and other colleagues need to know about this.' Diana had remained standing and he saw her eyes widen. She had already guessed what Sisson had done. Blackmer went on, 'I'm afraid the facts are rather tiresome.' Then he told Welcroft everything.

Welcroft remained silent for a while. His face for once had gone almost ashen. Blackmer got up and went to pour himself a brandy. When he returned to his chair that enviable self-confidence of Welcroft's was already seeping back into his features. Welcroft turned to smile at Diana in reassurance, then looked back at Blackmer. 'Don't worry, David. I'll handle this.'

He shook his head. 'No, Patrick. I'm not having any deal with this man. If he carries out the threat – so be it – I'll deal with the situation as it arises. But I'm not having any deal.'

Welcroft pushed the letter back towards him and stared at the table for a moment. Then he stood up and put his prisons file under his arm, ready to leave. He gave them both another brief smile but this time his face was expressionless. 'You're right, David, absolutely right. No deal.' He seemed for once to be completely on board.

· Twenty-Two ·

Beyond the slope at the end of the vines, a group of cypresses grew. Happening to glance in this direction, Sisson saw foliage that seemed suffused with blue. In the gathering dusk the colour shone with a curious intensity.

He switched his gaze elsewhere for a moment. When he looked again at the cypresses, as he had expected, the blue had gone.

He had begun noticing oddities of vision before the trip to Dublin. There had been no unlikely colours then, just the occasional eruption of jagged light into the lens of one eye. In the alternating moods of bleak depression and almost uncontrollable anger that had followed Blackmer's statement to the House of Commons, minor discomforts of a physical kind had beset him, but had usually disappeared after a day or two. He had supposed the flashes in the eye would do the same. But on the journey to Dublin, they had seemed to be getting more frequent; he had speculated on whether this was a sign of a retina becoming detached. After his successful search for the death certificate, he went to an oculist, who told him the eye seemed healthy enough, but was ageing. Since then, warmed by thoughts of the revenge to be taken on Blackmer, he had found he could almost ignore the condition.

He started the tractor again and moved towards the vines. Driven by a compulsion that now required he should occupy himself unceasingly, he had worked all day among the vines, first on tying-in, later turning the soil with the help of the tractor. He had refused to stop for lunch, had broken off now only to swallow a little dry bread and wine. Progress had been very slow, the ground hard even for the tractor to break up. Occasionally, seeking a respite from the continual seething of his mind, he had thought of Virgil, imagined his comments on the state of the vines. Labouring with just a hoe, Virgil would perhaps have given up for the day by now. He tried to picture him, drinking last year's wine in the arbour, under the wisteria. But Virgil was no longer quite real to him.

Where the rows of vines stopped, a dried-up water course, divided his land from a hillside. Approaching it, he saw several large stones in his path. Puzzled at their appearance, he got down from the tractor to heave them away. It was then he realised he was not alone.

Three men were crossing the water course. He was sure none of them were from neighbouring farms. They could have been tourists who had wandered off the slip road that served the main part of San Donato. The man leading the way, the tallest of them, was wearing a designer-labelled shirt, well-cut slacks and loafers. His companions were younger, one with cropped blond hair, the other heavily moustached. These two wore jeans. The blue of the jeans was the colour he had noticed earlier in the foliage of the cypresses.

He asked if he could help them, first in Italian, then in English. For answer, the man with the moustache thrust a knee deep into his stomach. As he began to crumple, another kicked his legs away. He was dragged into the bed of the water course, where the man with the moustache sat on his back. When, in bewilderment, he tried to ask what they wanted, a handful of the turned soil was forced into his mouth.

For weeks now he had sensed his world was splintering. He heard the tractor being moved. It appeared alongside him, tilted precariously because of the slope of the land. The tall man had meanwhile picked up the largest of the stones he had earlier moved and was crouching by his head.

He knew then he was about to die. His head would be crushed with the stone and afterwards the tractor toppled on to his body. Whoever found him would conclude he had attempted to turn the tractor too near the water course and had struck his head as he fell beneath it: an unfortunate accident.

In his terror he was still conscious of a craving to know who was doing this to him. They were not Italian, he was sure. Their general appearance as they approached had seemed North European. He could best believe them to be British, sent by Blackmer because of the threat of exposure with the birth certificate. But they could also be American, especially the blond one with cropped hair, who had grunted in what might have been an American voice. Washington, getting wind of his campaign against Druitt and Goble and suspecting more shots to come from his locker, might have its own reasons for wanting to silence him. Or perhaps the attackers had been sent by powerful interests whose nature and concerns he could only imagine. Managing to spit out enough soil to free his tongue, he twisted his head so that he could focus on the tall man's face. 'Tell me who you are! *Who sent you?*'

The other uttered words that were impossible to hear above the tractor. Sisson tried once more. '*What?*' The tall man was raising the stone. He paused for a moment, the stone held high in both hands, as though in celebration. He seemed about to speak. But then he brought the stone down and an answer no longer mattered.